Shiromi Pinto was born in London in 1971 and raised in Montreal. She has written numerous short stories, one of which was published in *Kin*, the Serpent's Tail anthology of new fiction by black and Asian women, and one which was nominated for the 2005 Pushcart Prize. She lives in London with a percussionist partner. *Trussed* is her first novel.

D1825210

Dear Alison

Enjoy! – A racy

read for your

delectation x S.

Trussed

Shiromi Pinto

A complete catalogue record for this book can be
obtained from the British Library on request

The right of Shiromi Pinto to be identified as the author
of this work has been asserted by her in accordance
with the Copyright, Designs and Patents Act 1988

First published in 2006 by Serpent's Tail,
4 Blackstock Mews, London N4 2BT
website: www.serpentstail.com

Designed and typeset at Neuadd Bwll, Llanwrtyd Wells

Printed by Mackays of Chatham, plc

ISBN-13: 978-1-85242-913-3
ISBN: 1-85242-913-5

10 9 8 7 6 5 4 3 2 1

For my family

nomenclature *noun* **1** the selecting of names for things in a particular field. **2** a body or system of names. **3** the term or terms applied to someone or something. ORIGIN Latin *nomenclatura*, from *nomen* 'name' + *clatura* 'calling, summoning'.

Compact Oxford English Dictionary of Current English 2003

'The obsession with the media and focus groups is making us look as if we want power at any price and don't stand for anything.'

Clare Short, August 1996

1 Trussed

Who is she that looketh forth as the morning, fair as the moon, clear as the sun, terrible as an army bearing shields and banners?

My arm. My arm rises and falls, rises and falls. I can feel the sweat building under the skin of my thighs. My arm. It refuses to tire. It falls with mechanical regularity, like a well-wound metronome.

'Vinda', he says, 'Vinda, you're a – 'He is trembling. *I am a wall and my breasts are towers.*

'Shut up!' I am standing over his cowering body, knees apart. His pale flesh shivers. He is moaning. I force a stiletto heel into his forehead and hear his knees crack against the laminate floor. He whimpers.

'Feels good, doesn't it?' I whisper. 'Like a cold, hard silver bullet.' His belly-button dilates and constricts in time to my mental metronome. I remove my foot, sneering at the vague, trapezoidal hollow left on his skin. His eyes are wide, almost panicked. He is moaning and slavering and telling me he wants to suck my heel.

I turn around and thrust my buttocks toward him. 'Tell me I have a nice arse,' I growl. I can feel his eyes roaming over the leather seat of my pants, devouring the mottled flesh which squeezes out from underneath and through my netted tights.

His voice is tearful. 'It's gorgeous,' he says. I feel something wet touch my right buttock.

'Don't touch,' I shout, snapping round to face him. I thrash my whip on the floor, sending tiny dust motes scrambling. *Every man hath his sword upon his thigh*. He blanches. 'Did I say you could touch me?' Another crack of the whip. 'Did I?' He knots himself into a foetal tuck. His blue-white skin is creased pink and is as slick and fragile as an unbaked meringue. 'Answer me.'

'N-n-no.'

'Say you're sorry.'

'I'm sorry.'

'Louder.'

'I'M SORRY.'

I pat his head with a gloved hand. 'Naughty boy,' I say, pouting. 'And if naughty boy stays naughty, Vinda will be back.' I glance at my watch – a few minutes after 9.30 – and peel off my gloves. I can feel the muscles in my cheeks tensing as my lips pull apart to form a grin.

He staggers toward the couch where his trousers are lying and fumbles through the pockets. 'I have to give you something,' he says. 'Something for …' His breath is laboured. The air in the room is suddenly cool and his skin prickles with tiny studs like a plucked chicken. I nod, counting eighty pounds before folding it into my wallet.

I make my way to Holborn tube, kit bag swinging from my shoulder – that metronome again. The rubber lips of my blue suede trainers glow thick and white against the grey pavement. I come here every week – twice a week – to see Derek, the lawyer from Lincoln's Inn. Derek Fernley, I should say, though we don't bother with last names. Amrik is always asking me whether he's my boyfriend. What kind of question is that?

Now and again I catch sight of Derek in Safeway or Hart's. I scarcely recognise him in his navy suit and wool cashmere overcoat. We ignore each other on such occasions. Too embarrassing, I suppose. I can't get that image of him – that more familiar image – out of my head. His slack flesh and sweaty knees. The white towel. Perhaps it's the same for him, too. Perhaps all he sees is my jellied arse or the silver tip of my stiletto.

I'm standing in front of Holborn tube. A torrent of people runs in and out. They're in a hurry, all of them, and annoyed by my presence. I can't blame them. I'm standing right in front of them, parting the stream of incomers and outgoers. I can't help myself. I'm always getting in the way. And tonight, well, tonight, I can't make my mind up. Do I really want to go home right now? I consider hopping on a bus to Hackney to see Jason, but realise a visit from me would only make things worse for him. I take a step back and hear someone's tongue skinning teeth. I turn my head and see that I've pulled out right into a woman's path – am just about shoulder to breast with her, in fact. She's carrying a large shopping bag with a jack-o'-lantern on it, reminding me it's only a few more weeks to Halloween. Not that I care. Narrowing her eyes at me, she makes a grand display of changing direction. I shrug. *Mea culpa. Expiare.*

Expiation. I was once a soldier in the army of the Virgin Mary. A member of the Legion. Inducted into it by the Queen herself. When I was little, my parents sent me to Canada to stay with Aunty Queenie over the summers. She said we were all part of a great war against the world's evils. She let me share her handbook and we recited the *Magnificat* every day – and the rosary. The *Magnificat* is based on the *Song of Solomon*. I only discovered that a few months ago. I looked it up on the web.

The pavement is sliding by. It's a grey blur – a concrete conveyor belt conveying me forward. For no apparent reason, *Waterloo Sunset* wells up from my belly. It starts out muted but gains strength as it passes my breastbone until the words 'Waterloo sunset' soar from my lips in a great cloudburst. Actually, no one hears them. My mouth is moving and my inner ear hears the meandering melody – guitars, drums, voices going 'ooo-ee-ooo' – but outside, there's nothing. Just that wet-pavement sound of my lips sculpting words.

I turned away from Holborn station a while ago, but the crush of people is relentless – like flies swarming roadkill. I've missed the sunset, though sunsets – whatever the Kinks say – never make me think of paradise. Paradise is something else. A state of mind. A euphoria that, yes, can be brought on by natural phenomena as experienced by the Romantics, but even more exalted if achieved through pure meditation. Pure thought. Pure concentration. My mouth is chewing lyrics and blowing them out like bubblegum.

I've been walking head-down for a while now, careful not to tread on any dog turds. My neck is starting to ache and I realise I don't even know where I am any more. I look up and find myself standing by the steps of St George's. A man is sprawled by the side, just a little way up, a can of cider inching slowly from his grip. In another hour, the can will be clattering down the steps, slurring its contents in yellow dribbles.

I'm not sure why I'm here, but I go in anyway, surprised that the door has been left open. I dab my forehead with holy water as I enter. It feels cool against my skin, and somehow calming, so I edge into a pew and sit down. I bow my head and last night's dream enters me like a virus. It's always the same one. Actually, it isn't. Each time it's a little different. Me, lying in a pothole, hair soaking in a petrol rainbow; me, smeared in oil, surfing an endless parade of strangers. Each time there's a new clue, another dot in the matrix. But the overall picture is still broken up, like it hasn't finished downloading yet.

I feel queasy. I get up and light a votive. As I do, I whisper, 'paradise'. I don't know why. Obviously something to do with 'Waterloo Sunset'. But I can't be sure of what I really mean by it. Perhaps I mean: 'pair of dice' or 'parodies'. My eyes are drawn to the flicker of the candle – its blue centre and white halo. I search my coat pocket and pull out a little paper tube. Bowing my head toward the flame, I light the roll-up. Immediately, the air smells sweeter. I inhale deeply, ignoring the slight constriction in my chest, recalling that marijuana is meant to be good for asthmatics. Then I say it again. Paradise. As soon as I say it, I realise it's time to go.

The streets are almost empty when I finally emerge from South Harrow Station. I could murder a kebab right now. Crisp carrot and purple cabbage under a silky yoghurt sauce, lamb steaming below it. Already my tongue winces with anticipation. But I can't. Eighty-five pounds or no eighty-five pounds, I can't afford to drop two quid on a kebab. Everything I earn goes into paying the rent or for better kit. Not that I have much kit. The rest of it goes into the bank. Last year's trip left me near penniless. I can't afford to go into overdraft again. Now that I'm no longer a student, it just isn't worth it. I don't believe in debt, anyway. Debt is a sign of weakness and greed. I make a point of living within my means. So, no. No kebab tonight.

'I've spent it all, Vinda. I'm broke.' Amrik's voice is faintly strangled but composed. He's lavished yet another dinner on yet another young blond with no success.

I take a bite from my apple – an Egremont Russet – and make soothing noises into the telephone. 'Next time,' I say.

Uncharacteristically, he seems satisfied with this offering. 'Yes. Yes, of course. There's always a next time, right?' He's being sarcastic.

'Right,' I say, then change the subject. 'It's been a long night, Am.'

Amrik's curiosity is piqued. 'Oh? How's Derek?'

'Well,' I say, between mouthfuls of Russet, 'he's the only guy I've ever met who gets off on my stretch marks. Not only does he get off on them, he pays me for it, too.' I swallow the sweet-sour flesh. 'But what about you? How's the thesis going?'

'Never mind the thesis, Vinda. I need a man.'

I roll my eyes. 'Oh god, not again. What happened this time?'

Amrik is whimpering now. 'I took him out. I took him to an

Italian restaurant. I paid for everything – *everything*. We even had dessert. And then he left. He ate, gave me a hug and said he'd call me.'

'Well, he did give you a hug. That's something, right?'

'No.' Amrik is emphatic. 'No it isn't. It's nothing. Meaningless. Casual. He doesn't like me.'

The apple core is nestled in the palm of my left hand. It's turning brown. 'It was your first date, right? Perhaps next time.' As soon as I say the words, I want to reel them back. I want to press the undo key. I even type it mentally: ⌘ + z. But Amrik's voice has turned to ice.

'Yes,' he says, over-enunciating. 'There *is* always a next time.'

Silence. I watch the apple core go from sepia to walnut in the quiet. I can hear the click of computer keys. Amrik is typing. I resist the urge to hang up, and ask, 'So, what're you doing tonight?'

More clicks of the keys then a sigh. 'I'm going to Russell Square. It's either that or King's Cross. Maybe I'll let some gross old man feel me up for money.'

'Oh god! Come on,' I chuck the apple core into the bin across from my bed. 'You're being silly, now. You know you can't get it up for the old men anyway.'

He sniffs. 'That's true. The last time I was offered money, I went with this old guy to the toilets and nothing worked. I should have taken the money first, then at least I would have had twenty quid instead of cheap humiliation.'

I can't help smiling. Amrik's midnight wanders are legendary. Or so he says. He claims there are web posts and even toilet graffiti testifying to his prowess. I haven't bothered to find out. And why should I? His accounts of dark and fellatious encounters are achingly lurid. Every so often, there are slapstick moments – like this incident with the old queen. But usually the story will begin in a park or loo somewhere and end in a bush or urinal or even his room. I can't help myself. I'm engrossed and grossed out at the same time.

'Amrik,' I tease, 'honestly, I expect more from you. Anyway, you really shouldn't be encroaching on rent-boy territory. You'll get into trouble doing that.'

'Excuse me?' Amrik's indignation pierces through the receiver, prompting a triplet of + z's in my mind. 'Exactly who are you to preach to me madame? You spend half your evening whipping some poor sod and come home to dictate to me?'

'Poor sod?' I kick a pillow off the bed. 'Listen, Amrik. He's a lawyer. He's loaded. But all he can spare is eighty-fucking-quid—'

'Eighty quid! He gives you eighty quid!' Amrik's words tumble through the receiver. 'I get offered twenty if I'm lucky, and even that's not often.'

'Get off it. This ain't no shake and stain, darling. What I do is art, nothing less. Like a geisha, you know? There's nothing trite about it.'

Amrik draws a sharp breath. I brace myself, preparing for an onslaught of hysterics, barbs and, if his mood collapses, a litany of self-pitying, contractionless pronouncements. 'I am very lonely', is a popular one, followed closely by 'I do not have anyone. Nobody loves me'. If he starts on the dogs and bears, then hanging up will be my only option. But Amrik does none of these.

'So,' he says, his voice lowering a register; it's the tone he reserves for mischief and seduction. 'Who's next on your books, then?'

My ears fill with blood and my head suddenly feels very tight. Damn him. 'Shut up,' I say, and am immediately treated to a close-up of Derek's quivering backside. I jam my eyelids shut. 'I'm not a prostitute.'

Amrik is unmoved. 'One client is all it takes.'

'Look, he's not a client, ok? I told you. He's sort of my boyfriend.'

'Since when do boyfriends pay?'

My ears are still pounding. 'In a more civilised world they would.'

'Get real, Vinda.'

My lower lip momentarily bunches to the left. 'Ok, so he's not exactly a boyfriend. We just have this agreement, yeah? He's got this need. I need some cash. Sorted.'

'Ooo my, sounds ideal. Do I hear wedding bells?' Amrik's voice is so cold my earpiece bristles with icicles.

'Oh for God's sake. Why am I trying to justify myself to you of all people? You know I didn't just pick him up off the street.'

'What then?'

I grit my teeth, 'Damn it, Amrik—' but as I gulp my next breath, a fruity, rotten scent rises from the bin and coats my tongue. The apple core has chosen this precise moment to start to decompose. I stop speaking and throw a wad of tissues into the bin, smothering the core. 'You know what your problem is, don't you?' I say, clearing my throat. 'You hang out in all the divey places. How can you expect more than a twenty when you're prowling around King's Cross?'

Amrik lets out a long breath. 'You're right,' he says. 'But where am *I* going to find a big-bucks lawyer? … Hey—' he snaps his fingers, 'why don't you ask Derek whether he knows anyone?'

'What?' I try to imagine the conversation, picture Derek's snicker, the prurient glint in his eye. I shudder. 'I can't ask him something like that.'

'Why not? When you're putting the pliers to his nipples you can just ask him whether he has a friend—'

'I WON'T.'

'Fine. Don't help your friends. Be like that … SADIST.'

I go over it again in my mind. This time, Derek looks earnest and helpful, and only temporarily smug. I sigh. 'Ok, ok, I'll see what I can do. God …'

Amrik seems placated. He hums gently to himself, tapping out a rhythm with what sounds like the point of a pencil.

I look at my watch, surprised that it's nearly half-twelve.

'Shit!' Amrik gasps. 'I need to get to Russell Square now before all the cute boys are taken.'

My stomach gives a feeble yowl. I yawn in response. 'Yeah,

yeah. Go for it. But remember, if there are only old ones left, take the money first.'

'Oh please, Vinda, what do you take me for?'

I chuckle. 'Nothing less than eighty quid.'

When I slink into the kitchen to forage for leftovers, I find my uncle standing by the kettle swinging a tea bag over his mug. His eyes squint over flaps of cheek. He hasn't seen me yet, so I attempt a retreat when my stomach emits a gurgle. Uncle Aloy swivels his head like a barn owl surveying its territory. 'I say, niece! Are you going to make tea now?'

I shake my head. 'No, I'm just going to eat something.'

'Anhh,' his eyes widen for a moment. '*My* God, only now you are eating? Why so late? Where have you been?' He giggles, 'Must be with some bloke getting tickled under the covers, no? Maybe with some ahz-hole?'

I purse my lips, imagining what it might be like to cane his bony posterior. I open the fridge and take out some plastic containers. 'Did you have supper, Uncle?'

Uncle Aloy watches the steam spurting from the kettle. 'Supper? No, no. My wife is punishing me.'

'Punishing you?' I open a tub of Dairylea spread and scoop fried aubergine onto a plate. 'Why? What have you done this time?'

'I? Nothing, *men*. Your aunty, don't you know. She's mad.'

This is true. But it is only true because Agnes Aunty lives with Uncle Aloy. If she shouts at him, it's usually for a good reason.

I watch the old man stirring sugar into his tea. He's a diabetic, but instead of taking his medication, he fries *karavila* – bitter gourd – once a week, proclaiming its healing properties. If not for Agnes Aunty, Uncle Aloy would have gone into diabetic shock long ago. She goads him into taking his insulin and slips his pills into his food when he's not looking. In return, he winds her up with endless, inane prattle.

'Go on, Uncle, why is Agnes Aunty punishing you?'

'Shh,' he holds the spoon in mid-air. 'She'll hear you.' He cocks an ear toward the doorway.

I drum the counter with my fingertips. 'Ok, so do you want me to serve you some rice while I have everything out or not?'

Uncle Aloy shakes his head. 'No, no. I have already eaten.'

I can feel my nostrils flaring as my front teeth search out my bottom lip. My uncle is contrary, not only with those around him but himself as well. Three and a half minutes into our conversation and he has already contradicted himself. And not with philosophical matters – no. Facts, reality – these, too, are slippery and inconsistent in his addled world. Agnes Aunty is right. Not only is he going blind, he's going senile as well.

He giggles. 'I had some dried fish and *karavila* just now.'

I sniff the air. It pongs of fat and frying. I fancy I can still hear Agnes Aunty's bellows bouncing off the walls. 'No wonder she's punishing you. You could at least have opened the win—'

'Quiet, *men*. You sound just like her.' He shakes his head. 'You De Zoysa women are all the same.'

I glare at him.

He chuckles. 'Bad with the good, no? My wife had very nice thighs in those days. That's why I married her.' He studies the rim of his cup, then looks up at me, his eyes travelling across my chest. 'I can still please a young woman, you know.'

In one fluid movement, I turn away, remove my plate from the microwave and exit the kitchen.

He calls after me, 'Oy, niece, aren't you going to—?', but I am up the stairs and in my room before he can finish his sentence.

Mouth watering, I fan the plate of rice and aubergine with my hand, cooling it to avoid burning my fingers. Whether it was the joint I had earlier, the whipping or a combination of both, I'm not sure, but I'm exhausted and famished at the same time.

'I do it for the money.'

Trussed

I have to tell myself this from time to time, otherwise I forget why I keep seeing Derek. I begin to wonder whether he isn't my boyfriend, after all. Whether the money is only an incidental part of our relationship. Then I remind myself that we don't have a relationship as such. Or, we do have one, but it's the purest kind – based entirely on exchange: pain for pleasure, slap for tickle, money for services rendered.

And I need that money. My parents stopped sending me regular cheques after I graduated from Uni and went travelling. My rent is due at the end of the week, and I like to be prompt with my payments. I give the money to my aunt, of course. Never to Uncle Aloy. He would probably take it as an investment in his import-export business. He doesn't really have a business. He just likes to send old cars to Sri Lanka part by part. Once, he tried to get a stranger to carry a tyre in his suitcase. He hovered around the Air Lanka check-in queue at Heathrow for hours, scanning the crowds, looking for an amenable 'mule'. It was, like so many of Uncle Aloy's ventures, a failure.

No one knows what happened to that tyre. Maybe he got it to Sri Lanka, maybe not. The Benz, however, is still sitting somewhere in some godforsaken warehouse along with two Morris Minors and a 1987 model BMW. Uncle Aloy is, as Agnes Aunty says, mad. He just can't help himself. When I was a teenager, I used to catch a ride with him into central London. We would sit side by side – me messing with the radio dials, he hunched over the steering wheel – and his leathery palm would curl and peel over my thigh like smog. I would pick it up, as I would a crab on the beach, and deposit it by the gearbox. Once, he even told me to say a 'Hail Mary' and ask God's forgiveness. I stopped taking lifts from him years ago.

Later, as I creep up the stairs after visiting the kitchen for the last time, my aunty calls out to me from her bedroom. 'Is that you, Asma?' I stamp my foot on the landing, flinching at the sound of that name.

Asma. Some kind of cruel trick played on me by my father, lover of things Greek.

'Why did he have to name me after a chest condition?' I whined to my mother once I was better acquainted with our family's chronic health problems. 'And where were you anyway? How could you let him do that to me?' Mum just shook her head and stroked my hair. She kept saying something about Asma meaning 'song' in ancient Greek before it ever became associated with a breathing disorder.

Revenge – and a touch of irony – led me, years later, to seize on the garish nickname given me by a spotty boy during a shag between classes. 'You're hotter than a … a … a …', Ryan, the boy in question, was pushing into me, clutching my sweating backside away from the teacher's desk. 'A VINDALOO.'

'Vindaloo?' I said, wrinkling my nose. 'As in … the curry?'

'Yeah,' he smiled, kissing me gently on the cheek and hugging me close. 'You're my little spicy curry girl, my sexy Vindaloo.'

I smiled weakly, and within a week let him go, spitting, 'Next time you want a curry, order a bleeding take-away.' I should have known better.

But I have taken that name and made it my own. I am Vinda the invincible, Vinda the inflaming, Vinda the dominatrix. And yet my aunt persists in calling me Asma, the name itself a wheeze in the throat.

'Asma? Why are you so late?'

I stand in the doorway and put on a mock accent. 'Anh, don't you know?' I chuckle. 'So, how's things, aunty?'

'Oh, all right,' Agnes Aunty turns her head toward me. 'I was feeling a little chesty earlier, but I'm fine now.'

I peer at my aunt: the doughy swell of her belly, the plump density of her cheeks. Despite her size, she is a female version of my father, his features unmistakable though distributed across a broader plane. I, too, bear his blueprint: his small nose, the overzealous cheekbones, his tendency toward constipation. I'm also a chronic wanderer, and the older I get, the more I realise this has more to do with him than growing up a Catholic or my parents' warped relationship.

I walk in and flop down at the foot of the bed. 'What's the family goss like these days?'

'What?' My aunt laughs. 'Well, nothing much really.'

'Any news from Angel?' His name sticks in my throat. 'How's things going for him in California?'

'*Aney* I don't know, *men*. He rang the other day, talking about some nonsense …' Her voice tapers off as she heaves a long sigh. 'My son … He's mad, no?'

I want to add 'just like his father', but refrain. I haven't seen my cousin in years, not since he left to 'go Elvis' in LA. He's always been a little 'touched'. If not for his voice – a 'gift from God', apparently – no one in the family would tolerate his behaviour.

A thin wheeze rises in Agnes Aunty's chest. 'Annie is having another baby.'

'Really?' I've never actually met my cousin Annie. 'But I thought she got divorced.'

'She is.'

'Does she have a new boyfriend?'

'A boyfriend?' Agnes Aunty scratches her elbow. 'No, *men*. What boyfriends for her? She's decided she's a less-bian now.'

I stifle a giggle. 'Oh … so, where does she live?'

'In her flat, I suppose.' She sounds irritated. 'She and her *friend* are going to bring up the baby. *Ayyo*, what that child will be like, God only knows.'

'But who's the father?'

Agnes Aunty shrugs. 'She won't say. No one knows.' She sighs. 'What to do? She says she's happy.' She searches her scalp with the tip of an index finger. 'Just like her father, she is. I give this new one a year, like all the others.'

'You mean there were other women?' I stare at my aunt.

'No, no. But there were so many others, *men*. One must have been the father.'

I nod, then roll onto my back to stare at the stucco ceiling. I think of Annie's dad. 'Whatever happened to Uncle Nimal anyway? Is he still in California?'

'Oh yes. He's a Hari Krishna now. A holy man. He told Annie that no meat-eaters are allowed to enter his house.'

I recall my cousin's fabled love of beef burritos. 'So, does Annie see much of him then?'

'Yes, very often. Anyway, this Nimal is mad. He has a new woman now, an Indian. A vegetarian I suppose.' She giggles and her entire girth trembles beneath the duvet. 'When he wants a nice steak he'll have to leave this one and find someone else.'

'A Hari Krishna,' I chuckle.

Uncle Nimal, with his super-flared jeans and mutton-chopped sideburns, left Flo, Agnes Aunty's sister, years ago – much to everyone's relief. It was Uncle Nimal, they said, who had led my father, Martin, down the path to perdition, dragging him to nightclubs to dance with English birds. I've seen old photos of them wearing aviator shades and sharp ties, and can imagine them grinning over pint glasses, pulling girls. My parents had only just sailed in from Colombo, but Uncle Nimal wasted no time in spreading his corruption. And now Uncle Nimal is a Hari Krishna, and Dad is moored somewhere off the coast of the Aegean, bimbette in tow. Typical.

'And Annie? Is she still Church of God?'

Agnes Aunty pulls absently at a strand of black hair. 'That one? I don't know. One day she's Church of God, another day she's a Hari Krishna, another she's Muslim, and the next she's a devotee of Sai Baba. Now she's a bloody less-bian. What to do, child?'

I yawn and the stairs behind me creak. I quickly bend to kiss my aunt on the cheek. As I do, Uncle Aloy appears in the doorway.

'Oy, what are you two ladies up to? You-all are the same. Without a man you go mad.'

'Just shut up, *men*.' Agnes Aunty shifts her weight abruptly. 'You have a bloody filthy mind.'

He giggles. 'Calm down, Agnes.' Turning his eyes on me he whispers, 'Your aunty has a fiery temper ...' he approaches the bed, murmuring, 'and good thighs.'

'What?' Agnes Aunty sits up in bed. 'Get out of here without talking your damn nonsense.'

I jump from the bed, taking my cue to exit. 'Night all.' I slip quickly from the room and up the stairs. As I open my bedroom door I hear the distant warbling of my uncle: '*Love bells are ringing for me and my cow*.'

The phone rings three times before I pick it up. It's Derek, calling just two days after our last appointment to cancel the Tuesday and confirm Thursday. In a rare breach of etiquette, he asks me to meet him at a bar instead of the flat. 'Wear something nice,' he says. I bring my gear as usual, this time in a patent-leather backpack.

As I walk into Village Soho, I stare at the walls, searching for Derek among crowds of immaculate young men. They talk easily with one another, shifting their eyes constantly to follow the movement of well-fitting 501s or a ribbed torso. I see Derek standing by the bar, sipping from a martini glass. He waves me over, pointing to his glass and crooking his head to the side. I nod. As soon as I reach him, he pushes a fresh Martini toward me. 'Thanks. Why the special meeting?'

Derek's mouth grows tense. 'I'm fine, and how are you?'

I dismiss him with a flip of my hand. 'I don't usually drink Martinis, but thank you.' I sip tentatively. 'Glad to know you're fine, so am I.'

'Do you want to go upstairs? More interesting, I should think.' He winks. 'You know – more women.'

'Isn't it Dyke Night up there?'

Derek nods.

I sneer. 'Dying to check out the women even if they're not interested in you?'

We make our way up the stairs. 'Why not?' Derek cups the air with up-turned palms. 'Some of them are very sexy.'

I tip my head to the side, conceding. We carve out a space by the bar and order another two drinks. Both of us scan the room.

'What do you think of her?' Derek points to a dark-haired woman in a fitted blue T-shirt.

I stare for a moment. 'Not bad. Like the T-shirt.' I exchange a quick look with the woman and smile to myself.

Derek nods, ordering another drink. 'Have you eaten yet?' He plays with the cuffs of his shirt.

'Not really.' I slit my eyes. 'Why?'

'Stop behaving like a caged animal, Vinda.' He puffs hoarsely. 'I'd like to go out to dinner with you, that's all. How about Soho Soho? It's on me.'

I frown for a second, then sigh. 'Ok. Why not.'

Leaving Brewer for Old Compton Street, we walk in silence. I glance at Derek. This is the first time I've seen him in something other than a suit – or towel. Without a tie, his neck seems somehow gelatinous – like a marshmallow threatening to engulf the collar of his shirt. That same neck will hang low when I pull out my whip, dimpling and contorting with each blow. He will weep like a desperate drunk, sweat running down his temples. It's an odd picture, incongruous with the man walking beside me right now.

Derek is a human rights lawyer. After our first meeting, we rarely spoke about ourselves, but this piece of information emerged by accident a few weeks ago. In a moment of indiscretion, Derek simply told me, hoping, perhaps, to extract something from me in return. I gave him nothing. What could I have said? That I was unemployed? That was obvious. That I was a recent college graduate? Also obvious.

I shake my head. Maybe Amrik is right. Derek really is just a client and I'm nothing but a whore.

But then here I am on what seems to be a date, and I'm

annoyed. Derek insists that tonight, he is going to treat me first; we are going to have fun. But 'fun' was never part of our agreement – not this type of fun, anyway.

We stop in front of the restaurant. Smiling, Derek holds the door open and ushers me through. I take a deep breath, step inside and am absorbed into the glittering crowd.

Voices bounce incoherently against clay tiling and glass panes as I insert and withdraw the tines of my fork from a square of lasagne. I watch Derek's mouth moving as he speaks, the way his lips curl around words and spittle pools at the corners. There's a fleck of basil stuck in the cleft below his lip. It's shiny with olive oil and seems to have fused with his skin like dark green glitter. His mouth continues to move, oblivious to the graffiti below it. I notice his voice dipping down to close a thought, and tune back in.

'… don't you hate it when that happens?'

I peer at the tiny shred of green. 'Yeah, it's really embarrassing.'

Derek scowls. 'What?' He shakes his head and grunts. 'You haven't been listening at all, have you?'

I figure I'm not paid enough to listen. 'Can you blame me?'

Derek flushes, his face trembling like a baby's. 'Still thinking of the woman in the T?'

'Who?' He's really desperate now, making up things to justify my dead expression. He can't bear the fact that I actually find him boring. I kiss my teeth. 'Listen. Do you mind telling me what this is all about? I mean, I know you said you wanted to treat me, but why exactly are we here? Aren't we supposed to—'

Derek averts his eyes, holding up a palm. 'Later, later. Can't we just have a chat, right now?' He pauses. 'And if you must know, I haven't eaten since 11.30 this morning, so I thought … and anyway, why are you complaining so much?' He glances at my excavating fork. 'What's wrong? Don't you like it?'

I jab the fork into the lasagne and sit back in my chair. 'Like, don't like – what the fuck does it matter?' Actually, it does matter. To me, I mean. And it is rather good – a perfect balance of flavours: creamy béchamel, woody porcini mushrooms and a tart tomato sauce. Divine. Calmly, I reiterate, 'What the *fuck* does it really matter?'

Derek opens and closes his mouth, then lowers his eyes. He picks up a piece of olive bread and nibbles at it. He tries to change the subject. 'What did you study, Vinda? In college, I mean.'

I fold my arms across my chest. 'And why do you want to know?'

Derek gets this desperate look, like he's being strangled. 'Just *tell* me.'

I glare at him for a full thirty seconds, watching the sweat prickle his forehead. 'English literature,' I say finally, keeping my arms crossed. 'I did it for the enjoyment, but it ended up being a bit disappointing. Too much theory, not enough literature. What do I know about "terror" and the "colonial encounter"?' My lips pinch into an elaborate pout. 'To tell you the truth, I've gone off reading. I stick to the papers these days. Current affairs and that.' I tap the metal handle of my fork which is standing exactly perpendicular to the surface of the lasagne. I'm hungry and regretting my earlier mutilation of my supper. I sigh. 'So what are you working on these days?'

Derek sits up in his chair. He taps the side of his nose. 'It's confidential, you know.' I nudge him with a look. 'Well, I'm sure you're not going to blab to anyone, are you?' The idea of me knowing someone important enough to compromise his career is so preposterous he laughs. I watch the basil fleck stretch and jig on his skin. His face is red when he finally stops.

'It's a discrimination case,' he says, wiping his eyes. 'Council tenant. Some poor woman with little taste and even less money living off the state.' Derek rolls his eyes with disgust. 'At least she speaks English – like a Yorkshire lass, no less.' He gurns. 'Anyway, it's a good case – good for my career. A win would put me in excellent standing. I'd be rather surprised if I didn't make QC as a result.' He caresses the napkin. 'I can almost feel it.'

'It?'

'Silk, Vinda. Soon I shall have the ear of the Queen.'

'Are you sure that's all you'll be wanting from her?'

Derek smiles a lizard's smile. 'Oh, you vulgar thing. Bravo.'

I laugh. 'So, you enjoy being a lawyer, then?'

Derek smiles. 'Of course. I like dealing in semantic minutiae.' He leans forward, casting a shadow over the table. 'It's not about morality, you know. It's about manouevring your way through the law. It's a chess game: trap, dominate, fuck … Of course, the money is also good.' He looks straight at me. 'It allows me a few luxuries.'

I want to roll my eyes, but raise a querying brow instead. 'You're a human rights lawyer; you *can't* make that much money.'

Derek rubs an index finger against the table, 'I have my ways.'

So that's it. I'm an object. Of course I am. Something to be collected, packaged and stored away until required. At least he's honest. We're honest. 'Well, good thing there are a few dull idiots like myself around to keep you amused for a small price.'

Derek lights a cigarette. 'Amusing? Yes. Dull? … Never.' He trails his gaze vertically, billowing smoke down my chest as he speaks. 'After all, darling, if you were dull, I'd find someone else, wouldn't I? Dull is not a fetish I'm willing to pay for.' He puffs out another cloud, this time squarely in my face. I sneeze.

'I suppose,' I say, clearing my throat, 'I suppose I should be flattered to be counted amongst your luxuries.' I glance at the table next to ours where two middle-aged, wine-faced men sit drinking with a young woman.

'Let's go to the O Bar,' the larger one says to his colleague.

'The O Bar,' pipes an American voice. She is blonde, and her lips slide along the top and bottom of the 'O' until they meet, sending it up like a soap bubble. 'That's a great idea.'

The large man winks at his friend.

I turn away. 'So, to the flat, then.'

Derek places his hand on mine. 'Yes. I've got a treat for you – some excellent grass.'

I cringe, snatching my hand away. Derek is not allowed to touch me – whether inside or outside the boudoir – unless I tell him to. 'Right,' I back my chair away from the table and stand up, 'let's go.'

As we step out onto the street, Derek clears his throat. 'I hope you don't mind walking a little.'

'Didn't you bring the car?'

'I left it by the flat, actually.'

I rub my hands together. 'No worries. A walk would do me good right now.' We head down Frith Street toward Soho Square. I turn to Derek. 'Don't you see a contradiction between your business and your pleasure? Don't you get tired of splitting yourself in two?'

'Don't you?'

I knead my palm with a thumb, annoyed at myself for this clumsy, self-inflicted breach of my own defences. 'Everyone has two lives,' I say. 'It makes things interesting, at least.'

'Does it?'

'It pays.'

Derek places a conspiratorial hand against his mouth. 'And are you claiming?'

I slow my gait. 'What do you care?'

He shrugs. 'I don't really.'

I pick up the pace again, peering at the brittle steps of St George's, its grimy columns. Beloved St George's. The church is, as ever, a squalid beacon in Centrepoint's shadow – a gathering place for all manner of detritus, human and otherwise. I'm tired, nursing regretful pangs for that luscious square of lasagne I so wantonly stabbed not thirty minutes ago. G & Ts slosh about in my skull, casting soft-edged shadows that oscillate and blur like a Bacon painting. I can almost see the three-dimensional outline of an invisible cubicle building around me.

Trussed

This part of London really is a giant toilet, its denizens no more than turds floating about in its murky waters. And ambling next to me, the biggest turd of all. Amrik asks me why I keep seeing Derek. I'm not sure I can tell him. Not in words he will understand. It certainly isn't to watch Derek writhe at my feet, his flesh lolling. Maybe it's his tears, as plump and yielding as his thighs, that bring me back, week after week. Or hope – hope that one night, I might feel something, compassion even, for a man who needs to be brutalised to feel anything at all.

I remember our first night: Derek's sweating back rippling with welts, me standing over him, shaking inside. And yet, I wasn't as frightened as I'd expected. Nor did I enjoy beating his pale, babyish skin. In fact, I felt nothing, tuning instead into the rhythmic slap of leather upon muscle. I focused on pace and force, recalling years of piano and, later, cello practice. I imagined the notches on a metronome, choosing a different tempo each session. Sometimes I would begin at *andante*, concluding with a breathless *vivace*. Other times I favoured *allegro* throughout, occasionally varying it with an excruciatingly *largo* movement. But always, I end with a crescendo, Derek's tears cadencing my thunderous finale. And through all this, through all the whipping and crying, I am locked into metre and pulse, a staccato figure in a room filled with the stink of unstaved desire.

After that first night, I knew I was not just his punishment; I would be his salvation. As the hours went by, I meditated on the true meaning of the *Magnificat* and I was transformed. When I step into the room, I *am* she that looks forth as the morning, fair as the moon, clear as the sun, and terrible as an army dressed for battle. He is false and wicked, but he will feel my wrath and know truth. He will experience epiphany. And he does. And so he pays me for it. My service is my art. My art is the grace I shower upon him with every thrash of my whip. I purify that stink so that the perfume of truth fills his lungs and spews from his loins.

And yet he pays me a pittance.

We are approaching Queen Square, just minutes from Derek's. I look up at him, wrinkling my brow. 'I know you make quite a bit of money, but how can you afford two flats?'

Derek seems pleased by the query, smiling and winking at me. 'I share it.'

'I see.' I nod. 'So you all have your little bit on the side.'

'Not all. I share with one other guy. It makes things much cheaper.'

'I can imagine.' I yawn as I dig my hands into my pockets. 'By the way,' I say, watching the pavement slide by beneath me, 'do you know anyone who's into boys – men boys, I mean?'

'What? Why?'

'I've got a friend …' I watch two women kissing by the traffic light. One is in a leather jacket and jeans, the other wears a long, flared coat.

'Interested?' Derek prods me.

I roll my eyes. 'Well? Do you?'

'What? Know anyone who's into boys?'

I nod.

'Sure. Do you want me to arrange something?'

We are approaching his flat. 'Maybe. I'll let you know.'

As soon as we're inside, I take my bag and head for the bathroom. Derek catches my arm. 'Hey, wait.' I pull away and he removes his hand. 'I … I thought we could have that joint first.'

I scratch the back of my neck. My head is still swimming with vodka and gin. 'Derek, look, how am I supposed to work if I'm stoned?'

'Don't worry about it. I don't know if I want that tonight.'

I feel a throbbing at my temples and a tremor of rage. 'Why didn't you say that in the first place? Look at how much time you've wasted. Damn it, Derek.'

'Why?' Derek seems surprised. 'What's wrong? You haven't had to pay for anything, have you?'

'That's not the point.' My hands are clenched against my hips. 'This is supposed to be a professional exchange. You're complicating things unnecessarily.'

'What complications have I created?' Derek rubs his chin. 'You'll get your money, don't worry. Why don't you just enjoy the break?'

I stare at Derek, sensing an opportunity. 'All right, all right. But I'm charging you double for this.' I hold my palm out. 'Eighty-five now and the other eighty-five before I leave.'

He blinks at me.

'Well? What are you waiting for? … Now!'

Derek jumps, then shoves a hand into his pocket and brings out his wallet. 'F-fine,' he stammers as he places the bills in my hand. 'F-fair enough.'

I deposit the money in my bag and grin. 'Good boy,' I say, patting him on the cheek. I look at his chin. 'It's still there, you know.'

He frowns. 'What is?'

'The basil, it's been there all night.'

Derek digs a finger into his chin. '*Now* you tell me.' His face darkens. 'You know, sometimes you can be a right – ' He purses and unpurses his lips, struggling to keep in his breath, then lets it out in a huff,' – bitch.'

'It's what you pay me for, darling.' I grin, throwing my bag on the ground. 'So, where's this joint, anyway?'

We pass it back and forth wordlessly. My knees go lax, and my shoulders droop. What would Amrik say to this? I've had free Martinis, dinner and now a joint – *and* I'm getting paid for it – double. 'Too good,' I say out loud, 'too good.'

Derek nods at the smirk on my face. 'Premiere quality, isn't it?'

I give him a wobbly smile. 'Mmm … yeah.' This is so hilarious, I laugh and Derek laughs with me. We're lying on the floor, knees up and swaying from side to side. 'I was expecting my lips to start itching,' I say, pulling at my lips. 'They often do, some allergic reaction.'

Derek giggles. 'I've never heard of that before.'

I roll my eyes toward him. 'Never? But I know loads of people who've had a similar reaction.' No I don't. 'Ok, maybe not loads. But I'm sure there was at least one other person …'

'Vindaloo,' Derek croons, 'Vindaloo, who are you?' I snort. Derek turns over and places his mouth against my ear. 'What's your last name, Vinda?'

Our rules about touch are fast becoming a fiction. This fails to upset me. 'Loo!' I cry, before a wave of high-pitched screeching falls from my lips.

'Shhh, shhh.' Derek clasps a hand over my open mouth. I bite him. 'Ow.' He inhales sharply. 'Mmmm. That was … nmmmm. Please, do it again?' I frown, then grind my teeth into the flesh of his hand until his mouth flies open in silent pain. He lets out shivering moans, then twists the butt of his hand hard against my teeth. I jerk my face to the side. 'Oy!' I gasp, 'get … get your … h-hand … off.'

Derek doesn't move. He stares at me with red-rimmed eyes, swallowing. 'I'm getting pasty,' he says. 'I need some water.' He removes his hand and gets up.

I remain still, trying to catch my breath. I replay the previous scene: Derek forcing his hand against my mouth, wedging its edge against my nostrils. I couldn't breathe. He tried to suffocate me. I know he did. And now I'm thirsty. Derek hands me a glass of water. How does he know I'm thirsty? How long has he been standing there? I reach out for the glass and drink.

Eyes open, I see waves of water rolling toward me. They go down with loud gulps. Derek's face looms like a jellyfish through the bottom of the glass. I close my eyes and keep drinking. When I open them again Derek is lying by my side on the carpet. My anger recedes. I can't remember why I was angry. 'You have a very low ceiling,' I say, blinking at the white space floating above me. It has lost its delineation and seems to hover over us like a slowly falling bedsheet.

'It's not low. It's high. It's a high ceiling,' Derek lifts his arm and points upward.

'It's high, see?'

I squint at him and see that he is balancing the ceiling on the tip of his index finger. I, too, reach my arm up, but feel nothing. 'There's nothing there.' My arm drops. 'Is this real?'

Derek turns over and puts his arm around my waist. 'Everything is real.'

Except the rules, I think. I sigh. 'De Zoysa,' I say, finally.

'What's that?' Derek's breath is dampening the inside of my ear.

'My last name.'

His hand, warm and firm, is lying on my bare stomach; my muscles unnumb beneath it. Closing my eyes, I imagine the path of the hand. It seems to be sliding under my pants and between my breasts at the same time. *Every man.* Blood collects just under my skin. *Every man hath his sword.* His whispers turn to ice in my ears. *Every man.* I want to open my eyes. *Every man hath his sword.* My body goes cold.

I open an eye and see Derek's neck straining above me. With a jerk of my shoulders I try to topple him, but he is too heavy. *Every man.* My lips part with the effort, letting loose a gush of air. *Every man hath his sword.* 'Get off,' *Every man.* 'you bastard.' My voice hits the ceiling and splits into waves. My eyes roll back as he moves into me, slamming the base of my spine against the rug. *Every man hath his sword.*

'Nmmmm ....nmmmmm ....nmmmm,' he is whimpering. Something dribbles into my ear. 'Nmmm ... nmmmm ... nmmmm—'. My face is wet, but I am not crying. *Every man hath his sword.* I am not crying. Derek is weeping, weeping. *Upon his thigh.* I cannot move *upon his thigh.* Every man every man hath his every sword upon his his his.

Darkness. My eyes are open but I cannot see. I blink. Still nothing.

I blink again. The room begins to take shape. Slowly, objects gain definition: a dresser there, a chair here, the end of a bed at my feet. I am on the bed. A chill. Fragments of ice have fused with my spine. My clothes. I am not wearing any. *Every man.* An ache – dull, dislocated – gathers within me like the crimped waistline of a taffeta skirt.

My body is like a block of lead. I am weighted to this bed, chained to it by the hem of a taffetaed wound. *Every man.* I force myself to roll over and throw my legs over the side of the bed. My feet fall into a puddle of clothes. My clothes. Stiff-limbed, I pull my underwear and trousers on. I notice how wrinkled my shirt is and want to iron it. I even glance round the room for the appliance, but find none. I smooth the shirt with my hands, pressing my palms firmly against the sleeves. As I finish dressing, I notice my patent-leather bag by the foot of the bed. A roll of paper protrudes from one of its pockets. I take the roll and smooth it to length, much as I did with my shirt a moment before. It's an envelope. The words 'As promised' are written in a fine hand on its creamy bond surface. In it is exactly eighty-five pounds.

Every man hath his sword. I bite my lip, counting the notes carefully. 'Son of a bitch,' I spit, and fold them into my wallet.

2 Angel

Angel returned with God and Elvis tattooed to the inside of his shades. His complexion was toned with an even coat of foundation so that his eczema remained hidden beneath layers of panty-hose brown. Strapped across his chest was a holster for wallet and keys; a thin, Colonel Sanders tie hung in black prongs from his neck.

For two years he had spent his evenings taking telephone orders for Wilkinson knives, and days selling Electrolux vacuums door to door. Weekends he crooned Elvis tunes at the Pineapple Ring, dressed in black leather jacket and wide-cuffed blue jeans. The morning after he dreamt of walking hand in hand with Elvis through the gates of heaven, Angel walked into the first Catholic church he came across and volunteered to lead the choir.

Sunday mass at Santa Evangelista would never be the same as Angel took its congregation through a tear-inspiring version of 'In the Ghetto'. With quavering throat and arching brows, Angel sang, and people in the church almost forgot the colour of his skin. They closed their eyes against his untamed hair and deep tan, believing instead that the King Himself had seen fit to grace the inside of Santa Evangelista's stained-glass paned precincts. Los Angeles lost Angel when Santa Evangelista closed its doors forever. With a roll of bills in his holster and no alibis, Angel waved gratefully at the steel doors of the church and caught the first flight to Vegas, eventually ending up in London.

At precisely midday, Angel knocked on the door of No.3 Moat Farm Lane, pausing midway to adjust his sunglasses.

'Angelus!' Agnes could not believe her eyes.

Angel bent down to hug his mother. '*Ammi*.'

'Come.' Agnes pulled away quickly, catching a hair in the hinge of Angel's shades. She rubbed her scalp. 'Take off those damn glasses, *men*, this isn't California. Do you see the sun anywhere?'

Angel removed his glasses. 'They're Ralph Lauren, you know.'

'I don't care what Lauren they are. Why didn't you tell me you were coming?' Agnes led Angel into the living room and settled into the burgundy couch by the window. 'How long are you here for?'

Angel curled up next to her. 'I've come back, *Ammi*. I've had enough of America.'

Agnes began massaging his head with her fingertip. '*Ané bolé*,' she sighed. 'Didn't you like your job there?'

'No … no job satisfaction.' Angel rested his head on Agnes' lap and closed his eyes. 'And Santa Eva closed down, so …'

Agnes' finger froze. 'Why? What happened?'

'I don't know. Ran out of money, I guess.' He nudged his mother slightly, reminding her of his needy scalp.

'Did you see Annie before you left?'

'No, no time.' Angel yawned. 'I saw Rita and Mikey, though.'

Agnes frowned. 'Who's this Rita and Mikey? Some new friends?'

'No, *Ammi*. Rita is Annie's girlfriend—'

'*Ay-yo*.' Agnes kissed her teeth. 'God only knows what that child will be like when it gets older.'

Angel laughed. 'He's really cute. Good head of hair – strong and black.'

'Did she tell you who the father is?'

He shrugged. 'Could be anybody, I guess.'

'*Chi!* Dirty girl. Running around like a … like a bloody ….' She paused, losing momentum. 'Still, with a father like that, what can you expect of the children.'

'Uncle Nimal?' Angel grinned. 'He's ok now. I think Padma – his new girlfriend – has really sorted him out. I went to the temple with him—'

'What?' Agnes jerked forward, knocking Angel's head off its roost. 'You went to that cult temple? What for?'

'I had a nice curry. Vegetarian of course. The people there are really nice, *Ammi*.'

'Of course they're nice. You're lucky they didn't try to drug you.'

Angel shook his head. 'Lots of people go to the temple to eat. The food is free as long as you attend the service.'

'Stop. Stop now.' She pinched his ear. 'I don't want to hear any more of your nonsense.' She stopped, drew a finger along his cheek. 'Angel, what's all this on your face?'

He pushed her hand away.

'Go upstairs and wash instead of babbling here like an idiot. Go on.'

Angel slid off the settee and stretched out on the carpet. 'What a long flight,' he sighed. 'I'm glad I'm home for Christmas.' He rolled onto his side, leaning on an elbow and looked at Agnes. 'Otherwise, *Ammi*, I'd have had a very blue Christmas without you.'

Agnes blushed. 'What Christmas? It's only November.'

Angel leapt up onto his feet, drawling out 'Blue Christmas'. He circled his mother, singing and holding a hand out to her, then trotted from the room, the words still flowing from his lips.

Upstairs, Angel came flush against a locked bathroom door. Before he could knock, the door swung open. Wrapped in a thick towel and dripping watery sequins onto the carpet was Vinda. Her eyes widened. His mouth fell open. She yelped. He whistled. She slammed the door. He closed his eyes.

She emerged a moment later, smiling. 'You scared the shit out of me,' she said, slapping him on the shoulder. 'When did you bloody get in?'

'About half an hour ago.' He tugged on the hem of her towel.

'Stop it, you pig.' Vinda tightened the knot at her armpit as she hurried toward her room.

Angel followed. 'Someone's been going to the gym.'

'So, what of it?'

Angel shrugged. 'Still, nothing beats those California girls.' He was several paces inside the room.

'Pee off, will you?'

'Excellent calves.'

Vinda glared at him.

'Ok, I'm going.' Angel backed away.

Vinda squinted at the stubble on his cheeks. 'By the way,' she grinned, 'don't bother looking for any Neet; I don't use that stuff any more.'

'Neither do I.'

'Oh,' Vinda raised her brows, 'graduated to Immac have we? And what's that on your face? A little Clinique, perhaps?'

Angel sneered, ignoring her last comment. 'I use razors, like everyone else. Gillette if you must know.'

'We are a big boy, aren't we?' Vinda sat on the edge of the bed and crossed her legs. 'Try not to cut yourself too much.'

Angel shivered, his eyes wandering from knee to ankle over Vinda's shins. 'Asma—'

'—Vinda—'

'Asma, do you have a razor I can borrow?'

Vinda threw a pink Bic at him.

'Thanks.' Angel strolled out of her room, clasping the razor to his chest.

Despite the steamy mirror, Angel patiently wound licks of hair around his fingers, coaxing them into a coherent set of curls. His chin and neck were blotted with flecks of tissue; the pink Bic lay in a bed of suds at the bottom of the sink. Angel opened his mouth. *'We're caught in a trap. I can't walk out.'* He thrust his pelvis toward the sink, and snapped his fingers into a point. *'Because I love you too much babé.'* There was a knock. He turned and pointed toward the door. *'Why can't you see? What you're doing to me?'* A voice called from the other side. 'Angel? Aren't you finished, yet? Hurry up!' Angel closed his eyes. *'When you don't believe a word I—'* There was a loud banging on the door before it flew open, catapulting Vinda against the sink '—*say.'*

Vinda pushed Angel aside and lurched toward the toilet. 'Go,' she gasped as she leaned over the bowl. Angel quickly left the bathroom, closing the door behind him. He turned away, then thought better of it and placed an ear against the door. There were whimpers followed by a loud retching 'arghhh'. He frowned, shaking his head.

Back in his room, Angel resumed grooming himself. Standing in front of the mirror, he put the final touches to his hair, then rubbed dollops of emollient into his skin, pausing to massage in a little cortisone where it was needed. Finally, he applied a thin film of brown cream to his cheeks and forehead, evening the tone of his face. He took a breath and surveyed his reflection. He was ready now. It was time.

He turned to his suitcase which, until this moment, had remained untouched, by his bed. Freshly bathed, he now allowed himself to open the case. In it lay his precious cargo: the object that had unleashed everything and vindicated everything at the same time. He put out a trembling hand and touched its cool nylon covering. His heart raced as he pictured it nestled beneath the thin tarp. Already, he could read its topography with his fingertips. Not yet, he thought. Not yet. He picked it up and placed it gently – so gently – in the cupboard.

He unpacked the rest of his things, concluding the exercise by placing a framed print of Elvis on his dresser. The King's smile, so broad and deep and sincere, took everything with it. It was as if his eyes, his cheeks, even his hair, were all swirling out of that smile, reaching out to Angel and pulling him into its vortex.

Angel basked inside the smile, engulfed by its loamy embrace. Something sweet and mellow rose in his stomach. Everything would be all right. That's what the smile kept saying to him, whispering in its soft, Tupelo accent. Boy, it said, it's all gonna be OK.

Angel was grateful for the opportunity he'd had to go to Memphis. True, he'd had little time, had almost missed his London flight, in fact. But the few hours he'd spent there – those few hours at Graceland, felt like home. He felt like he'd come home. Like all those years before had been empty – the aimless wanderings of a prodigal son. But walking in Memphis, with the one thing that would save him tucked under his arm, Angel knew he had been chosen. Elvis had chosen him. Everything else was illusory, meaningless.

It was late when Angel knocked on Vinda's door. 'Asma?' He knocked again and let himself in. Vinda was lying face down on her bed.

'Are you all right?'

She didn't move. Angel sat on the floor, his back against the side of her bed. 'Hard night at the pub?' He chuckled. 'I bet *Ammi* gave you a right telling off when you got in. What happened? Did you mix drinks? You wally.'

Vinda groaned.

He angled his head up and to the side. She hadn't moved. 'Hair of the dog, that's what you need. And some Panadol. Or Horlicks. How about some Horlicks?'

'Nn-mm.'

Angel sighed. 'So what was it all in honour of? Was it a work do or something?'

Trussed

Vinda blew gusts into the mattress. With a great effort, she rolled onto her side and looked at Angel. 'Work do?'

Surprised by the clarity of the two words, Angel swung round and stared at her. Her face was red and creased by the quilt, and there were tears at the corners of her eyes. 'Yeah, a work DO. Night out with the office crowd. That sort of thing.'

Vinda took a long breath and shifted onto her back. 'No ... work ... do,' she said softly. 'No ... work ... period.'

Angel nodded slowly, thrusting out his lower lip. 'No work yet, Asma?'

Vinda closed her eyes.

'Ah well.' Angel stretched out his left arm, letting it rest on the mattress. 'It's always hard to find work. But listen. Where'd you go last night? Was it a party?'

No reply. Vinda lay silently, eyeballs twitching beneath closed lids. Angel thought she might have fallen asleep. His eyes roamed her walls, pausing here and there to take in a picture or unusual fixture. Above the length of her bed was a large print of some ghoulish crucifixion, like something out of *Aliens*. And above the headboard, two postcards of what looked like Japanese inks: details from Oscar Wilde's *Salomé*, Vinda had once explained to him, drawn by Aubrey – or was it Audrey? – Beardsley.

Angel was fascinated by the second image: Salomé floating above a pool of black water, John the Baptist's severed head clasped in her hands like a lily. The bitch, he thought. Evil, scheming bitch. The postcards were arranged one above the other, and next to them hung a two-pronged candle holder, its copper oxidized to a cool, minty blue. But dominating the room, though it was across from the bed and not immediately noticeable when you walked in, was a set of shelves crammed full of books. Several dictionaries lined the top shelf, including an Anglo-Saxon/English dictionary, accompanied by two ponderous Norton anthologies. There were books on art, evolution, a few studies on Buddhism and reams of fiction. Angel shook his head. Ever since he knew her, Asma had had her nose screwed into a book.

'It was a mad night,' said Vinda, finally. Angel jumped. 'Mad. Met up with some mates and one pint led to another.' She paused. 'Then two pints led to a G & T and some tequila and whiskey and—' she clutched her stomach. 'Mad,' she whispered.

Angel chuckled softly. 'You know, after living in North America for a few years, you lot over here look like a bunch of alcoholics to me.'

'Oh come on,' said Vinda. 'You were in LA. There must have been clouds of cocaine out there – blizzards even.'

Angel shook his head vigorously. 'Coke? No way. Not me, anyway.'

'Yeah, right.' Vinda squinted hard at Angel. He looked sheepish. She rolled her eyes. 'No worries. As long as you're not sporting a long pinky nail and your nasal cavities are intact, I won't be telling anyone.'

Angel laughed. 'I didn't do it often. Only a few times. Parties and all.'

'Whatever.'

They were silent for a moment, and Angel continued to scan Vinda's bookshelves. The thick, gold spine of *A Suitable Boy* caught his eye. '*Thathi* is still up,' he murmured, almost to himself. 'He's watching the cricket.'

Vinda snorted. 'Cricket my arse. He's usually watching blue movies round about now.' She lolled her head from side to side. 'He's expert with the remote.'

Angel grinned. 'So the old man is still at it then.'

Vinda sat up in the bed. 'Remember when he used to 'read' the Bible downstairs while we watched videos?' Angel laughed. 'The only things pointing at the pages were his glasses. His eyes were always well into the telly.'

'Yeah, *Ammi* always used to shout at him.'

'She still does.'

'Not tonight though, she's gone to bed.'

'Then it's up to us.' Vinda's eyes flashed. 'Shall we see what the old man is up to?'

Angel and Vinda crept down the stairs, moving slowly so as not to be spied from the sitting room. They crawled on hands and knees through the corridor, sinking low to avoid Uncle Aloy's twitching eyes. There was no need to worry. Uncle Aloy was immersed in the women on the screen, bathing in the blue glow of their naked bodies.

'So what was the score, *Thathi*?' Angel stood up quickly by the side of the couch.

Uncle Aloy reached instinctively for the remote control, but stopped short. 'Anh. You're here. I was just switching channels.'

'Oh really?' Vinda strolled over and sat next to her uncle.

'You too?' Uncle Aloy's eyes widened. 'Here, Angelus. Come *men* and tell me what this is? I was just switching the channels and suddenly I came to this. There are three girls here, and I don't know what they're trying to do. No knickers even.'

Vinda stifled a giggle.

Uncle Aloy continued to scrutinise the screen. 'Now see, that one with the light hair. She had a boyfriend. The black-haired one is in love with the other one. Now they all work in the same doctor's office, and he is in love with the black-haired one. He just went out for a minute, and now all of these young nurses are kissing each other in his office. What is the meaning of this?'

Vinda crossed her arms. 'I thought you said you were just switching channels.'

Uncle Aloy turned to her. 'I was.'

'Then how come you know the whole plot of the film?'

Angel patted his father on the knee. 'Come on. Why can't you just admit you were watching a blue movie?'

'I?' Uncle Aloy was incredulous. 'Blue movie?' He looked from Vinda to Angel with ever-widening eyes. 'I?'

Vinda couldn't resist and let out a bellyshaking laugh.

Uncle Aloy grabbed her thigh firmly. 'Here, keep it down, *men*, I don't want you to disturb my wife.'

Vinda immediately clamped her mouth as Angel ran to shut the door to the sitting room. She took a deep breath, quelling the rising laughter. 'Sorry,' she whispered. 'Mind if we join you?' Angel sat next to his father, so that Uncle Aloy was sandwiched between son and niece.

'Anh. But this is dirty *men*, we can't watch this with my niece here.'

Vinda rolled her eyes. 'Why not? Can't I have a laugh as well?' She winked over her uncle's head at Angel.

'Yeah,' said Angel, winking back at Vinda, 'she might be able to explain things which I can't … so—'

Uncle Aloy nodded gravely. 'Ok, ok, now be quiet. I think the doctor fellow is coming back. My God, look! What is he doing to her? And what are they doing to him? That blondie is holding a false member. Anh, like those ancient Greeks, no? And—' Uncle Aloy took in a sharp breath. '—My God *men*, see where she is putting it, will you?' Uncle Aloy began to giggle. 'Is he a homosexual then?'

'No *Thathi*,' Angel shook his head, 'I think some men like to have—'

'—What?' Uncle Aloy sat up in his seat. 'But it must give the chaps haemorrhoids, no? Dirty buggers.'

'Shh,' Angel admonished his father, 'look.'

Uncle Aloy studied the bodies on the screen intently, twisting his head forty-five degrees to either side. He watched as two women (Blondie and a ginger-haired one) used the 'false member' on one another. 'Hooo!' he cried, unable to contain his mirth. 'They have become experts. Do you think they are really—'

'What's all this?' It was Agnes Aunty. She was standing by the door, television still out of sight, staring at the guilty trio. Her nostrils were flaring. Angel fumbled for the remote which was wedged on Vinda's side beneath Uncle Aloy's right buttock. Vinda pulled at it desperately, but her uncle had frozen at the sight and sound of his wife. Agnes Aunty took a step toward them – seconds away from seeing the screen. Vinda nudged the old man again. 'Uncle Aloy,' she whispered harshly, 'come on, move.' Angel's father stared helplessly at his wife. She took another step. Vinda jabbed her uncle's behind. A moan echoed from the television set, and Agnes Aunty swung her head toward it. Uncle Aloy shifted his buttocks.

'Cricket?' Agnes Aunty stared at the figures in white, running almost gently toward one another, arms reaching out to the ball. 'You and your bloody cricket. What is this? Can't you get to bed in time? It's nearly two o'clock, and you have to get up at six to go to work.' She turned to Angel. 'You.' She jabbed a finger at him. 'Don't encourage your father this way, hanh?' Relieved, Uncle Aloy leaned toward Angel. The screen immediately bloomed with a bouquet of nude buttocks and rasping breaths. Vinda grabbed the now freed remote and flicked the power button just as Agnes Aunty turned to leave the room. 'You people are mad.' She threw a glance at the blackened TV set. 'Now get to bed – all of you!'

Imperial Mini Cabs was little more than a bombed out Chinese take-away: the receptionist sat behind a singed counter taking bookings and giving fares. Behind her a door led into a makeshift kitchen replete with kettle, toaster, fridge, sink and wooden table. Angel had been back in London just one week, but he'd already managed to find work. The morning after his mother had almost caught his dad, Asma and him watching porn – the very morning after he'd arrived, in fact – he had found himself at Imperial, signing up for shifts that ran from 4pm to 4am four days a week. His approach to the job was functional – a way of getting out of the house and beyond the eye of suspicion. At the same time, he hustled for a better job. To keep his voice well-oiled, he sang while waiting for fares, and if they didn't mind, while taking them as well. It was during a particularly inspired rendition of 'Love Me Tender', that Angel met Carla.

Shiromi Pinto

'But you sing so nicely,' she whispered, as they drove up Essex Road. 'Where did you learn?'

Angel smiled. 'Nowhere. Everywhere. I've been singing since I was very young.'

Carla looked surprised. 'But you should sing in a club or something like that,' she said, shaking her head. 'You must not waste a talent like that. It would be a … well, it would be a *seen*.'

The way she said *sin* made Angel shift in his seat. He felt the stressed *i* insinuate itself into his lower belly. He stared at her through the rear-view mirror. 'Where are you from?' he asked, studying her short, curly brown hair and full lips. 'Your accent sounds European.'

'Guess.'

'Portuguese?'

She shook her head.

'Spanish?' He felt sweat building up in the creases of his neck.

She shook her head again and laughed. 'No, no. Of course not. Italian. Was it so difficult?'

Angel sighed with relief. 'Of course, Italian.' He grinned. 'Yes. It should have been obvious.' He drew his sleeve across his throat, wiping away the dampness. 'I'm Angel, by the way.'

Her smile widened. 'Angel?' She lowered her gaze to her lap. 'I'm Carla,' she said finally, 'I'm so pleased to meet you, Angel.'

They turned onto Aberdeen Road in silence. Darkened, tree-fringed houses lined the way.

'The third one up on the left.' Angel slowed in front of a red-brick Georgian house. He felt his heart throbbing as he turned to collect his fare. Carla handed him exactly seven pounds and paused. 'You must be tired.' She looked him straight in the eyes. 'You should come in for a drink. Perhaps an espresso?'

Angel hesitated for a moment over the wheel. 'Your flatmates must be asleep. I shouldn't.'

Carla giggled. 'Flatmates? Why should I have flatmates?'

'Oh, um …' Angel chewed his lip. 'I shouldn't have assumed.'

'When does your shift end?'

Angel glanced at the clock. It was 4.15. 'Uh … well … that would be now, actually.' He could feel his chest thumping.

'So then?' Carla had one leg out of the car. 'Are you coming?'

He drew his lips into an exaggerated 'o' and let out a quick breath. 'Ok, sure. Why not?'

Angel found himself sipping espresso in a pristine, white-tiled kitchen. He stared at the enamel sink and pine cupboards, and thought of Venice Beach. Only a month ago he had basked by the North Pacific, trying to calculate the distance between himself and the next chunk of land. He sighed, thinking of the sun and space, but shook it away as the spires of Santa Evangelista appeared in his blue sky. He scanned the kitchen again and realised that Carla was not there.

She had said something about 'the loo', but Angel had been too distracted by the blood welling in his ears to hear much more. She had just finished pouring coffee into two miniature cups when she turned to look at him. Angel saw her mouth open, saw it flare at the edges, preparing for speech. But he heard almost nothing. Each time Carla's lips moved, lust and panic crackled in his chest sending blood thrashing through his body like a mob of desperate groupies. Her lips, as fragile and full as the peeled segments of an orange, overwhelmed him.

He was relieved when she left the room, felt himself receding, falling gently back into the rhythmic waves that sloughed the shores of Venice Beach. But that had been about twenty minutes ago – enough time for Angel to lose himself in watery thought – and she had still not returned.

'Carla?' he whispered, stepping into the hallway. He frowned and continued down the corridor, into the sitting room.

Even in the darkness he could appreciate the design and layout of the space. Two chairs, one straight-backed, the other reclining, sat beneath an enormous window. Geraniums, aloe vera, cyclamen, creeping ivy and various ferns framed the window, sometimes spilling onto armrests. A pale and inviting settee was placed with its back to the door, facing the now bluing sky. 'Ca—,' he tried again and stopped. A lock of hair appeared over the edge of the settee. He approached the curl and peeked over it at the head below. He could see Carla's thighs, round and covered by gray tracksuit bottoms. Her feet, stretched forward, were swathed in red socks and crossed at the ankles. Angel walked around the front of the couch. He felt an itch rising along his hairline. Carla was unbearably still.

In the dim light, he looked at her lips, still as potent and delicate as citrus. And below her right nostril, a red thread cut a clean line from cheek to ear. Angel pulled back in horror.

'Oh shit.' He rubbed his hands. 'Oh my God. Ok, calm down.' He took two deep breaths, patting his chest. He crouched at her feet and looked directly up her nostrils. 'Carla,' he whispered. 'Carla—,' he covered his face.

This was the last thing he needed. A dead woman and him – a stranger – found by her side, his fingerprints all over her kitchen. Now he would definitely be caught, no longer just a thief but a murderer, too.

'Oh shit shit shit shit SHIT.'

Carla opened her eyes. She blinked and smiled. 'Angel—'

Angel gasped and dropped his hands. 'Carla?' He leaned toward her and put his hands on her knees. 'Carla are you all right?'

She lifted her head. 'Oh yes. Yes. I'm so sorry, Angel. I fell asleep.'

Angel shook his head. 'But—?'

'I had a nose bleed—' Angel noticed a tissue crumpled in her left hand and sighed. '—and I just sat down for a moment until it stopped, and I fell …' she laughed. 'I'm so sorry.'

'It's ok.' Angel grinned. 'I'm just glad you're ok.' His eyes fell on her gray sweatered thighs. 'I'd better go now.'

'Did you like your espresso?' Carla dabbed at her cheek.

'It's dry. You need some water.' Angel stared at the red line. It was so sharp and straight. He wondered how heavy the drop must have been. How steep the angle of her head. He shook himself. 'I should go. It's late.'

Carla looked at him. 'You really want to go? I have been very rude, haven't I?'

'No, not at all.'

Her eyes were open and he was falling into them. He felt the *i* of her *'seen'* flinch and curl in his intestines. 'Your place is charming,' he heard himself say. He saw now that he was kneeling in front of her, his hands resting on her inner thighs. She tilted her head back and closed her eyes. Her knees parted a fraction. Angel's fingers worked up between them to her hips. Her breath quickened and she let out a little sigh. Angel untied the knot of her trousers and pulled them down gently with her socks. He kissed her knees, his fingers already slipping through elastic, and glanced up to see sunlight breaking over her chin.

The first thing Angel saw when he woke up was his wallet. Snug in its holster, it sat propped against his jeans by the bed, neatly bisected by a shaft of sunlight. While trying to recapture his dream of Elvis, Angel inadvertently opened his eyes and caught sight of its leather lip. He half-expected Carla to be there with him. But he knew he had left her on the couch, in her living room, sleeping beneath a red-checked blanket.

He sighed. He couldn't remember leaving Aberdeen Road. Driving west. Falling asleep in the car in front of his house. Dragging himself up the stairs an hour later, spilling his clothes as he crossed the threshold of his bedroom, and finally collapsing in his bed. He didn't know what day it was, let alone the time. But at that moment, he knew something wasn't quite right. He should have been basking in contentment – after all, Carla had been unexpectedly obliging. Instead, he felt something like guilt. Not exactly guilt, but the shadow of it, casting a gloom across his spent loins.

He pulled a forearm over his brow in an attempt to keep the sun from fading his mind's sketch of the King. It was no use. Santa Evangelista loomed in the background, as did a pneumatic, dark-haired Theresa. Theresa. Now there was a woman with an amazing voice. When she and Angel sang, the congregation went into rapture. Sunday services brimmed with Christian and non-Christian alike, such was the pull of their crooning. There was something deliciously forbidden about the way they belted out their hymns. If the *Kyrie* was inspired, then the *Alleluia* was almost sinful in its evocation of blissful relief. So it was best that no one knew how Theresa knelt in the confessional with Angel behind her and muffled her voice with her sleeves.

Theresa. Angel couldn't help the regret now washing over him. It was she who had welcomed him the day he walked into Santa Eva. She who had led him up to the choir, knowing nothing about him except perhaps that he looked 'touched'. She who later organised the choir practices and – coincidentally – oversaw the service collections. She who instructed Angel in all of this and more. For they did not, as some would assume, make love in the confessionals after hours. Theresa was too good, too pure for that. She knelt with Angel behind her in prayer. Thrilled at the touch of his groin against her backside. And never allowed a movement to betray her desire. Then.

With voices like molasses, Angel and Theresa seduced their listeners, trapping them like ants in sticky, sensuous notes. And, as their moments in the confessional grew longer and longer, Angel took to seducing Theresa. At first he only leaned, casually and with pure intent, into her ample behind.

'Holy Mother of God,' he would whisper, and she would reply, 'Pray for us.' On another day he bent low so that his lips were against her ear. 'St Louis de Montfort,' he said. 'Pray for us,' she replied. Still a week later he kissed her gently on the nape of her neck. 'St Anthony of Padua,' he breathed.

Theresa's resolve crumbled.

Eventually the confessional was too small to contain their lust. They took to the choir loft, the basement, the vestry. And in time, Theresa handed responsibility of collections – including chequebook and safe – to Angel. And what collections. Angel and Theresa's fame spread far and wide, resulting in significant revenue for Santa Eva. Forget the bake sales and Christmas bazaars, Sunday services made a killing with Angel's Elvis tunes and the couple's hymns. For the first time in a long time, bills (and not just of the one dollar variety) outnumbered coins in the collection baskets. Oh yes. Business was looking good, and Theresa talked of donating fifty per cent to the Christian Children's Fund. But Angel saw things differently. It wasn't that there was anything intrinsically wrong with donating to the CCF. It was just that so much of this new-found wealth had been encouraged by him. By his voice.

The answer was obvious. Of course Angel didn't trouble Theresa with his conclusions. They kept meeting in the vestry or the church basement, or, if nostalgia came into the picture, the confessional. And Angel kept collecting and multiplying and singing. And one night, after leaving Theresa in the confessional, Angel stole into the vestry, opened the safe, and wrote himself a cheque (under the name of Santa Eva) for most of the money in the collection account. In the expenditure ledger, he wrote: 'Christian Children's Fund (cash donation),' then returned to the confessional to make love to Theresa for the last time.

The next day he withdrew the money, dropped by the CCF and handed over a fifth of it – two hundred thousand dollars – then made his way to the airport to catch the first flight to Vegas. That was his mistake. But it didn't matter. He made it to Memphis and then London in spite of everything.

And now, with his nose buried in the crook of his arm, Angel felt something like regret. Not for the money, of course. Money was money. It was his right, really. Proper recognition for services rendered. And anyway, that money went towards a higher purpose. Higher even than the CCF. No. The regret he felt was for Theresa. Theresa of good heart. Theresa of true intentions. Theresa of passionate song and desire. He didn't love her, but he did admire her. And in some ways Carla, with those big eyes and silent sighs, reminded him of her.

In spite of himself, he began to compare the two women. Personality. Theresa he knew more about: strong, sensual, smart, sexy. Carla: silent, enigmatic, passionate, direct. Face. Both beautiful, though Theresa more conventionally so. Body. Angel lingered on this one. Theresa was round, full-figured, strong – but not in a gym and aerobics way. Her legs were muscular from walking, her arms honed by years of waxing and polishing church pews by hand. Theresa would have been happiest as a mountaineer, thundering across ranges with operatic force. Carla was small. Silent and wide-eyed as a fish. A swimmer with small, demanding breasts. And a mole – almost an extra nipple – tucked into the crease of her upper ribcage, like a spare button sewn into a shirt hem.

A door slammed. Carla's mole evaporated as did visions of Theresa's languid eyes. A groan came from the bathroom forcing Angel toward his door. Turning the handle quietly, he peeked into the hallway to see Vinda stumbling toward her room. 'Asma?' Vinda looked up. Her face was pale, her eyes red. 'It's Vinda,' she croaked, then lurched into her room muttering, 'How many times do I have to tell you people?' She flung the door shut.

'*Mé*. What is all this banging?' It was Agnes Aunty shouting up the stairs. 'You two behave like hooligans. Sleeping until God knows what hour. No decent jobs even. I don't …' Her voice trailed off.

Angel tiptoed across the hall into Vinda's room. Without a noise he slipped into the bed and snuggled up to his cousin.

'Eh, get off me,' Vinda whispered hoarsely. 'What do you think you're doing?'

Angel pulled Vinda closer to him. 'Just tell me what's wrong.'

She heaved and jerked him away. 'Please. Don't squeeze me like that.'

'Aw, you used to love it when I did that. Remember? We used to have a cuddle all the time.'

Vinda glowered at him. 'Look, not now, ok? I'm not feeling so great, and squeezing me isn't going to improve things.'

Angel relaxed his grip. 'Ok. Sorry.' He rolled onto his back. 'Another heavy night out?'

Vinda turned toward the wall. 'Yeah, something like that.'

Angel crooked his head toward Vinda. 'You know, you need to slow down a bit. Otherwise you'll end up with a beer gut and bloated thighs. No man'll have you, then.'

Vinda jabbed a heel into Angel's shin. 'Shut up, Angel, or I'll kick you right out of here.'

He frowned. 'Look, I'm just telling it like it is. You're turning into an alcoholic.'

Vinda sighed, tipping onto her back. 'It's none of your damn business, Angel.' She cocked her head to the side and looked at him carefully. A smile creased her face. '*You* look like something's jumped into your pants. Who is it?'

Angel raised his brows. 'No one really. I don't know her. She was a fare. Can't even remember her name.'

'Bollocks.'

'No, really. She invited me in.'

'And you went?'

'Yeah, what else could I do? She invited me. And she had this sexy Italian accent. And she offered me espresso. I mean ...'

'Oh well, if she offered you an espresso, then—'

Angel laughed. 'Yeah, she made a nice espresso.'

'So what happened?'

'She's got a nice place. Really nice. I wonder what she does for a living.' He paused. Vinda gave him a nudge. 'Anyway.' He stopped again.

Vinda cleared her throat. 'Yes?'

'Sorry, I was just thinking. She's got … I don't know how to describe it, Asma—'

'—Vinda—'

'—She's got these amazing eyes. It's not the colour. It's … It's like you get lost in them.' Angel closed his eyes. 'It's almost scary – how everything happens in her eyes. The rest of her is quiet, you know? But her eyes – they're like … you know when you dive into water and there's that foamy bit on top? Well it's that – that foamy bit, but it's also the bit just before. That bit when you actually hit the water and everything sort of shatters. It's both – one sort of flowing into the other. And she hasn't said anything – hasn't even opened her mouth. But you know. You *know*.'

Vinda shifted onto her side and propped her head in the palm of her hand. 'Wow. A real black magic woman. I'd watch out if I were you.'

'Yeah … I won't be seeing her again.'

'No—oh, look, I was only joking. Why not?'

'It was a bit of fun, Vinda. Nothing special. Anyway, she didn't even give me a tip.'

Vinda looked disgusted.

'Before. I mean before, you know? She only paid the fare. No tip.'

'Don't be an idiot, Angel.' Vinda slapped his arm. 'She gave you one hell of a tip. You're being stupid.'

'Whatever.' Angel stared at the ceiling. Vinda followed his gaze. They lay like that for a while, blinking and thinking, listening to the clock ticking by the bed.

'So what's her name?' Vinda broke the silence.

'Carla.'

Vinda giggled. 'So you do remember her name then?'

'Yeah, so?'

'So?' She sighed. 'Nothing, I guess. Nothing at all.'

The telephone rang. Angel bounded from the bed to Vinda's

phone. He picked it up before the second ring. 'Hello?' He heard the sound of breathing, then the phone went dead.

'Who was it?' Vinda was sitting up.

'I don't know.' Angel ran a hand through his hair.

Vinda swung her legs over the side of the bed. 'Well, what are you waiting for? Dial 1471 before the damn thing rings again.'

'1471?'

'To trace it, idiot.' She made a grab for the phone, but Angel had already dialled the number. He glanced up at Vinda and motioned for a pen. She shoved a pencil toward him.

'0181 272 3545. Mean anything to you?'

Vinda's face skewed into a wrinkle. 'Nothing. You?'

Angel shrugged. He crumpled the piece of paper and tossed it in the bin.

'Right,' said Vinda, 'it's time for you to get out of my room.'

'Why?'

'I've got to change my clothes.'

'So?'

Vinda stared at Angel. He ambled toward her, and pulled at her T-shirt. 'Come on As—Vinda.' He winked. 'For the hell of it. You know.'

Vinda slapped his hand. 'You'll end up in hell, if you're not careful. What is wrong with you? Go find your Carla, if you're so horny, and leave me alone.'

He shrugged. 'Are you jealous?'

Vinda cast a stern look at Angel. 'Jealous? No. I just don't fancy a shag right now. Particularly not with you. Is that all right?'

Angel's eyes widened. 'You are jealous. I can tell. Your nostrils are flaring.'

'Fuck off Angel. I told you, I'm not in the mood. And even if I was, I wouldn't be doing it with you.' She pushed him toward the door. 'Now go. NOW.'

Exiled to the hallway, Angel made his way back to his bedroom. He tried to recall the telephone number. Was it Carla? Had he given her his number? Or was it someone else? He cast a glance at his cupboard. The doors were still closed, sealed. Sweat broke out across his back. His eyelids and earlobes prickled, beckoning him to itch. Angel resisted, knowing that even the smallest drag of a nail over the skin would set off a trail of pin pricks that would criss-cross his scalp and run down his neck. He had given in before, delighting in the scratching, digging his nails deeper and deeper until mucus and then blood pearled on his skin. But until then the euphoria would be intoxicating, building in his brain like an orgasm, forcing his eyes to roll back.

Angel ignored it, trying instead to focus on the telephone call. He wished he hadn't thrown the piece of paper away. He thought of trying to trace the call again, but decided against it. What if it *had* been Carla? He really didn't want to see her. Not yet anyway. His mind was too full of Theresa. And finding gigs.

This was a matter for concern. He hadn't sung in weeks now – not since the Pineapple Ring over a month ago – and then he'd gone and got himself arrested two weeks later. All because he wanted to be closer to Him. And now that link with The King was falling away. He cleared his throat. *'We're caught in a trap ...'* It was no use. Singing in his bedroom just wasn't enough. He needed a stage. He needed lights. He needed an audience.

He examined himself in the mirror. His face was full of stubble, his hair standing up, his teeth unbrushed. He was a mess. Today was his day off. He resolved to shave, shower and book a gig by the end of the day. And maybe, just maybe, find Carla.

3 LAX—LHR

He was sweating. The seat was cramped, and the child next to him, blonde and cherubic, had just farted. Regis didn't like kids. He couldn't imagine what this particular child, a four-year-old girl with pigtails, had eaten to cause such a stink. He clutched at his nose, trying to breathe in as little as possible, then felt an annoying tickle somewhere around his neck. Reaching into his pocket, Regis broke out a fresh handkerchief, mopped his brow, and dug a nail into his collarbone. He sat there for a good minute, searching out the itch, pinching it, extracting it like a splinter from a thumb. The lady in the aisle opposite flashed him a reproachful glare. He ignored her.

Five more hours, he thought to himself. Five more hours, breathing in this cabin air now polluted with the insides of a living Barbie doll. It was all too much for him. He punched the little button with the stick-person icon on it, scrawled something onto a piece of paper, and within minutes, a smiling stewardess was bending toward him. 'A rum and Coke and a large glass of water please,' he said quietly, then cleared his throat and pushed the piece of paper toward her. She looked down, her green eyes darting across the perfectly formed letters, then nodded and was gone. Two minutes later she and a colleague were striding down the plane's aisles, leaving a lemon-scented spray in their wake.

Regis sipped at his rum and Coke, trying hard not to look at his watch. He examined what looked like fine white powder on the backs of his hands: dry skin. He felt himself dehydrating, felt his eyeballs shrinking in their sockets. He put down his drink and picked up the water instead. Some six hours had elapsed since he'd left LA. And exactly six weeks since he'd left Audrey. He sighed, rubbing a hand along the back of his head, feeling the bristles prick his palm. Audrey Kim with her short bob and short legs and expert manipulation of seaweed and glutinous rice. He had left her in their Burbank apartment wound in white sheets next to a shaggy-haired surfer named Finnegan. When he found them crouched against one another, deep in sleep, he thought his skin would fall off. Without a word, he closed the door quietly, wrote a note to Audrey which he blue-tacked to the bathroom mirror, and left. He spent the night in a bar in North Hollywood, staring into a single glass of rum and Coke. He blamed himself.

When he returned to the apartment she was gone – her clothes, her creams, her hand-blown glass bong – everything was gone. The bed had been stripped, the place aired out. It was as if she had never been there. Regis slumped on the couch, felt embers in his eyes. Through the pale, muslin curtains – the one thing she had left behind – the sun shone unbearably bright. He stared at the little cactus across from him, rising plumply from a white porcelain pot. And then it happened. Everything around him cracked like ice, splintered into jewelled fragments, glinting shards. Regis' head fell back against the sofa. His chest tightened, rocketed with spasms. And tears spilled over the tops of his big cheeks, into his ears, down his sideburns, into his collar.

' … with this, sir?'

Regis looked up to see a row of white teeth. He blinked, creased his forehead, blinked again.

Trussed

The stewardess motioned toward his hands. 'Your drink, sir. Shall I take it?'

Regis followed her gaze to the near-empty cup on his fold-out table. He was confused. He couldn't recall drinking that much. But there it was, just a millimetre of rust-brown liquid remaining in its plastic depths. He picked up the cup mechanically and handed it to the stewardess. 'Thanks.'

'How about some bourbon creams?' She proffered a foil packet of biscuits. He took them, smiling. She seemed nice, whatever her name was. He shrugged. It was her job to be nice.

Reaching inside his jacket pocket, Regis withdrew an old Discman. He slipped a CD – Tupac's *Makaveli* – into place, then leaned back and drew a deep breath. The air had finally cleared. To Regis, the CD was a triumph. He'd managed to pick one up within a week of its release, despite the anxious, occasionally hysterical, hordes. It was Tupac's last recording – a brilliantly timed, posthumous release. Regis shook his head, extracting a cookie from the neat packet on his lap. He had been in Vegas with Audrey just a week after Tupac's murder – stayed at the Luxor, in fact. He, Audrey, Finn and a girl called Darla had booked two pyramid suites months before the attack. They could hardly cancel. In spite of the pall that had fallen over Vegas – slight, almost unnoticeable – they had had a brilliant time.

The Luxor was unreal: a gleaming, glass pyramid rising from the desert. Boarding the hotel tram, Audrey, Finn, Darla and Regis sat back and ogled as it rolled through the paws of a replica Sphinx, one of the Luxor's many entrances. Tiled walls and sweeping halls left them speechless. They felt dwarfed by the hotel's stature and opulence. Serious gamers headed straight for the tables, but Regis and his friends were happiest sipping champagne, chilling in the jacuzzi. One night, they got drunk and squeezed into one tub, Audrey and Darla sitting on Regis and Finn's laps.

'So Darla,' slurred Finn, 'was your mother, like, a fan of, like, the *Little Rascals*, or what?'

Darla's face screwed up to match her auburn curls. 'And what does that make you, Finnegan? Alfalfa?'

Finn was undeterred. 'Sure,' he smirked, aiming a mischievous wink at Audrey. ''Cept my spike ain't made of hair, and it sure as hell ain't sticking out of my head.'

Everyone had laughed. Ever since he had known him, Finn had always been the crude one. Regis was the large, quiet teddy bear. They were an odd pair, Finn and Regis: one blonde, the other bald; one wiry, the other thickset and huge. They met years ago in Malaga Cove. Regis had been trying to photograph a seal; Finn, with surfboard upright, was surveying the waves. They started talking about seals and SLRs, and later they met for a beer and admired the passing women. It was an easy friendship, relaxed and uncomplicated. When Regis started dating Audrey, Finn was always there to listen, particularly when Audrey made it clear to Regis that he could never meet her parents. Regis had expected that, though it was difficult to hear. But he buckled his pride, and accepted Audrey's numerous conditions to the metronome of Finn's approving nods.

He had wanted to kill Finn when he found out, wanted to pull out his revolver and pump him with a succession of bullets. But Audrey looked so happy, lying there. And Regis knew that she had done it only because he hadn't been there for her. So he spared his friend's life for Audrey's sake. And let her go.

Regis' head bobbed gently, keeping time with Tupac. Doing time, he thought. If this wasn't doing jail-less time, then he didn't know what was. Lack of time had ruined his chances with Audrey. And lies. He was a workaholic; that much was obvious. But he could never tell her where he went in the dead of night, or disappeared to over weekends. He was a mechanic – a damn good one at that. He also freelanced for Hector's Bail Bonds in Van Nuys.

He started working for them a while back, when he was about

thirty-one. He was a security guard then, bored and eager to court danger. It was a natural progression: he already had a permit to carry a gun, he'd done his Power of Arrest training. There wasn't much more that he needed to do. In fact, California state law didn't require him to do anything. But Regis was a thorough man. He did everything possible to prepare himself for the job. In doing so, he sealed tight his chances, leaving no room for excuses. Anyone who turned him down, he knew, would be doing it for only one reason.

Regis ran his tongue over his teeth, feeling between the grooves for cookie crumbs. Shit, he thought. Just applying to be a security guard had made him feel like a criminal. They had taken his prints, like they took everyone's, but later when he'd walked down the street with indigo-stained fingertips, he felt horribly conspicuous. People seemed to shrink from him. Maybe that happened every day. He couldn't tell. That was the eighties, he mused. The shit was bad then. His size didn't help either. He'd walk along South Fairfax Boulevard and white women would, unconsciously, squeeze their handbags against their hips. Occasionally he'd get hassled by the LAPD. Nothing serious, but consistent enough to light a slow rage in the pit of his stomach. And then there was Rodney King.

Regis had been lying on his living room floor doing stomach crunches while listening to the radio when the verdict was passed. Holliday's video footage hadn't been enough for the jury. Koon, Powell, Wind and Briseno had all been let off. Regis had been incredulous. King wasn't dead, of course, but he might as well have been.

A chill ran through Regis. When he was seven, Watts had caught alight. He'd overheard his parents talking about it in hushed voices: the beatings, the arrests, the bodies rolling like potatoes under the force of the hoses. Back then, it had been exciting to Regis, a welcome distraction, even. Only later did he realise that he had lost family to the chaos: his Aunt Sally, who used to look at him with stern eyes, and his older cousin Frank, who always carried around two playing cards with women in bikinis on them. When

Regis had found out, the only thing he could think of was those cards. He imagined them floating endlessly through the streets of Watts, bearing the two blondes on their backs like lily pads carrying flowers.

Without thinking, Regis picked up the telephone. He hadn't spoken to his cousin, Rudy, in years, had just about forgotten his South Central buddies. But something compelled him now to make contact.

'They let those motherfuckers go. Shit, Reg.' Rudy was close to tears. He didn't bother with the wherefores and what-the-fucks. 'There's no justice for the black man, Reg. No justice at all.'

Regis, sitting in his Venice Beach apartment, shook his head. 'Can't argue with you there, Rude. It's like Malcolm X never lived.'

Rudy was sobbing. 'Denied … our … dignity.' The words came out strangled.

Regis kept his voice low. 'I know. I know—'

'No … dignity.'

The phone went dead. And before he could fully digest his cousin's words, LA went up in flames. The riots started in Westwood and spread like contagion across the county. Nowhere was off-limits; from Long Beach to the San Fernando Valley, fire and frustration rained down. Regis spent those five days rivetted to his couch. The television was on twenty-four hours a day, and after a while, Regis thought the video feed must have been on a loop. Looting, shooting, physical assault. It seemed endless, the faces generally black or Hispanic. And that infamous footage of the Korean store-owner brandishing a gun, firing, it seemed, willy-nilly. He saw that again and again. Then there was the black trader from South Central, crying, demanding to know why people were destroying his livelihood. And a looter, looking desperate, shaking his head saying, 'God forgive us. We can't help ourselves.'

Lying there, almost catatonic with anger and disbelief, Regis felt like he was drowning. Perhaps the couch would just swallow him up, deliver him from this conflagration. Was this what Baldwin was talking about? Was this the Fire Next Time? Regis didn't think so. From his perspective, the only people getting hurt in all this were his brothers and sisters. Black people tearing into black-owned businesses, destroying their own neighbourhoods, their own communities. Why didn't they vent their rage in the Hills? Or in god-damn Malibu? This was a total fuck up. No revolution here, just a maelstrom of anger. A spontaneous combustion. An implosion.

Months after it was all over – after Crenshaw Square had been reduced to cinders and most of the area gutted – Regis drove down to South Central. He didn't have the heart to go into Inglewood, and certainly no stomach for Crenshaw. Instead, he stopped his car at Florence and Normandie, and got out. It was a weekday afternoon. The sun was bright, sapping everything in its path of colour and depth. Regis scanned the intersection, taking in the surprisingly unscathed exterior of the Liquor Store. He crossed over to Art's – a short, blue, homely looking shack – and ordered one of his Famous Chili Dogs. He took up a stool and stared out the small window. The gas station, the Liquor Store, Art's – they were all still standing, survivors of the riots' worst.

When Regis returned to the same spot years later, South Central had been deceptively peaceful. The houses, low to the ground, were small and in faded pastels. People – very few – moved slowly down the sidewalks, hair alive and springy. There were no gang bangers or knuckleheads loping about. An old man was selling equally aged fruit by the side of the road. Everything was calm, lazy even. But the Liquor Store still had its iron door, most places had bars on their windows, and despite an average of two churches per block (including the Universal Christian Miracle Centre not far from the intersection), there was no real evidence of grace.

Regis didn't bother to stop in on anyone. His cousin, Rudy, had shrivelled up into a statistic, his life raked together with the other fifty-one claimed by the riots. His other friends and family, he could do without. By then, Regis had effected the desired transition. He had moved from Venice Beach to Burbank. He had a decent job, a Korean girlfriend and a surfer buddy. Life was sweet. At that moment, he just couldn't face Aunty Alice's two-bed bungalow with the Chiclet-sized windows. Couldn't bear the sight of her weedy lawn or the smell of her fat tabby. After all, his parents hadn't moved to Crenshaw, and later Fountain Valley, for nothing.

Regis had been a good kid. He worked hard, studied hard, and generally stayed out of trouble. But after he graduated from university, an idleness overtook him. Much as he tried, he couldn't get the jobs he wanted. So he settled for less. He signed up to be a security guard. Later, he took a predilection for cars and engines and turned it into a lucrative profession. And in between all that, he satisfied an urge for risk and the unknown by freelancing as a bounty hunter.

He was smarter than the average bail recovery agent – quicker – an expert at securing trust (and, more importantly, the skip who was attached to it). Regis was always sympathetic. No guns-blazing, door-kicking cowboy, he. No. Regis was patient and methodical. He spun his web slowly, stickily. If he did his job right, his skip would come to him. From time to time, he'd have a partner come along to cover his back. More often than not, he worked alone.

His first gig had been straightforward: a low-level drug dealer, sprung from custody by his pimp with a promise from Hector's Bail Bonds. Of course the guy never showed up for his day in court. Within hours of his release, he'd jumped on his bike and gunned it to Mexico. Regis caught up with him in Tijuana. The skip had inexplicably stopped there – waiting for word from his pimp, perhaps. Regis found him at the XXX bar, doing tequila body slammers with a wide-hipped San Diegan peroxide blonde. Regis slid in next to them, joining in with the applauding crowd. When the blonde eventually disappeared out back to puke, Regis bought four shots, and invited the guy to share them with him. The skip could barely keep his eyes open, but he accepted happily, knocking them back with unexpected energy. The blonde never returned and Regis continued to ply the guy with drinks until he lost consciousness. Regis told everyone not to worry, that he'd take care of his friend, and escorted him gently to his car. He cuffed him carefully, then laid him to rest in the back seat. When the skip finally woke up, he was in a jail cell, his cheek nesting in a puddle of drool.

Not all Regis' contracts were as easy as that, otherwise he would have given up long ago. There were times when he did have to knock down a door, or pull out his gun. In his seven years of bounty hunting, he'd been stabbed three times, concussed twice, shot once and frequently bitch-slapped. But he never returned empty-handed. Which meant he never *left* empty-handed either. Often, he ended up with at least twenty per cent of the retrieved bail money – anywhere from five grand and up. And though he was careful with his money, he didn't see a problem with allowing himself – and those around him – a little luxury.

But Regis was not ostentatious. He had a modest, though elegant, Burbank apartment. He drove a deep green convertible 300 series BMW, and on some days, a Harley Davidson Soft Tail. And he had a masseuse come over every Sunday to work on his neck and shoulders. Regis was also generous. He gave money to his parents and to his sister in New York. He even gave money to his Aunty Alice. The rest he tied up in investments and tax shelters. He was saving for his children.

At thirty-eight, Regis didn't have any kids. As much as he didn't like them, he liked the idea of being a father. He'd even broached the subject with Audrey. But she just laughed and said she was too young to think about things like that. That was true. She was only twenty-five. But the real truth was that her parents would never accept it. Regis and Audrey were doomed from the start.

His own family were no better. His aunty, his father, even some of his friends stitched their lips and narrowed their eyes, calling her 'a piece of Soon Ja Du', and saying, if he wasn't careful, she'd shoot him in the back, too, for a dollar seventy-nine. No one had forgotten that day, just two weeks after the King beating, that Soon Ja Du shot Latasha Harlins, 15, in the back of the head. The old Korean lady had claimed Latasha had been trying to steal a bottle of orange juice. The 51-year old never served her sentence – got let out on probation, proving that a black girl's life didn't even amount to two dollars. Of course, in the end, Audrey did shoot him in the back. Not for a dollar seventy-nine, though. Money hadn't been the issue.

She had brought her car to him for an engine check. That's how they met. Audrey's face glowed when she smiled, and her hair, cut into an asymmetrical bob, was almost blue in the sunlight. Later Regis discovered that some of it was blue – she had dyed the tips indigo.

Their first date had come perilously close to disaster. Regis took Audrey to Santa Monica for mussels. They'd gorged on bouillabaisse, and within twenty minutes, began frowning at one another across the table. It was a case of mild poisoning. Not serious enough to require hospitalisation, but distressing enough to call an early end to the evening. Regis thought he'd blown it. But Audrey surprised him by phoning the next day. She liked him.

Audrey was a cartoonist. Some weekends, Regis and Audrey would browse the numerous comicbook stores in Burbank, searching out her work. She was a fan of R Crumb, Ralph Steadman, HR Giger and Miuchi Suzue. Audrey's art was deceptively cute: big-eyed mini-dolls and teddy-bear hamsters abounded. But what these charming creatures got up to was not just unexpected, it was unholy. Everyone was expendable in Audrey's world. And each ended in such gruesome, scatological circumstances, most readers waited a long while before coming back for more. Regis preferred not to examine Audrey's creations too closely. They made his knees go stiff. Yet, surprisingly, Audrey had a decent cult following. It wasn't enough to make a living, though, so to supplement her income, Audrey wrote erotica. The contortions thrown up by her brutal imagination gained her good money from magazines like *Hustler*. For a while, Regis and Audrey were happy.

Even if Finn hadn't turned up, things would have failed. Regis worked constantly. So did Audrey, for that matter, but she always managed to make Regis feel like he was the negligent one. Perhaps he was. Moving in together improved things somewhat; it meant they saw each other at least once a day. But their schedules conflicted to such an extent, often this meant nothing more than sleeping back to back. Audrey became bored and withdrawn. She sulked or went out with friends, sometimes returning the next morning. On occasion, she disappeared to spend a few days with her parents.

From time to time, Regis made an effort to take Audrey out to dinner or on short holidays. They went to Vegas, San Francisco, Mexico. When the mood seized them, they would drive out into Death Valley or up to Santa Barbara. But it was never enough. Somehow, Regis had lost her interest. So when Finn came along, with his sea-green eyes and super-chilled lifestyle, Audrey must have been relieved.

Regis considered the empty foil packet on his lap. Hollowed of its bourbon creams, the casing seemed suddenly fragile, prone to the slightest release of breath. He repeatedly smoothed the wrapper against his thigh, pressing out the wrinkles with a thumb. He got lost in the convex patina of his nail, coasting up-back-up over metallic blue. As it moved, a shaft of light travelled along its arc, like a time-lapse image of the sun crossing the sky. Regis stopped, and covered the object with his palm. It felt warm and oddly alive. He let his head drop against the rest behind it, and closed his eyes.

The contract had come to him like waffles on a Sunday morning. Butter-scented and steaming, sensually demanding. Regis threw himself onto it like a half-starved homeless man, every bite cauterising the wound in his gut. Never mind that he had decided, weeks before (the very day he found out about Finn and Audrey, in fact), that he was giving up the freelance stuff. It hadn't been about Audrey, though she, of course, played a part in it. It was really about Regis getting older, getting tired, wanting to enjoy his life a little more while working a little less. But suddenly idle time meant pain.

Regis opened his eyes. The CD had run its course long ago, and it was sitting, now, balanced on a wheel, ready for another spin if he was so inclined. He was not. Instead, he replaced it with some acid jazz, a gift from one of his buddies down at the garage. Piano and trumpet knitted together, pouring into Regis' ears. In his mind: street lights, red and yellow, bleeding into one another; pavements slick with rain and run through with tyre tracks; everything disintegrating into a pointillist dreamscape. Regis' eyes drooped. Somewhere, sailing beneath the whispering sax, thoughts of his contract, the need to revise his notes, all drifting gently away like sheets of newspaper over traffic.

A flute shivered over a rolling drum beat. Regis melted into his seat, fell through a gap in the cushion onto the floor of the aircraft and rolled between passengers' feet (running shoes, stilettos, loafers) until he slipped through a crack that sent him clear through the belly of the plane. He emerged from its navel like a worm from an apple, his head wriggling and squirming in the freezing air. One moment he was gasping for breath, squeezing through an impossibly narrow tunnel, the next he was airborne, wind gusting through his body, clouds disappearing down his gaping mouth.

The ground was still far away, still looking like a giant map. Regis panicked, hugging the air and swallowing dirt. He was falling faster now, hurtling forward with a speed that ripped against his skin, threatening to flay him. He could just about make out the country he was falling onto. It was El Vez, its pompadour and thin moustache unmistakable, despite the speed with which Regis approached it. El Vez: north of Charo and west of Tupelo. And just his luck, Regis was headed straight for its red-rimmed nostril.

Trussed

There was a juddering sound. A voice announced something about turbulence and seatbelts. Regis yawned and found himself sprawled inelegantly on his seat. The woman across the aisle was darting short, sharp glances at him. He smiled sheepishly, and she jerked her head away. Regis rolled his eyes. She had red hair, swirled and pinned up like a fat cinnamon danish. Regis felt his mouth begin to water.

At that moment, as if reading his mind, two stewardesses appeared at the far end of both aisles, rattling meal trolleys and proffering trays. Regis collected himself into a more dignified pose, awaiting service. He opted for the roast duck, and, using a series of careful gestures, managed to eat it without causing injury to either himself or the pig-tailed kid beside him. As he sat back, sipping a cup of red wine, Regis turned his mind to his contract. The skip was in London. Regis had discovered he had flown out of Memphis some days ago, though precisely why from Memphis he couldn't say for sure. He shrugged. Perhaps it had something to do with Elvis.

The skip had a velvet voice, apparently – or so he'd heard from Ms Aviliera, and there were several in the former congregation who backed that up. In fact, many had expressed consternation when they heard that Angelus Peries had abandoned Santa Evangelista, helping himself to a fair amount of its collection fund on his way out. Theresa Aviliera wept openly when Regis spoke to her, telling him that at least Angel had been thoughtful enough to give a substantial donation to the Christian Children's Fund. Regis concluded that Ms Aviliera had been in love with Peries, but though he let slip some of the rumours about Angel's night in Vegas, she only wept harder and insisted he was a good man.

Regis nodded through her tears. The sight of Theresa's swollen lids and washed-out face sent twinges of recognition across his scalp – sent him falling back, as if bruised by the recoil of a rifle butt.

'Ms Aviliera, when was the last time you heard from Mr Peries?' The question came out hollow and metallic. Theresa had a tissue bunched into her fist which she rubbed against her right temple aimlessly, letting the tears flow unchecked. 'Ms Aviliera,' Regis held a tissue box in front of her. She ignored it. 'Ok, how 'bout we talk about when you first met Mr ... Angel.'

Theresa sniffled and blew her nose. 'It was a long time ago. Maybe a year and a half?'

Regis nodded. His eyes gravitated toward her nostrils, which were pink and raw. 'And how did you meet him?' Again, a tinny echo.

Theresa bent her gaze to her lap, almost dropping her chin to her chest. 'He ... he came to us. He just opened the church door and I was there, collecting the missals. And he told me he wanted to sing ... for us ... for God.' She looked up, smiling. 'He was so good, Mr Watts. You must understand. He sang like ... like ... an angel. Members of our congregation – well, they were so shocked. They couldn't believe what they were hearing. I mean, one day we have the old woman playing organ – playing *Jesu Joy* or something – the next we have this strong, handsome man singing like ... like ... Elvis.'

'And what about you, Ms Aviliera. Did you sing?'

'Yes. We sang. Angel and I, I mean. Both of us. Together.' She gave a weak laugh. 'You could say, we became quite popular. Father Peter was very happy. Our church had been struggling, Mr Watts. For many years. But after Angel came to us, things changed. Suddenly, everyone wanted to celebrate with us. Our collections got bigger and bigger. It was great. Our governors thought we could expand. With the money we were getting. But ... but ...' Her chin sank forward into her breast, muffling her voice. 'But, we couldn't. We had to close down after ... after ...' Theresa stopped and stared at her knees.

Regis bent toward her, lowering his voice. 'Has he tried to contact you since he left you last?' She shook her head slowly, from side to side, eyes eternally fixed on her lap.

Theresa's forlorn figure, hunched and brooding on the couch, caused something to unravel inside Regis. Much of what she said came to him as if through the womb of a seashell. Regis had a vague feeling that Theresa had just lied to him. But somehow, thoughts of Audrey snagged his brain like fish hooks, leaving a loud, scraping sound reverberating in his skull. Regis watched Theresa's mouth open and close, but caught nothing. His ears filled instead with white noise. He heard nothing of what he said to her on his way out. Perhaps he had thanked her – perhaps even shouted it, given her startled expression as he reached out to shake her hand. He had very little memory of actually returning to his car. By then, his head had begun a furious throbbing, and everything around him had gone spotted and blurred.

Even now, memories of that migraine beat a tense path up the base of Regis' neck. He had spent the following eighteen hours in bed, blinds drawn and a bag of frozen corn on his forehead. He had temporarily lost partial sight in his left eye. From time to time, he would cast his eyes across the room, trying to focus on an object. But in that hole where the rest of the lamp or chest of drawers should have been, Regis saw gray. He almost decided to abandon the case, hand it over to someone else. But two days later he realised it was the only thing left in his life.

So Regis spoke to Theresa again. She was less weepy this time, and more helpful, though Regis still had the feeling she wasn't telling him everything. She did tell him that Angel was from England, that he had, most probably, been working under the table. Of course no one at Santa Eva had asked to see Angel's papers; after all, he started as a volunteer. When he eventually took up an administrative position at the church, the transition had been natural, expected even. Grand theft aside, Angel had been an exemplary employee. He seemed very committed to Santa Eva's ideals and to raising money for the church's building extension fund. Anyway, any lingering doubts about Angel dissipated as soon as the first note sprang from his gold-balmed throat. According to Theresa, a lot of women had found Angel irresistible, but he had been a model of chastity. A few hours later, she admitted she had had an intimate relationship with him. 'I couldn't help myself,' she said, blushing and averting her gaze.

Regis went to Vegas. His initial inquiries had been half-hearted, conducted by telephone or over the internet. But he knew that long-distance tinkering would amount to little, so he flew there instead. Unfortunately, he couldn't avoid the Luxor. This was the last place Angel had been before the police caught up to him, so Regis had to brave its glaring interior once again, this time friendless and with a soughing hole in his stomach. He questioned the clerks at reception, the bar staff and the gaming crew. Most were eager to help, but had nothing to add to the case. The rest were just gormless.

When presented with a picture of a mutton-chopped Angel, one fresh-faced blonde bellhop shrugged, 'Like, I don't know. There are *so* many Elvises in Vegas.' And a green-eyed waitress had stared and stared at the photo only to declare, 'Oh m'god, that's not, like, a picture of Tupac *before* he was famous, is it?'

Eventually, Regis found someone who actually remembered seeing the skip that night. 'Oh yeah,' said a barmaid, 'he was real cute, if you're into weird cute. He had this foundation on his face? But you could tell he was kinda handsome underneath.'

'Was he with anyone?'

'Not at the beginning. But he was revved up, you know? He had this weird smile on his face. I think he left with a woman. I'm not sure.'

'What did she look like?'

The barmaid frowned. 'Like anybody, I guess. Pretty, blonde, long legs, high heels.'

Regis nodded.

A light leapt into the woman's eyes. 'Why do you want to know, anyway? Did he kill someone?'

'Did you see him again? Since then?'

The woman shook her head. 'What did he do?'

'And the woman? Have you seen her since then?'

'Maybe. It's hard to say. Like I said, she looked like anybody … What did he do?'

Regis thanked her and found other staff members to question: the croupiers, the security guards, the busboys. It was the same story each time. No one had seen anything particularly untoward. Everyone wanted to know what Angel had done. The Blackjack dealer, on the other hand, recalled that Angel had lost a substantial amount of money – about a quarter of a million dollars – but, he added, there were a few high rollers out that night; it wasn't unheard of. And no one had seen Angel since.

Regis paused to stare at the cavernous interior of the casino. Its 120,000 square feet were still mind-blowing, even more so this time around, without the distraction of champagne and jacuzzis. An ersatz Nile river cut through the hall, flanked by Egyptian-styled sculptures. Some seventy tables, plus a bevy of slot machines fanning out from a BMW centre-piece, filled the room. But there was a curious languorousness that pervaded the space, any nervous energy diffusing in the vastness of that underground universe. Regis was not surprised that few remembered seeing Angel. He could have wandered anywhere within the labyrinthine interior of the hotel, and chances were, he would have remained unobserved. Still, Regis told himself, at least he'd managed to get a better idea of Angel's disposition that night.

Of course, he knew a fair amount about this already, having consulted the police notes on the case. He knew, for instance, that Angel had been high on coke when they found him, that he had lost a substantial sum of money at the Blackjack table. But there was no mention of his having been with a woman that evening. Patience had brought Regis this tiny reward. Still, he had to find her. Regis suspected that Angel had hidden most of the money in Vegas, and had returned to collect it before leaving for England. Perhaps Angel had seen the woman again on his way out of the country. Regis decided to give the barmaid one last try.

'So, the woman – the one who left with Mr Peries,' he said. 'Would you recognise her if you saw her again?'

The barmaid shrugged. 'I dunno.' She stared hard at the bar, as if trying to draw the woman from its reflective surface. 'Wait.' She looked up. 'You know, I think she comes in most evenings … Hangs out here at the bar. Yes!' She grinned, meeting Regis' dubious gaze. 'No, no. I swear.' She placed a hand on her breast. 'Seriously. I really do remember her.'

'So, what's her name?'

'Name? You're asking me for a name? Listen, buddy. Just come back here tonight, and I'll point her out to you. All right?'

She wasn't lying. Later that night, Regis sat by the bar, drawing his thumbs down the sides of a glass of rum and Coke. He studied the pattern of condensation on its surface, the fat welts where his thumbs had been. His notepad was buried inside his jacket. Then the barmaid came over and asked him whether he wanted another drink. He followed her gaze to an area just behind him. As he turned, he saw the woman loping up toward the bar, a thin blonde in jeans and stilettos. He smiled, inviting her over, and offered her a drink. She accepted.

Regis didn't ask her about Angel right away. Instead, he asked her what she liked about the casino, whether she was a regular, what was the most money she'd ever won – and lost.

The woman played with her glass, chewing on her tongue. She was in her twenties, face a little drawn. Her lipstick blurred over the edges so that her mouth looked like a bright red tulip. After a few minutes, the tulip opened a fraction. 'What are you? A cop? What's with all the questions? I thought you wanted to have a drink?'

Regis affected embarrassment. 'Aw, listen, I'm sorry. I'm sort of … new at all this.' He gave her a meaningful look. 'I … I just want to talk, if that's ok. Talk a little, you know?'

The blonde looked at Regis. 'Talk?' She shifted in her seat, about to get up, but slumped back down with a sigh. 'Buy me another drink and I'll think about it.'

Regis ordered another round – a Martini and a rum and Coke – and smiled. 'Happy?'

She seemed to relax, flashing him a wide, white-tiled smile in return. Fake, thought Regis, as he extended a hand toward the woman. 'I'm Bill, by the way.'

'Pleasure, Bill, I'm Carol.'

They nodded at one another, swilling their drinks in their glasses. Carol rubbed her nose gently, batting her eyes at Regis. 'So, *Bill*. Start talkin'.'

It took another three Martinis to thaw Carol. By that point, the tulip was in modest bloom, letting slip the occasional giggle. But it was Regis who was doing most of the talking, laying his failed relationship on the bar like a piece of fly-blown carrion. Carol shook her head and made comforting noises, knocking back yet another Martini. 'That's fucked,' she volunteered, pinching her nostrils. 'You know, I see a lot of that crap around. Usually men cheating on their women. But your ex-lady was somethin' else.'

Regis shrugged at the blonde. 'Bad luck,' he said, signalling the barmaid for another round. 'But do you know what the worst thing was?' He leaned forward and jabbed a finger in the air. 'Do you?'

Carol shook her head.

He stared at her, struggling to keep his face still. 'She … she left me for some Elvis geek.' Regis scoffed, 'Some freak with so little personality he had to borrow someone else's.'

Carol blinked at him, then threw her head back and hooted.

Regis slapped a palm on the bar. 'Can you believe that?'

'Believe it?' Carol had tears in her eyes. 'Of course I believe it. This is Vegas, man: Elvis capital of the goddamn world.'

Regis grinned. 'Bet you've seen a few Elvises in your time.'

Carol nodded. 'Shit yeah. Have I ever. Fat Elvises, skinny Elvises,

Elvis on stilts, female Elvis, Japanese Elvis, black Elvis – no offence.'
She looked up at Regis.

Regis waved a palm and shook his head.

Carol affected a preacher's lilt.'Uh have sayn Ayl-vis and uh aym
a *believah*! Praise the Lawd.'

Regis raised his hands, joining in. 'Praise him now!'

'Allelujah.'

'Ay-men.'

They laughed, shaking their heads at one another. Regis ordered
more drinks while Carol nipped to the bathroom. She returned a
minute later, pulling gently at her nose.

'So … which was her Elvis?' The tulip was now in full bloom,
showcasing those gleaming white tiles again – this time sincerely.

Regis gave her a deadpan look. 'Surfer Elvis.'

Carol chuckled while offering him a compassionate glance.

'So,' Regis raised a brow at Carol.'How about you?'

She stared at Regis.'What about me?'

'Well, you said you've seen a lot of Elvises. What was your
weirdest?'

She rolled her eyes.'Canine Elvis. Hands down.'

Regis nodded. 'Yeah, yeah. That's obvious. But what about the
others? What was the strangest guy-Elvis you've seen?'

Carol pinched her nostrils firmly between thumb and forefinger.
'Oh shit, I don't know.' She paused. 'There are so many around, you
know?' She looked down, tapping her temple with a finger. Her
forehead crinkled and uncrinkled like a caterpillar in motion. She
looked up and frowned. 'No. Nothing. Like I said, Canine Elvis. The
rest are just a blur.'

They finished their drinks. Regis had been sitting with Carol for
almost two hours, and still he had nothing. He thought of walking
away, but this was the first time since Audrey's departure that he
had actually laughed. So he stayed. They drank one more round
before Regis invited Carol back to his room.

He wasn't sure why he did it. It wasn't motivated by desire, though that, too, seemed to be doing a dance in his belly. It was something else – loneliness perhaps. It didn't matter. Carol was obliging and Regis was drunk – much too drunk to care. He lay back and let her do whatever she wanted. It all felt good. Regis' mind toppled into Audrey's embrace: her hair against his chest, her gravelly laugh, her perfectly formed fingernails – he conjured all these, could almost feel her surprised breaths upon his face. He didn't want to open his eyes.

When he did, Carol was sitting on the edge of the bed, reaching for her top. Regis wanted her to leave. 'Don't go. Not yet.' The words were unexpected. He frowned. It was Bill talking.

Carol shook her head. 'I have to,' she insisted. 'I've spent way too much time with you already.' She looked at Regis, her face softening. 'You all right?'

Regis nodded.

'Not thinking about Elvis, are you?'

Regis looked wounded. 'Why'd you have to go and mention that, now?'

Carol flung a palm forward, giving the air a limp slap. 'Forget him. He's just a freak. I see them all the time,' she lay back on the bed and drove her legs up into a pair of jeans.

'Yeah?' Regis rolled onto his side, and watched the denim swallow her thighs.

'Yeah. Like this guy I saw – I dunno – a while back.' She paused to pull up her zip. 'Yeah … he had all this make-up and shit on his face. Shades, leather jacket, the works,' she let out a tight, tinkly laugh and propped herself against the headboard. 'Oh God, he looked so *weird*. Anyway, he was fucked up on coke and losing money big-time, but when he came up to the bar, he saw me and bought me a drink. He was all fired up, saying he didn't care that he'd just lost all his money, and that he was going to Graceland some day. He said he was going to win the battle of the Elvises. I was like, what? I mean, no offence, but he didn't exactly look the part, if you know what I mean.'

Regis cocked his head to the side, fixing her through the corner of his eye. 'Uh, no. I'm not sure *what* you mean.'

Carol breathed out roughly. 'Look. All I'm saying is he didn't *look* like Elvis. Like, his skin was sort of bumpy, for one. And not exactly a normal colour like you or me. I couldn't really tell with all that make-up.'

Regis gave a slow nod.

'Anyway, it got even weirder later. Because, you know, I thought I had to see what else this guy was about, so when he *invited* me to come up with him to his room, I went, you know? I mean, I made sure he hadn't lost all his money first, of course. And then I went. And *then* ...'

Regis leaned towards Carol.

'Well, this is going to sound strange, but ... he *sang* to me.' Carol paused for effect. 'When we got into that room, he took my hand, looked me in the eyes, and started singing 'Love Me Tender' ... The thing is, he sang it well. Really well. So I was like, wow. And then we danced. Can you believe it? Me – dancing with that freak,' she heaved herself off the bed.

Regis raised his brows. 'I hope he paid you well.'

'You better fuckin' believe it.'

'So ... you danced.'

'Yeah, we danced.' Carol stepped carefully into her stilettos and raised a foot onto the edge of the bed to do the buckles. 'He sang like an angel. He really did.'

'So, what happened to him?'

She frowned, standing up and smoothing her hair back. 'I don't know. I left an hour later. Do you think I give a shit, anyway? Just another traveller. It's always the same. You meet someone, step inside them for an hour or so, and then they go, and it's as if you're standing on the beach, watching the waves rushing away from you.'

At that moment, Regis felt like he was the one left standing on the sand while an angel with sideburns went surfing into the sunset. He looked up at Carol. 'Well, I guess it's like Elvis says.'

She puckered her brow. 'Why? What does he say?'

"'That's the way it is.'"

Carol shifted her gaze sideways in thought. 'No,' she said finally. 'I think that was someone else. Bruce Hornby or something.'

Regis smiled. He thanked her, slipping her several hundreds for her time, and left Vegas the next morning.

Regis was exhausted. He felt like he'd been airborne for days. Everything had happened so fast. Angel hadn't shown up for his trial, Hector's had called the next day, and, within forty-eight hours of his migraine, Regis found himself on a flight to Vegas, and now London. The plane began a slow descent. He sighed. Theresa may not have told him much, but she had, during the course of one of her dewy-eyed recollections of Angel, mentioned the skip's father's name: Aloysius. A quick search on the British Telecom website revealed only one 'A Peries' listed. But as the plane landed, Regis felt a weight slide forward in his skull. He had the address, but had forgotten to bring the telephone number with him. As soon as he had cleared customs, he headed for information and asked to take a look at the white pages. They only had the central London directory to hand. Unfazed, Regis referred to his notes containing the Peries address. He asked the clerk for a map, memorised the exact location of the house, and booked into the closest hotel. Before leaving the airport, he rang directory inquiries, noting the telephone number hastily on a scrap of paper.

Regis slept for sixteen hours, waking up the following afternoon bug-eyed and brain a buzz. An hour later, he was standing in a phone booth outside, searching his pockets for the slip of paper inscribed with the Peries' telephone number. He pulled it out and paused. Peering through one of the booth's glass panes, he saw the sky – yellowish-grey, low and indifferent. Tree branches, naked and ashen, seemed to claw at it, like fingers scrabbling for attention. The pavement, even the streets, were strangely desolate. Regis let out a slow, measured breath, lifted the receiver from its cradle, and dialled the number.

4 Hunger

The phone is hunched in its roost, silent and impassive. I can still hear it ringing. Angel pounced on it like it was a roach. And it was, flying in on clumsy wings, dropping shrill notes like debris. The phone number – an anonymous pencil scribble – lies wadded like gum in my bin.

I sit on the edge of the bed, staring at the door. Why did Angel come back? What does he want? I slouch back and draw the quilt to my chest, shivering at the thought of him lying in my bed. I curl up, pulling the duvet tightly around me. Angel likes to cross lines. He's the brown Elvis, only he never actually says 'brown' out loud. Ever since he stood up and sang – what was it? – 'Love Me Tender' to Delia Aunty, the whole family went mad, lighting candles and giving him prominence on the family altar. Never mind that he's never actually done anything with his life, that he's no better – if not worse – than I am. After all, I joined the Legion. I was a soldier in the Holy Virgin's army. I defended her honour and that of all women.

Until I lost mine.

My throat is dry and my stomach hollow. I swallow air.

I rub my forehead, trying to fit the telephone number to a face. Maybe it was Jason. Maybe he's moved and wants to get in touch.

I am tempted to retrieve the number from the bin, rise up on my elbows, in fact, preparing to get out of bed. I frown, recalling our last night together, months ago, and slump back again.

It couldn't have been him. Or that bastard, Derek. It's been a month since … it's been one month. Exactly four weeks. I haven't seen him since.

There's a shushing sound, like cold breath, coiling into my ear. The notes he left me were so smooth, crisp, dry. All the qualities of a very fine white wine. I took them because I had to. I took them because I wanted to. They were mine.

My eyes fall on the rubbish bin and its crumpled contents. I yank the phone cord, bringing the cradle and receiver within arm's reach.

'Hello?' Amrik answers in a hushed tone.

'It's me.' I, too, lower my voice. 'How's things, Am?'

There is a pause, followed by a long sigh. I can hear the drawl of Amrik's breath against the receiver, dragging back and forth like a slipper over laminate. When he speaks, it is with the voice of a child. 'I am very lonely.'

I bite my lip. Amrik has entered the contractionless zone. I'm not sure I can minister the appropriate dose of compassion. I try, anyway. 'Why are you lonely, Am?'

'Nobody loves me.'

I shake my head. Derek's scowl, his spit-glossed lips, suction to my ear. Amrik's drooping lips and wounded gaze vie concurrently for my attention. There is no contest. 'You know that's not true,' I say, 'I mean, you just shagged someone the other day.' My voice is as flat as my arse.

Amrik is subdued but emphatic. 'That is not love.'

Derek left me eighty-five pounds in an envelope: four twenties and a five. I spent those notes as quickly as I made them, sliding them out of my wallet with a licked thumb, transforming them into another month's lodging. They went from one envelope into another, Agnes Aunty innocent of their journey.

'Hello?' Amrik's voice rises a notch.

I stall, trying to regain the thread of our conversation. 'Well,' I say finally, 'you were pretty happy about it. He was floppy-haired, remember? You said he looked like Ronan Keating.'

Amrik releases a triplet of nasal squeaks. 'He did not love me. He did not ring.'

I resist the urge to kiss my teeth. 'Did you call him?'

'I did not.'

'So?'

He pauses, sniffing to himself and emitting another triple squeak. 'It is no use. No one will ever love me.' He draws a long, dramatic breath. 'You must buy me a bear.'

'A bear.' I flop back onto the bed with a huff. Derek is no longer a sucker fish on my ear, but his breath has left icy stalactites behind it. My voice drones on. 'Right. Ok, Amrik, I'll buy you a bear. How about Winnie the Pooh?'

'He is a bear of very little brain.'

'All right. Paddington, then.'

Amrik offers a nasal assent.

'Paddington Bear,' I say, absently. I lift a leg and rotate my foot, stretching out my toes at the same time. Irritation overcomes me. 'Well, are you even going to ask me how I am?'

Amrik sniffs. 'How are you?'

'Am, I …' The words don't come. They cling to my tongue, unformed and skinless. It is an open question with complicated answers. There are no guard rails to hold on to, no anti-slip mats.

Amrik drops his maudlin tone. 'Have you heard from that arsehole?'

'Which one?'

'You know, the D-man.'

I sit up and take a sip of Lucozade. 'No … thank God. But you know, I keep thinking about what happened … Christ. I'm so pissed with myself. Why did I go there?'

Amrik takes a deep breath. 'You weren't to know, my dear. You did what you had to do.'

'But there has to be a way.'

'What do you mean?'

'To make him pay, Amrik. I have to make the fucker pay. I've sat on this for a month now hoping it would go away. But it hasn't. And you know I can't go to the police – not now. I couldn't before, anyway. So, I have to do it. I have to find a way.'

Amrik is silent.

'Well?'

'Well, now that you've brought it up, I have been giving it some thought. Shall we say dinner tonight? My place?'

I trawl my cupboard, searching for something suitable to wear. There are stripy turtlenecks and two-toned T-shirts. Amrik is cooking his special – creamy linguine with smoked salmon. He says it will help set the mood. There will be wine and fine music. So I have to dress the part. Plotting revenge requires certain accoutrements. Elegance, both gastronomic and sartorial, are a must.

Amrik. He's my one real friend: solid, even as he weeps and moans about this or that fresh-faced boy. When I met him in college, almost four years ago, he seemed shy and vulnerable. But I soon realised that he was a brilliant student with a talent for decimating what he called 'charlatan academics'. His sharply-timed, abstruse questions shamed many an obnoxious postgrad. When he made presentations or dined with senior colleagues, he was all charm and wit. But with me, all that grace and swagger often disappears, leaving a mawkish, lonely, sometimes petulant boy.

I settle on two charity shop bargains: a fitted, black, wide-cuffed shirt and an A-line skirt. Amrik would approve. As I step into a pair of knee-high boots, I feel my insides knotting. My heart quickens and my breath skips. I am standing in the middle of my room, but Derek is at my feet, kissing the toe of my boot. As his lips touch leather, his mouth withers, as if afflicted by some necrotising disease. His entire body desiccates in minutes, reduced to a tongue of cured flesh hanging off the end of my foot. I stare at it. At this flat, dry piece of meat. It goes from pink to red to black. I close my eyes then open them. A black skirt of leather is pooled around my ankle. I gather it against my calf and zip it up. My ears are filled with ice.

It is seven by the time I make it to Amrik's King's Cross flat. My head is spinning and my stomach convulsing, in spite of the cheeseburger and chips I scoffed on the way. I am nibbling on some salted crisps when Amrik answers the door.

'But you'll ruin your supper,' he cries, kissing me on the cheeks. 'Great skirt, by the way. Fabulous with those boots.'

'Thanks,' I grin, stepping inside. 'Mind if I use your loo?' I surge ahead, dropping my coat as I go, and lock myself in the bathroom. A few minutes later I emerge, sweating and shaking.

Amrik inhales sharply. 'Vinda, you look terrible. What's going on?' He puts an arm around me and leads me toward the settee.

I shake my head as if trying to dislodge what I want to say. 'I ... I don't know. I just feel awful. I'm not sure what it is ... I ...' Something hisses in my ears.

Amrik stares at me with widening eyes. A shadow crosses his face as he surveys me from head to foot. 'Oh my God, you're pregnant!' He bites his lip. 'Oh, Vinda. You poor dear. What shall we do? Have you seen a doctor?'

I want to cry, but am so shocked by Amrik's accurate diagnosis, I don't. 'Oh God, is it *that* obvious?'

'No-no, Vinda. No. Not really.'

My heartbeat accelerates. 'Oh, shit. If *you* can tell, how the hell am I going to keep this from my aunt?'

Amrik flicks the air with a palm. 'Never mind your aunt. She has enough trouble with that addled uncle of yours to notice.'

I clench my fists. 'You don't know Agnes Aunty. She has the eyes of a hawk.' Anger unknots inside me, strikes a match.

Amrik waves an impatient hand. 'Yes, but she's a distracted hawk, isn't she? Don't worry. Now, have you seen a doctor?'

I see myself, closing my hands around the match, rage blistering my palms. 'No. Yes. Yes, I have. But they can't do anything for another month.' Something hisses in my ear – smooth, crisp, dry. 'They said they don't have any appointments before then.' There is a hammering in my chest. My hands are alight. 'Amrik—' My breath comes quickly. 'Amrik … I— I—'

'What? Vinda? Wh—'

Amrik is saying something to me, but I can't hear him. A gale has unleashed in my ears. My breath tightens in my chest. I brace myself against a brocaded armrest, nails digging into it. I see Derek's stomach yielding to a knife-blade like a wedge of brie.

Rage lashes my tongue, scalds it. I dig deeper into brocade. Warm cherry jam oozes from Derek's flesh. He is looking at me, blue eyes pale and accusing. The hissing in my ears gets louder. I want to open my mouth against it, launch my voice over it. But my tongue is tied up, trussed to the back of my throat. My throat is burnt, raw. I look down. There are dark patches on my lap. I have spilt a drink. But there is no glass in my hand. There is no glass nearby. My chest convulses. I feel a splash of something on my wrist and realise my cheeks and chin are wet. My palms fly to my face, cover it, absorb brine.

I lean back in my chair and look at Amrik. His expression is still, almost serene, but his cheeks are colourless. I wipe my face with my hands and breathe slowly. The hissing subsides, replaced by the sound of Amrik and me breathing. We inhale and exhale in staggered time. The room seems to retract and expand with each breath. Everything is quiet. Amrik and I face one another, but neither of us sees the other. We say nothing, loosing thoughts, instead, to mingle in the silence like cigarette smoke.

Eventually, footsteps clatter beneath the living-room window. And then all the sounds flood in – revving engines, wheezing pigeons, distant sirens, someone's TV.

'I can't take it,' I say finally. 'I can't taste anything any more. It's just food, going down my gullet to feed this … this … parasite. If I don't eat when it commands me to, then I throw up. It made me eat a cheeseburger. Can you believe it?' I look at Amrik. He doesn't seem to be listening. 'A cheeseburger! I don't even eat beef. I haven't in years.'

Amrik nods. His gaze is preoccupied, as if reading a transcript of what I've just said. A moment later, his eyes are fixed and attentive. 'But can't you have it sooner?'

'No. If I wanted to, I'd have to do it privately. Which means I'd have to pay. I won't know anything for sure – I mean, I won't have a proper date until I have my ultrasound next week.' I wring my hands. 'I just can't believe this is happening. I don't even know how it bloody happened.'

Amrik's lips tighten. 'Now Vinda, you know damn well how this happened.'

I shake my head emphatically. 'No, Amrik. I don't. I really don't know.'

Amrik sighs and stands up. 'I think it's time for a drink –' he disappears into the kitchen and emerges with two long-stemmed glasses. 'Now that the hysterics are over,' he says, handing me one, 'let the plotting begin.' He raises his glass.

'Here, here,' I say, raising mine in return. My voice is iron.

I sip a sweet, sparkling wine that is cold on my tongue but warm as it reaches my throat.

'Asti Spumante,' says Amrik. 'I had an Italian lover once, you know.' He drinks from his glass. 'Dark and hairy – Oh that's such a cliché – but this time it was true. It ended badly.' He studies the liquor in the glass. 'It's a dessert wine. But I had nothing for an aperitif, so … I hope you don't mind?'

'It's fine – lovely.' I am grateful for the break from Lucozade. I take another draught.

Amrik is by the stereo, going through his CDs. Within seconds a chorus of tightly choreographed male voices sweeps through the room.

I cringe. 'Boyzone, Amrik?'

'I know, they're rubbish, but they're so cute.' He switches CDs. 'I was only joking, dear.'

A ream of sensuous accordion notes banishes Boyzone from the room. Amrik is playing his favourite Astor Piazzolla. He beckons me to his side and puts his hand in mine. His touch is so warm and open, I feel suddenly weightless. We fake-tango from the stereo to the window. With one great lunge, he dips me and I see the lights of an airplane shimmering in the night sky. It makes me giddy. We stride like panthers to the other side of the room, grinning madly. He grasps my lower back. As he dips me a second time, the scent of smoked salmon wafts up my nose, triggering a wave of nausea that sends me crumpling to the floor.

'Vinda?' Amrik is leaning over me, trying to lift me up.

I wave him away. 'No don't. It's—' My stomach retches. 'It's the fish. The fish.' I scramble to my feet and make for the window. Amrik closes the kitchen door. I lean out the window and gulp fish-free air, dissipating the choppy feeling at the back of my throat. I turn around to face Amrik, who is standing in the middle of the room, looking worried.

'What's wrong? Has the fish gone bad?' he asks.

'No. No.' I gulp.

I can still smell it – the smoked salmon, that thick odour of dairy, the garlic, the parmesan. The thought of belts of linguine coiled in cream makes my stomach lurch again. I return to the window.

'Amrik, the thing is, right now, some smells are … revolting. Fish, cream, cheese – all those thick, oily smells – I can't take them.' I swallow back bile. 'It's awful. I don't even know how I managed to make it here without vomiting. It's ridiculous, I know. I'm sorry. After all the trouble you've gone to.'

Amrik does his trademark flick of the palm, then pats me on the shoulder. 'Oh, don't worry. I can always eat the rest tomorrow. But what about you? What can I give you? You must be hungry.'

'I am. I don't know.' I let out a long breath and a vision of orange squares rears up in my mind. Tasty, orange squares. I can now think of nothing else. Nothing else will sate my hunger. 'Processed cheese,' I gush, mouth watering. 'Do you have any … Kraft Singles?'

Amrik recoils in horror. 'Processed cheese slices? Cheese *food*?' His mouth gapes. 'First cheeseburgers and chips, and now processed cheese. Whatever you're harbouring in there certainly has the most appalling taste. It's like some nasty little American.'

I grin. 'I know. I know.'

'So much for *la gastronomie*.'

'For now, anyway.' I watch as Amrik makes for the front door, zipping his jacket. 'Hey, where are you going?'

'To buy you some of that dreadful cheese, of course.' He pauses, considering his fez on the coat stand. 'Too obvious. How will I ever explain?'

'I'll buy it if you're so worried.'

'No, no. We can't have you throwing up in our local's aisles, can we?'

I laugh. 'Yeah, I guess it's safer in here. I really owe you.'

'No problem, my dear. And don't worry about repaying me. I'll find a way soon enough.'

I sit on the sofa tearing cheese slices, rolling the bits into little balls before eating them, between sips of sparkling water. I keep my gaze firmly averted, relaxing away from the smell of salmon while Amrik sits at the table, winding linguine against a spoon with his fork. 'This is ridiculous,' I laugh. 'I'm sorry.'

'Never mind, Vinda. Stop apologising.'

I press a pearl of cheese between thumb and forefinger, raise it to eye level and squint at it. 'I hope this doesn't give me weird dreams.'

Amrik pauses, swallowing a forkful of pasta. 'It's not even real. I wouldn't worry.'

'Yes, but all those chemicals; you never know.' I nibble the pearl. 'I had that dream again, you know. A few weeks ago.'

Amrik puts his fork down. 'Not again. What happened this time? – Wait, don't tell me. You were smeared in baby oil, right? And it all descended into some orgiastic ritual. An upmarket Annabel Chong.'

I wince. 'Good God, no. Nothing like that. Just the same thing: me riding the shoulders of the singing multitude ... And I was covered in some kind of oil. Really pungent. Definitely not baby oil, though,' I frown. 'I still can't figure out what they're saying, you know. It could be something really important.'

Amrik snorts. 'You've been eating too much garlic, Vinda. That's all it is.'

I tear another strip off a square of cheese. 'Maybe you're right.' Its naked, shiny surface is almost indistinguishable from the plastic sheen of its wrapper. 'You know, Angel came back a week ago.'

Amrik smirks. 'Yeah, you mentioned.' He grunts. 'Ersatz Elvis. God help us all.'

I roll my eyes. 'Come on – he's not *that* bad. At least he can sing. You've never even met him.'

'Only through you, my dear. And that's plenty.'

I nod, chewing on a piece of cheese. 'He's a pain in the backside. Shagged one of his fares last night and then proceeded to tell me all about it – like I wanted to know. He's so self-obsessed. It's always me-me-me – oh yeah, and Elvis, of course.'

Amrik puts down his fork for a moment. 'So, why is he here? Why did he leave LA?'

I shrug. 'Who knows? Probably bored or disappointed that no one was impressed enough out there. He gigged a bit, but I guess he thought everyone would simply fall at his feet or something. Not everyone is as gullible as my family.'

Amrik is huddled over his plate, busying himself with his food. 'Oh well', he says, and grates extra parmesan over his remaining pasta. I change the subject.

'So, what did they say at the local?'

Amrik slurps a strand of linguine. 'Nothing. The cashier just looked at me, you know, suggesting something like "ooo, how the mighty have fallen", and I stared back coolly without batting an eye. Why should I care what he thinks?'

'Indeed. After all, I'm sure he's no match for Blue Boy – is he?'

'Blue Boy!' Amrik's face lights up. 'I'd almost forgotten him. And such a good shag, too.'

'You shagged him?' My jaw drops. I jump from the couch and take a chair by Amrik, in spite of the salmon pasta. 'You never told me.'

Amrik draws his chin toward his right shoulder and flashes a coy smile. 'Come now, dear. I can't kiss and tell all the time, now, can I?'

'You tart!'

'Careful, Vinda. I wouldn't go down that route, if I were you.' Amrik shakes his head. 'Tart, indeed. What about you and all those boys – those *English* boys. Oh yes. And Jason. Poor thing. What about him?'

I look down and realise, with a jolt, how large my thighs have become. And so soon, too. I sigh. Jason. Yes, maybe he *did* ring after … how long was it? Two months? Maybe less.

'Yes. Jason.' Amrik cradles his glass in his palm, smiling. 'He was a nice boy. A bit thin, but sweet. Or should I say … sticky?'

I raise a brow, narrowing my eyes at Amrik.

'It's him, isn't it?'

I say nothing, pausing instead to consider the water in my glass. Bubbles rise and pop crisply along its surface, like butter frying gently in a pan. I look up. 'Shit, remember Butter Boy?'

Amrik smacks his lips. 'The one with the lovely, buttery lips?'

'Yeah, the flaxen sailor.' I click my tongue. 'His father owned an oil company or something. He left after only a few months here. Shame. We never got to – you know.'

'Oh please, Vinda. Do you really expect me to believe that?'

I laugh. 'What? I meant last names. We never got to exchange last names.' I close my eyes and Butter Boy sneaks up behind me, puts a pill on my tongue. Two weekends and then a chance meeting at the Notting Hill carnival. While the long weekend hurried on, we lounged in his Ladbroke Grove flat, rolling out of bed at midnight to shake the floors at Subterranea.

'That was years ago. Oh, you lucky bitch.'

I lift my glass and clink it against Amrik's. 'Ah, to Butter Boy. May his lips remain glossy and full.' Amrik giggles.

I smile at him, at his broad cheeks and bushy eyelashes. 'I really am sorry about the blonde at your local. You knew it was a risk, and you took it for me and I really appreciate that.'

Amrik grins. 'Of course. Anything for you, my dear.' He takes a long sip from his glass. 'And we still have the small question of revenge to sort out.'

I nod. 'Hmmm … what did you have in mind?'

The air is cold and damp as I make my way back to the tube. I rummage through pockets laden with crackers and Lucozade, eventually extracting two pounds. In the end, neither Amrik nor I could come up with a suitable strategy for revenge. Our plans were too far-fetched, contingent on too many variables. I yawn as the train carriage bullets through a tunnel. I hear the hiss of clean bills against my fingers. Close my eyes and see Derek's drooling mouth. His contorted face. My stomach heaves. I reach for the bottle of Lucozade and sip hastily.

I think of that unanswered phone call again. It couldn't have been Jason. Not after the last time, anyway. And the number. It's not his – not as I remember it. Unless he was calling from somewhere else? I shake my head. Jason always wanted more. It annoys me – his need: syrupy, cloying. Amrik is right about that.

I'd been seeing Jason on and off since university, more off than on really. When it suited us, we met for drinks and a film, sometimes more. It really depended on our mood … and the weather.

It was raining the last time I saw him. We met at his Hackney flat, opting for a simple evening indoors: a Chinese take-away and some beer. He looked so cute when he came to the door, his dreads sticking out from his head like twisted yarn. The evening started in the usual way, me complaining about my persistent unemployment, Jason placating me. It ended the usual way, too: me lying in Jason's bed, hoping he would fall asleep this time instead of moaning endlessly about whether or not he was my boyfriend. He even tried to call me 'Asma'. My mouth grows tense just thinking about it.

I rub an earlobe between thumb and forefinger. Fuck Jason. He always gave me more than I wanted. Never stuck to the agreement. That was the problem.

It wasn't always like that, though. Before Jason, during Jason, even as far back as Ryan in high school, there were so many others. Rosy-cheeked English boys, all eager to take a little bit of 'Vinda' away with them. In truth, perhaps I started before I ever met Derek. Of course they never paid me cash. They bought me dinners or drinks or gifts. Payment in kind. And I did them the favour of dumping them as soon as they showed even a hint of wanting something more. But Jason was different. He was the only one I went back to. The only one, then, who asked me what my real name was. There was a difference between the way he and Derek asked that question. A big difference.

'I'm sick of that shit, you know.'

I cock my head toward two figures sprawled in the set of double seats across the aisle from me. A young Bangladeshi man in midnight blue jeans snaps his fingers at the youth opposite him.

'Ratri is so passé. I mean, God. Been there, done that, kn'ah mean?'

His friend peers at him through a fringe of blond hair. 'Bu—'

'Ugh!' The teenager throws his hands apart in disgust. 'All those Chutney Queens in frocks and bells – too much dot orientation, if you ask me. I like mixed places, you know? Like the Jazz Café.'

I stare at my lap, flicking cracker crumbs onto the ground. The weeks ahead are an endless expanse. I'm not sure how I'll get through them without drawing suspicion to myself at home. Sooner or later, someone will notice my frequent loo visits and constant feeding. Uncle Aloy is harmless enough, but Agnes Aunty is shrewd. There's no fooling her once she detects an inconsistency. Angel, too, may realise soon enough. Even he can't possibly believe I drink that much. But no way am I discussing it with him or anyone else – aside from Amrik. As far as I'm concerned, this will all be over in a matter of weeks. It's best accepted and forgotten.

Later, as I lie in bed trying to fall asleep, I listen to the passing cars, counting them as they go by. I reach for my bottle of Lucozade and packet of crackers, checking they're still within arm's length. Each morning is a race against nausea, with fingers grappling in the dark for salted biscuits and carbonated sugar. Anything to outwit my stomach.

Moat Farm Lane is popular with the passing vehicles tonight. After an hour, I'm still blinking. By the second hour, I'm totally alert. I suck my tongue, which is sore and coated with a strange white film. Must be the Lucozade. I grimace at the thought of sharp little bubbles flaying the inside of my mouth.

Turning toward the wall, I stare at the leaves fluttering darkly along its surface. Shadows blur, coagulating like rain on a storm-swept window. I can feel my muscles settling, feel my body turn to velvet limb by limb. When I look at the wall again, the leaves are gone, replaced by a human relief – an army of people striding forward. They stop beside me, singing at full voice, shifting their weight from one foot to another. Bending as one, they nudge their shoulders beneath me and hoist me up. I can feel their inky bones pressing against me, slippery like ice yet somehow intangible. Every movement threatens to pitch me to the ground, so I cling to their crude-oil frames, drinking in their strange lullaby that is familiar yet hopelessly unclear. They march for hours, maybe even days, through silvan alleys paved with cobbles. These give way to a baroque clearing, vast and green and thunderous with voices. They are chanting and the ground shakes with their roars. Then a switch is pulled and the night is flooded in white light.

Wheat-flecked crumbs explode with the dawn inside my papery mouth. It is an odd feeling, like eating dried couscous. My stomach pulses and my head throbs. I heave, but manage to control myself until I reach the toilet. Hands clasping the sides of the bowl I retch, sweating with the effort to keep silent.

Stragglers from the previous night's visions crowd my mind, clinging to me like an oily shadow. I shake them off, staring out the window. From my vantage point, the sky is a sooty white, as still and uninspiring as dirty snow. I'm not sure what I want to do today. Go down to the Unemployment Agency looking for crap jobs? Trawl the *Guardian* media pages for impossible jobs? Derek comes to mind. 'Damn, that was good money,' I mutter, '… ok, not good enough – but what a jerk-off. What a fucking jerk-off.' I turn on the shower and kick off my pyjamas.

The water is hot, and I let myself drift with the steam. I imagine myself in a sweating Cameroonian rainforest, tracking and observing lowland gorillas. Or monitoring the behaviour of ring-tailed lemurs in Madagascar. I pinch myself for not studying biology at A-level. I showed promise – was actually intrigued by the subject – but I turned my back on it anyway. I've never been able to stick to anything. My mind whirrs and ticks and soon becomes bored. I sabotage every opportunity I come by so that my path is forever strewn with broken promise and recrimination.

I am overwhelmed by boredom, my restlessness subsiding only when I'm in motion. But to keep myself in motion, I need money. Here I am, living with my aunt, a BA in my pocket and no job in sight. Of course I've had interviews, but they never go anywhere. Maybe I'm not enthusiastic enough. And the thought of actually signing a contract – tying myself down to something for a whole year – I can't bear it. But I have to keep trying. As I wind a towel around my wet hair, this realisation gathers inside the cloth, twisting into my skull like a rusty screw. I examine myself in the mirror, addressing my reflection, 'Well, I guess it's going to have to be a *Guardian* day, after all.'

'Asma, you must get yourself a good job.' Agnes Aunty is sipping her tea, sitting at the dining room table. I chew a sour apple, watching the kettle from my position by the kitchen door. 'You have a good degree. You could go into government service or something like that, no? Make your mother and father proud.'

I cringe at the mention of my parents. Ten years ago, Dad finally pursued his passion and moved in with a Greek secretary ('a modern scribe' as he likes to call her) just outside Athens. After the divorce, Mum returned to her family in Sri Lanka, taking on a senior position at a hospital in Colombo. Not wanting to deprive me of the opportunities associated with a British education, my parents decided it was best for me to remain in England with Agnes Aunty. I've seen Mum and Dad twice in the past seven years. Twice too many times as far as I'm concerned.

I shake my head. 'It's not that easy, Aunty,' I say, ignoring the reference to my parents. 'You know I'm trying.'

I can tell that Agnes Aunty is regretting her previous words. She rarely brings up Mum and Dad. Maybe she's irritated with them for dumping me on her.

Trussed

'But for how long?' she says. 'It's been nearly a year since you got your BA. If you don't find something soon, it will get harder for you.'

I frown. She probably wants to get rid of me.

'You can't go on receiving benefits endlessly.'

'I know. I know. Don't worry. I'll find something. Of course I will.' I spot the kettle boiling and flee to the kitchen. I pour myself a cup of hot water and dunk a fruit tea bag inside. The scent of blackcurrants rises gently.

'Here, Asma, you've been looking quite pale recently. Are you all right?' Agnes Aunty approaches, empty cup in hand.

I stare at my tea in silence, blinking through the steam. Half a minute later, I smile. 'Nothing serious.' I look up, meeting my aunt's gaze. 'You know, I bought this fruit fool a couple of days ago. From Sainsbury's. It was on special? And since then … I don't know. My stomach hasn't felt right.'

'A couple of days ago?' Agnes Aunty stares hard at me, then nods. 'Yes. Sometimes these things happen. I remember eating some useless mousse once. My stomach didn't go right for a week!'

'Yeah?'

'Yes. It was from *some* shop. I don't know, some bloody filth they must have served.' She turns to the sink. 'Are you going out now?'

'For the day. Looking for work, as usual.'

'Will you be home for supper?'

'Don't worry about me. I'll find something.'

Agnes Aunty turns to face me. 'Just be careful what you eat. Eat plain foods. Even plain rice might be good for you.'

I smile. 'Thanks. I'll be fine. Don't worry.' I dart from the kitchen, mug in hand. Halfway up the staircase, I pause for a calming breath.

Out on the road I feel better. I blow rings of breath, watching them dissipate in the crisp air. I head for the library, but divert to the newsagents instead. Tucking the *Guardian* neatly under my elbow, I make my way to the tube. A film seems a good idea or perhaps the V & A. I figure I'll decide on the way, and walk through the turnstiles.

In the end, I choose the V & A.

Winding my way through the European and British galleries, I make for the musical instruments on the third floor. Pausing on the steps, I look up at the great domed ceiling above. This strange, dark, circular space is like a hovering island, beneath which crowds mill between cases of Elizabethan and Victorian costume. The striated wood of a lute-like instrument catches my eye. The swollen back is more like a belly, with its white pin-stripes on chocolate-coloured wood. I study a German baryton, an 18th-century stringed instrument similar to the viola da gamba, marvelling at the fingerboard of tortoise shell and ivory. It has twenty-five sympathetic strings, there to be plucked while bowing the other six. Cello was hard enough with its four strings. Bowing was fine, but I could never quite manage the vibrato. My wrist was always too stiff. I feel a pang of regret. I had talent, but lacked motivation. I abandoned it after only a few years.

I duck into an even darker patch of the gallery and am immediately surrounded by clocks. Bracket clocks, mantel clocks, long-case clocks, clock watches. They are all here – standing, sitting, squatting, reclining – all with the same quiet resignation on their faces. I study a 'month-going' long-case clock, its walnut body covered in floral panels and surprised-looking birds. And further down, in a case of German clocks, stands an unusually faceless example. I consider this unsubtle comment on time and existence: Christ nailed to the cross, a skull and cross-bones at his feet, and above his head, time twisting forward along the lip of a brass crown. I prefer the wind-up clock at the other end of the display. There, a bearded merman is sitting, splay-legged, atop a tortoise. With a trident in his right hand, its prongs barely touching the tortoise's face, the bronze-bodied merman should look formidable. But his body sags forward, his face a study of boredom and fatigue, and the tortoise, too, despite its claws, looks powerless.

My parents were undone by time. Dad was always prompt, Mum once told me, which was one of the reasons why she married him. And then one night he came home late. That was how she knew. That's what she told me, anyway. But they were never meant to be together – my parents, Martin and Amara, whose arguments were epic, taut, vicious. A spray of Sinhala swear words would pelt the air like spit: *huthi, balla, balli, musaleya*. Sometimes the abuse got so ridiculous Mum would laugh. More often, it ended in tears: Mum lying dazed on the bed while Dad swept out the front door. I would sit in the living room, falling deeper into the television yet unable to block out the sound of the family car. And sometime between two and four am, I would hear the click and roll of the lock, the footsteps that always stopped at my bedroom door. I would feel Dad's gaze in the darkness, hear his sigh, and know that one day he would never come back.

Mum and Dad divorced when I was thirteen. And Dad never did come back, though he invited me a year later to spend a week with him at his new home. He had soon tired of Athens, abandoning it within eight months for the wonders of the Dodecanese. The island of Patmos, that inspiration for St John's hallucinogenic visions, was now home to Martin and Maria. Given that the Book of Revelations was the only part of the Bible I had ever read voluntarily, Patmos proved an attractive proposition – in spite of Maria. Silent and sullen, I wandered through the airy rooms of Dad's house, offering the occasional amicable shrug to him and cold stares to Maria.

Dad took me out in his boat a few times. We never said much to each other, just sat on opposite ends, staring out in one direction, both of us mesmerised by the glinting water. Back at his place, it was much the same thing, except for Maria and her doe eyes and shrill voice. She would eye me up and try to braid my hair, saying it was so silky and straight and would look beautiful tied back. All lies. If Dad wasn't around at lunch-time, she scowled at me, slopping food onto my plate and pushing it at me. She hated me as much as I hated her. I didn't care that I was in their home, eating their food. Why should I? Martin is my father. Maria is a bimbo, a secretary, a nothing.

Eighteen months later, I discovered that Maria had had a baby. It was there, on a tiny square, folded into a letter from Dad. This child, with its wrinkled, blotchy face repulsed me. I threw the photograph and letter into the bin, not bothering to read the remaining paragraphs. Later I retrieved the items, took them into the bathroom and burnt them in the sink. I didn't even know whether it was a girl or a boy. I didn't allow myself the luxury of such detail.

Of course I never told Mum. Not that she didn't know. It was an unspoken secret between us. Just as all the other women had been. Not babies though. This was the first baby. We shared the flat in solitude. Mum was always working; I was studying or reading. Occasionally we took walks in Holland Park or visited Agnes Aunty in Moat Farm Lane. But there was always a distance between us. Something inexplicable which had grown and hardened ever since I, at the age of six, approached my weeping mother and said, 'You should get a divorce.'

In retrospect, she should have thanked me. She certainly couldn't have denied the wisdom of the suggestion. But back then it was more than blasphemous; it was evil. For the first and only time in my life, Mum slapped me. 'Are you trying to break up this family?' she cried. My cheek stung. I was a heartless child – one that cared for nothing and no one. At least, that's what she probably thought of me because that night, she made me drink concentrated orange juice diluted in Lourdes water before I went to bed. When I told her it tasted of plastic, she made the sign of the cross and lit a candle to the Virgin Mary.

I was sixteen when Mum told me she was going back to Sri Lanka. O levels successfully completed, I was looking forward to a break before continuing my studies. I'd been reading a book: Peter

Trussed

Straub's *Ghost Story*, and had thought that Mum was proposing a holiday. But something about the way she said 'Asma' made me look up. There were tears in her eyes.

Her words were disconnected when they finally tumbled out: 'I ... I can't live here any more. I'm going back to Colombo. I've been offered a very good position there.' She kept rubbing her eyes with a crushed piece of tissue, leaving tiny white baubles in her lashes. 'You know I'm alone here. There's your aunty, of course, but my family ... they're all there. Back home ... It's just ... you know we – your father and I – want you to study here. Get a good education. Not be torn from your friends. From your environment. And your father is only a short trip away. And I'll come and see you every year. Or you can see me. And Agnes Aunty is so fond of you. If you moved in with her? What do you think?'

I felt something burning under my eyelids, felt an invisible fist slam into my chest. They had planned it already: how to hive me from their lives. I nodded blankly, looking at Mum. I saw the terror in her eyes, the shame of choosing herself over her child, and I knew that this act was born out of desperation – that she wanted me to come with her but would not command it. And I knew I couldn't leave England to start a new life in a country I'd visited only once before.

Mum left within the year, leaving me at Moat Farm Lane before installing herself at a private hospital in Colombo. She and Dad wrote monthly – both sending me cheques as well, but I rarely replied. Instead, I focused on preparing for my A levels. To my dismay, however, I found my mind routinely unravelling during class time, hovering over The Smiths' lyrics rather than Milton's *Paradise Lost*. And it was on just such an occasion – not long after Mum's departure, in fact – that I cornered Ryan, my then boyfriend, after lessons. 'Come on, Ryan,' I said, 'I'm so bored.' And with that we locked the classroom door. Copybooks slid off the teacher's desk as Ryan and I laboured against its edge. It didn't matter that there were pupils gathering outside in anticipation of the next class. Only later would it become an issue. With five minutes to spare, we returned the copybooks to the desk and emerged from the classroom, looking hurried and purposeful. Thus did Asma become Vinda, and Ryan … history.

I stand before a row of case clocks, transfixed by the regularity of whirrs and ticks rising from them. They remind me of my old wind-up clock and its red arrowed hands and round, beaming face. The sweetness of its melody prompted me to an obsessive winding and re-winding so that its song never ended. It was a melancholic, yearning sound – or so it seemed to my eight-year-old ears.

There's a rustling in my bag – the newspaper I bought earlier. Sooner or later I'm going to have to sit down and trawl through those jobs pages. This inevitability depresses me, much as the eventual silencing of my childhood clock had. As I picture myself sitting, reading the ads, cementing my resolve, I feel a twinge in my belly. Shoving a hand into a pocket, I draw out a cracker and with one deft movement, push it into my mouth.

I head next for the South Bank, grabbing a sandwich along the way to South Kensington tube. I alight at Embankment, preferring to walk to the Royal Festival Hall, rather than navigate through crowds underground. Crossing the Hungerford Bridge, I pause at its centre to stare out onto the water and far into the horizon. I apologise to the young homeless man who sits at the far end holding a styrofoam cup in dirty, weatherbeaten hands. Down the stairs I step, and onto the terrace, lamp posts heaving upward to my left and the great panes of the Royal Festival Hall glinting on my right.

The walkway is almost empty. I feel vulnerable – like an antelope, caught unawares on an open stretch of the Serengeti. I give the Thames a quick glance before skipping down the broad steps of the Festival Hall. As I enter, a saxophone wheels out a centipede of notes above my head. I follow the music, eschewing the crowded bar for an empty table by the windows at the other end. I can't see the band, but I can still hear the music. And the window is throwing a rhombus of light onto my table. I pull out my sandwich – an innocuous combination of ham and lettuce – and the *Guardian* media pages.

I scan the ads, ticking and circling the relevant ones. But my mind keeps drifting to the previous week – the look on Dr Cho's face – the shock. I only went to the clinic because I had a water blister on my lip. I thought that shit, Derek, might have passed on an STD, so I submitted to a number of tests. The fact that I'd missed my period was an afterthought. I put it down to the trauma of that night, though I didn't mention it to my doctor. Instead, I said I'd been under a lot of stress. We agreed it would be best to do a pregnancy test, 'just to rule it out'. Neither of us expected it to be positive.

Dr Cho couldn't hide her surprise. Like Amrik, she'd taken one look at the gauge and gasped, 'Oh my God, you're pregnant.'

Stunned, I stared at the blue line, willing it to disappear. My tears were instant and almost emotionless. Minutes later, I applied for a termination. Now, I am consumed by the idea of it, desperate to have this pregnancy halted, exterminated, air-brushed into nothingness. But without a precise date for the procedure, my life is in stasis, caught up in a space-time reality that seems to expand as the days progress.

Something flips in my guts. It flails, like a fish caught in mud, then swims in a yellow haze up my throat. I swallow, take a deep breath, then abandon my paper and half-eaten sandwich and flee toward the bathroom. It is metres away at the opposite end of the hall, but I make it there without incident, and vomit squarely into the sink.

I am lucky. When I return to my table, I find my bag untouched, and just in front of it – beside my paper – a discarded copy of the *Camden New Journal*. I pick it up, then put it down again and sigh. My pen is gleaming in a shaft of sunlight, exactly where I left it, its blue plastic cap obscuring a BBC job ad. I resume skimming the listings, ticking, circling and swearing as I go.

The band has stopped playing by the time I turn the last page of the jobs section. Only the drummer is left, packing his gear into circular cases. I gaze at him absently. His head catches and reflects the light, as does his shirt buttons and cufflinks. He is like a soft-edged prism. The bar area has cleared, and the hall echoes with the clatter of cutlery as waiters bus tables. I gather my things and drop them into my bag. It is time to go.

With a small stack of brown envelopes piled neatly on my desk, I lean back in my chair and smile. I feel relieved. I have managed to rein in my thoughts and re-focus, creating bespoke cover letters to accompany my various applications. As always, I convince myself that each job is the right one for me. So, each envelope bears a sliver of hope that, despite my cynicism, bubbles to the surface of my prose.

But this search is endless – the chances of rejection so high. I returned from my travels in July, almost penniless, exhausted but optimistic. I'd saved up all those cheques Mum and Dad sent me and bought myself an around-the-world ticket. Of course I had to visit Mum and Dad – not great, but not so bad either. Mum has a fantastic flat in Colombo with views of the ocean. Patmos was a dud, though, with Maria's little brat always coming into my room, going through my things and calling me 'Sister Asma'. Still, I went to India, Thailand, Australia, South Africa. I expected I'd be safely installed in a decent, well-paid job shortly after my return to London. But it's been four months now and I'm still applying for work.

It was boredom that led me, that day in August, to trawl through the personals in *Time Out*. That was how I met Derek. *SWM looking for sensual Asian babe to keep him firmly in his place.* I was desperate. I couldn't resist.

Our first conversation was so vague – not what I'd expected. I left a message for him. He rang me back. We exchanged small-talk. Derek was well-spoken, polite, but cagey. I wasn't sure what he wanted. Did he want a relationship? Did he want sex? What exactly did he mean by *firmly in his place*? We were both nervous. I decided to be blunt.

'Are you looking for a relationship?'

There was a pause. 'Of sorts.'

I chewed on the inside of my mouth. 'Well … it seems to me like you're looking for a service. Why didn't you ring the speciality ads, instead? Or pick up a postcard from the phone booth? Why put an ad in the personals?'

'Phone booth!' Derek laughed, then went quiet. 'Ummm,' his voice was small. 'I … I'm looking for … uhhh… perhaps it would be better if we met. In person. If that's ok?'

We met at a café on Lamb's Conduit Street. I didn't allow for caution. I was beyond desperation now, and perversely curious. Who was this man? What exactly did he want? And could I deliver? We recognised each other immediately. When we sat down, an incongruous pair amidst power-lunching suits, we eyed one another openly. Derek looked visibly relieved. I considered him harmless.

'Are you a lawyer?' I was the first to speak.

Derek's face went pink. He blushed easily. 'Yes. That's right.'

We fell silent. My mind was racing. I couldn't afford to look like a novice. My credibility was probably already damaged. But how could I know what to ask and how to ask it? 'So, tell me … tell me about yourself. Your likes. Your dislikes.'

'I … I …' Derek looked like he was choking.

I took the opportunity to make my move, levelling a brutal glare at him. 'Stop it,' I spat. I kept my voice low but cold. 'Stop shaking and speak!' In truth, I was the one who was shaking. I was pressing my knees together to keep my legs from trembling.

A strange smile stilled Derek's lips. 'Yes,' he said, meekly. 'Yes.'

It took about an hour for me to learn that Derek didn't want sex but domination. I can do that, I thought. I had a little money left, which I could use to buy my gear. And more importantly, I had enough pent-up aggression to make it interesting for Derek. It wouldn't take much. Anyway, he seemed like a novice himself. He claimed he didn't want to go to a 'service', as I put it earlier, because he wanted us to be friends as well. I laughed at that. We never discussed money, but the first time I whipped him, he gratefully handed over eighty-five pounds. That was also part of the agreement. That I would never ask for money, and Derek would always hand it over – the same amount, each time. Even then, I knew he was getting a bargain. An introductory offer, I convinced myself, and made a mental note to raise my fee in due course.

I stare morosely at the brown envelopes, which are now splayed in a fan across my desk. I never had a chance to raise my fee. I was meeting him twice a week for a month when he – when it happened. That I'd charged him double that night was, in retrospect, a bitter irony. Days later, I wept, realising how naive I had been. I'd walked right into it – handed myself to him on a plate.

I pick out the envelopes, one by one, and read each address to myself. As I lift the last one, the masthead of the *Camden New Journal* comes into view. I flick the envelope aside and scan the paper. A story about the council's recycling programme, something about beating crime on the streets. I turn the page and stop. My head suddenly feels light, my guts twist and parry. *Council pledges to rout discrimination* runs the headline. I skim down the columns: *significant win against the Council ... Mrs Ahmed's right to be re-housed ... astute barrister ... expected to take silk next spring.* I begin to rock back and forth in my chair. My mouth is pressed shut, my tongue boring into my left cheek. I stare at the picture that takes up almost a quarter of the page. Derek's hair still flops over his forehead. His cheeks are still babyishly full. But his grin is all teeth, pearly and as bright as a newly minted coin.

5 Stake-out

It shimmered like water receiving the setting sun. Rhinestones, rubies, garnets swarmed into a lupine outline on black velvet. Red satin glowed like embers where the cloth wrinkled and showed its belly. The cape pulsated on Angel's bed, capturing and ricocheting light across the room. He was still stunned by its opulence, still forced to catch his breath. And next to it, fringed and carefully embroidered: the black and red jumpsuit. Part matador, part Cisco Kid with an Amerindian flavour, the one-piece was a triumph of fine needlework and intaglioed leather. Angel gazed at these treasures, sighing. He could see – feel – Elvis' breath rising from their jewelled skins. He hadn't tried them on. Not yet. Just admired them with a caressing fingertip.

Angel breathed Elvis for the first time in the summer of 1977. It was a hot summer, full of *The Muppets* and *Little Rascals* re-runs – this last, a show he didn't usually get to see except that this summer he was in Ottawa with his parents and his brothers, visiting his grandmother and two aunts: the spinster Queenie and the young and very pretty Delia. Angel was eight years old. He had been at his aunts' since the end of July, and only the other day, Delia Aunty and Uncle Percy, her husband, had taken him and the family to Niagara Falls where they poked their heads through a rocky crevice and screamed as water pummelled their eager faces. Angel grinned at Delia Aunty then, blushing at her perfect teeth and thick lashes. When she smiled, he felt something warm and slightly sweet flutter in his stomach, and imagined it was freshly baked white bread.

Then night turned into day and the 15th became the 16th August. Angel was playing with his brothers, Michael and Francis, in the basement, having retreated into its cool darkness to escape the rising humidity (Matthew, the eldest, was thirteen and didn't have time to play stupid games with his little brothers; instead, he spent most of his time slumped in front of the telly). They were running around in circles playing fireman, Angel taking up the part of the siren, Francis the part of the fireman, and Michael the fire. They did this for a full fifteen minutes before collapsing into a panting heap. Angel needed the toilet and excused himself, trying hard not to inhale the hot air that met him as he made his way up the stairs. When he opened the basement door, the harshness of the sunlight hurt his eyes. He paused, blinking for a minute, then frowned.

The house was strangely quiet. He peeked round the edge of the door into the living room, but no one was there. He peered into the kitchen. No one there either. Forgetting his bladder, he crept upstairs to where the bedrooms – and the television – were. The TV was in Delia Aunty's room, which was right at the top of the landing. Angel went up the stairs on hands and knees, digging his fingers into the chocolate shag of the carpet. When he got to the top, he slid to the right of the doorway, casting an eye into the room. They were huddled around the television – Matthew, his parents and grandmother, Aunty Queenie, Uncle Percy and Delia. And she was crying. Angel ran into the room and put his head in his aunt's lap. From the corner of his eye, he could see that Delia's face looked bruised. Tears ran from her chin onto his temple. Angel was speechless.

Trussed

'*Ayyo*,' she wept. 'Oh Angel. He's dead. He's dead.'

Angel was confused. Everyone else just stood, expressionless, staring at the TV. He turned to his brother.

'Elvis,' whispered Matthew. 'Elvis died today.'

Angel wanted to ask who Elvis was. But when he looked at the television, the words stuck in his throat. He saw a man in a leather jacket, juddering his hips and singing deep soulful notes into a microphone. It was electrifying. Angel was transfixed. His mouth fell open and notes started pouring into it, coating his tongue and tonsils like honey. He remained like that for hours, watching tribute show after tribute show, swallowing lyrics. When he went to the bathroom that night to brush his teeth, he closed the door against the sobs of his aunt, clasped the toothbrush to his lips, and sang. In the morning, he walked into Delia Aunty's room, stood at the foot of the bed and sang 'Love Me Tender'.

First Delia Aunty looked shocked, her red and swollen eyes bulging slightly at the sound of her nephew's quavering voice. Then a smile spread across her lips and she held a hand out to Angel, urging him to come to her side. Despite her red, creased face, Delia looked beautiful. Her hair spilled in dark curls down one shoulder, the straps of her nightdress a shiny pale green against the light brown of her skin. But Angel didn't move, delighting instead in that bready sensation that started to fill his stomach. He kept singing, until his mother and father and brothers and grandmother and Aunty Queenie were gathered around him, quiet, awed, incredulous. When he finished his song, Aunty Queenie declared it a miracle, lit a candle and made everyone recite one decade of the rosary. As Angel prayed he knew that something inside him had changed forever.

When he found the garments, wrapped in linen and hanging in the back room of a collector's Memphis home, Angel had actually felt aroused. This long-thought-lost costume that Elvis had worn once at one of his legendary 1969 Las Vegas performances. A Bill Belew original, provenance all in order … Angel had simultaneously stuffed a hand into his jeans pocket and dragged the other across his sweating forehead. He was in raptures. This was the only costume of its kind; the only 'Howling Wolf' suit he knew of. And it was his for a cool quarter of a million.

Angel didn't hesitate. He handed over a succession of brown envelopes stuffed with cash, watched Poppy, the old woman, count it, and gently slipped the items into a nylon garment bag. For her part, Poppy was happy to answer Angel's hurried questions, but studiously refrained from asking any of him. Two hundred and fifty thousand in cash would be difficult to explain to the bank. But Poppy was a resourceful woman. She would find a way to do it without attracting too much attention. She was also a woman of very few words. Angel wasn't worried. She would say nothing. Discretion was written into the crow's feet about her eyes, folded into the furrows of her brow. So without a second thought, Angel left that blue clapboard home the same way he came in: through the back door.

Once outside, Angel felt a brisk wind beat the back of his head. At that moment, the ground caught up with him. He ducked under a tree, pausing to get his bearings. He was exhausted. He'd spent almost forty-eight hours sprawled at the back of a Greyhound bus, and before that, half a day driving with a friend from LA to Vegas.

Ron, a sound guy from the Pineapple Ring, was going up there anyway, so when Angel asked him for a lift, he happily obliged. The drive had been a slow crawl through traffic, then a trek through the desert. They parted on the Strip, Ron heading to Circus Circus, Angel checking into a nondescript motel by the airport. The following morning, Angel caught a taxi to the Desert Pine Golf Club. It was still dark when he got out on East Bonanza Road. He walked parallel to the north side of the green, counting the trees and shrubs as he went. Eventually he came to a barren, bushy spot, a block away from the course. Clichéd as it was, Angel had buried his money under a rock by a withering plant. No one saw him extract four hundred and twenty thousand dollars from a hole in the earth. Wrapped in several layers of cloth, plastic and paper, the bills were slightly damp, but otherwise unscathed. Angel scooped up the bundle and hefted it into his backpack. Before long, he was lying on his motel bed, freshly bathed, cash stacked neatly in manilla envelopes on either side of him.

He stared at them, wondering how to pack everything into his bag without anyone noticing. He had to catch a Greyhound in an hour. He wasn't sure what kind of security they carried out. If he was lucky, they wouldn't bother to search his bags. If he was unlucky … well, Angel didn't want to think about that possibility. No sense in conjuring negative vibes. The bag had a zip-up lining – an obvious place to hide anything. He shrugged. There was no other way. So he inserted the envelopes, one by one, into the lining, breathing a prayer as he did so. His first stroke of luck swept all twenty-one envelopes snugly inside. Once his clothes were packed on top, the bag looked like any other. A cursory glance would reveal nothing. His second lucky break got him straight onto the bus without even a look. To Angel's relief, Greyhound was fairly lax about its security. He took a seat with his bag at the back of the bus. Plumping it up beside him, he laid his head on top of it and promptly fell asleep.

He dozed fitfully as the bus slipped through Nevada into Arizona. By the time it made it to Phoenix that afternoon, he was sharp eyed and anxious to stretch his legs. An hour and a half later, he was on a bus bound for Dallas, a trip that would take him some twenty-six hours. He watched, bleary-eyed, as Phoenix became Tucson became Benson; as Arizona fell away into New Mexico and then Texas. He fell asleep again somewhere between El Paso and Odessa, and stopped paying attention until he arrived in Dallas. By 7.30 pm, he was on another bus, this one heading, finally, to Memphis. Every bone in his body ached when Angel climbed down from the coach in Memphis. It was 3.30 in the morning and the air was biting cold. He found another motel, much like the one he'd stayed at in Vegas. As his head hit the pillow, he wondered whether the journey had been worth it, whether old lady Poppy's promise was genuine.

A few hours later he was in a cab, on his way to Poppy's. Angel would never have taken the risks he had, had she not described the pieces so meticulously. He came across Poppy's advert while surfing for gear on the Net. She didn't mention a price, but the picture alone was enough to tempt Angel. He phoned her then and there. That was mid-October. Thoughts of the suit and cape burrowed into his brain, bubbled in his intestines, caused him to empty his bowels more frequently than usual. They also steeled his desire, foisting him into breathy embraces with Theresa. Poppy and Angel agreed on a price before he had a chance to think about how he would come up with the cash. Once the deal was struck, Angel knew what he had to do. It wasn't a difficult decision. After all, this was bigger than Angel. Bigger, even, than Santa Eva. When he took the money, he was surprised at how easy it all was. He realised he had been planning to do it for a long time. Poppy was just the push he was looking for.

Vegas, of course, had been his big mistake. Greed and hubris had led him there, so it was inevitable that he would get caught. He should have gone straight to Memphis. Instead, he lost a tenth of his precious money to the Blackjack table. Put a few grand of it up his nose, and squandered several ten thousand on pure sensual gratification. The slim blonde, for instance. She had offered him coke and a blow. He paid her for a lot more. True, he sang to her and held her like a ballerina. But he also took her into his bedroom and held her astride him, eyes locked on the mirror above them. He was on fire. When she left, he cut a few more lines for himself and snorted them through an exceptionally fine Danish all-butter biscuit curl. He delivered a string of karate kicks to the air, made a few lunges at the ground, mimicking Elvis' splay-legged stance, then clutched at an unseen microphone, letting rip, *'We're caught in a trap/I can't walk out/Because I love you too much babé ...'* Angel rubbed his nose, returned to the discarded biscuit and popped it into his mouth. Immediately he felt something warm blooming in his stomach, smelt a dozen loaves of just-baked bread. He decided it was time to hide the money.

Stooping by a shrivelled bush, out on the edge of Vegas, Angel dug. The golf course sprawled in the distance, silent but for the shushing of a few trees. Angel slashed at the earth with a small spade, disgorging scalps of grass and clods of soil. Fire shot through his veins like venom, flooding his muscles. He worked quickly, filling the hole with the parcel of money and the spade, then topping everything off with as much of the dislodged earth as possible. Covering the spot with a large rock, he took the rest of the soil and discarded it, bit by bit, a few metres away. It was a tedious job, scooping handfuls of earth from plant to plant, but it left the spot bald and inconspicuous.

On his way back from the golf club, Angel asked the taxi driver to drop him at the near end of the Strip; he wanted to walk. Neon tubing twisted and glowed around him, crowds of men and women loped in and out of view. Everything started to slow down. Angel's responses seemed to him to be quicker than usual – so that everyone else looked sluggish in comparison. In fact it was Angel who had gone fuzzy. He never made it back into the hotel lobby. Two policemen came up on either side of him as he was about to enter, addressed him politely and cuffed him. They took him back to LA, where he was arraigned and released on bail.

Angel hadn't planned to skip – hadn't planned to go back to Vegas to get his money and then find Poppy in Memphis. But at night, wolves entered his dreams, sideburns rolled out before him like great shaggy carpeting, and rhinestones studded the firmament of his subconscious. As he slept, he could feel the leather and satin against his skin. Breathed in poppies and yeasty bread. With less than a week to go before his trial, he left, hitching that ride to Vegas with Ron. Only a few days later, he was standing under a tree in mid-town Memphis, less a quarter of a million dollars, but in possession of something that, to him, was beyond value. It had held Elvis. It would hold Angel.

Angel pressed a finger into the grooves in the leather. His mind was buzzing. For the past few weeks, he had been in transit, fleeing LA, Vegas and then Memphis. He felt like he'd been running for months, when really it had been a matter of days. He'd been in London now for about a week. So far no sign of the police, or worse, a bail recovery agent. After all, Hector's couldn't be happy about losing a million dollars. He thought again of the telephone call, and his stomach did a flip. Of course, it could have been Carla. But she lived in Highbury, an 0171 number. He pushed these thoughts to the edges of his mind, and touched the costume again. Perhaps now was the time to wear it. Angel's breath quickened. He shook his head. No. This was a uniform for success. He couldn't wear it to prance around in his room. Nor could he put it on to sing in some smoky, clapped-out pub. 'Howling Wolf' was a thing of beauty, worthy only of a real gig: one that commanded a rapt, uninebriated audience. Besides, Angel knew he wasn't ready to wear the costume. It wouldn't be right. Who was he to put on something that had lately graced the shoulders and flanks of the King? He returned it to its case and flopped back on his bed.

Again he thought of Theresa. The last thing he'd done – foolish, perhaps – was send her a prayer book through Ron. He gave it to him in an envelope as they parted ways on the Strip, asking him to deliver it to Theresa's address by hand. Angel couldn't be certain whether she received his gift. He hoped she had. It was the Confraternity of the Precious Blood's *Novena Manual*, a collection of prayers to Jesus, Mary and Joseph. Angel had marked out the 'Act of Contrition', underlining the words: 'I am heartily sorry for having offended Thee'. He knew she would have torn up any money he might have sent her, so he sent her a prayer instead. Perhaps she would understand. His actions were for the sake of art, after all. And Santa Eva's congregation was proof of the appeal of that art. Angel had pull.

Now he was in London. No one knew about his velvet voice. And so far, no one cared. He had a cassette – a recording of one of his Santa Eva performances – and a few video tapes. But on their own, they weren't enough. Publicity was what he needed, first and foremost. He would have to wear the costume, after all.

Regis was bored. Stuck in this godforsaken, grey part of London. Sitting in a rental, watching the Peries house, hoping no one would notice him. Someone might call the police, he thought. How long could he sit there making notes before a neighbour got suspicious? He tapped his steering wheel absently with a finger, thinking he was getting too old for this, too impatient. It was twelve-thirty, just half an hour since he had parked at this spot.

There was the slight clatter of metal against wood, and old man Peries appeared. Regis studied his squat figure. Buried under a tweed overcoat and cap, Peries shuffled down the walkway, jangling his keys. Eventually, he stopped in front of a creaky Bentley, opened the door and got in.

Regis reached for the paper bag on the passenger seat, opened it and carefully picked open a foil wrapper. The kebab was still hot, drenched in yoghurt and glistening with onions and cabbage. It hadn't looked particularly appetising when he'd ordered it at the little shop around the corner, but biting into it now he was surprised. It wasn't Art's. It wasn't McD's. It certainly wasn't McCormick & Schmidt's. It was a mixture of hot sauce and salad, lamb and bread. And it was good. Regis dabbed at the grease running down his chin, struggling to keep bits of onion and lettuce off the steering wheel.

He kept tilting the kebab, almost cupping it in his palms, trying to keep the yoghurt from dripping onto his trousers. Then the door to the Peries home opened again. Grated carrot and shredded cabbage tumbled in small tufts to his lap. Regis shoved the remaining kebab into the paper bag and licked his fingers quickly.

Angelus Peries strode down the walkway, a garment bag looped over his shoulder. Regis gave him a two-block advantage, then quickly left his car, and followed behind at a brisk pace. They headed for South Harrow station, Regis keeping to the right, Angel veering left on the platform. When the tube pulled into the station, Regis made sure to get on at the far end of the same carriage. He had a book with him, *Interview with a Vampire*, which he opened up to an arbitrary point. He'd been using the same book to hide behind for a few years. He'd read it so many times that now he simply went through the motions, predicting the words, in spite of himself, before his eye caught them on the page.

They got out at Ealing Common, taking the District line to Ealing Broadway. There they changed again, jumping onto a Central line train bound for Newbury Park. All this made Regis nervous, made him think that Angel might have suspected something. But a quick glance at the skip was enough to calm him. Angel was lost in thought, tapping out a rhythm with his toe, adjusting and re-adjusting his hair as he stared, very seriously, at his image reflected in the window opposite. The young man sitting directly in front of Angel, however, was getting annoyed. His head, no doubt, marred Angel's view, but Angel kept staring through him.

Regis turned a page. His eyes scanned left and right, following the lines of text which were blurred by the motion of the car. From time to time, he looked up, pretending to examine the tube map, but keeping track of Angel's movements on the periphery. By now, the man opposite Angel had shifted seats. But the skip was too engrossed in himself to notice, narrowing his eyes at his reflection, pulling a sneer. Regis saw with a start that Angel's face was covered in a layer of foundation, lending it a waxen sheen. He couldn't reconcile the skip's success with women. Yes, he seemed a good looking kind of guy: good bone structure, large eyes, etc. But at that moment, he looked like a drag act who had forgotten to take off his make-up. A lot like Little Richard, in fact.

The tube continued onward, past East Acton, White City, Shepherd's Bush. When they passed Holland Park, Regis saw that Angel had gathered his bag close to him, and was leaning forward in his seat. They got out at the next stop: Notting Hill Gate. Angel paused at the station entrance, looking a little disoriented, before heading up Kensington Park Road. Regis kept back, watching Angel from a distance, annoyed that he didn't have time to wander on his own through this ritzy part of London. Darting a glance up Kensington Park Gardens, Regis was struck by the age and grandeur of the architecture, the houses that swept upward, bold and white, like a flock of swans poised to take flight. And the trees, lush, green, rustling beneath the clouds. LA had nothing on London, this was plain to Regis. Except, perhaps, the weather.

Angel made a right and then a quick left. Regis let him round the corner, certain that by the time he caught up to him, he'd see Angel striding a couple of blocks ahead. So he paused in front of a terracotta church, its girth as soft and ample as the thighs of a pregnant woman. As he got to the corner and made a left onto Portobello Road, he saw Angel disappearing into what looked like a shop. Regis jogged up, slowing down once he got to within a few paces of the building. It seemed residential, though one of the ringers had a small piece of printed tape next to it: *f-stop*.

Regis retreated back down the stairs, and crossed to the opposite side of the street. A clothing shop selling psychedelic knitwear offered a convenient vantage point. He pretended to examine a top – tiny, for petite women. He smiled sheepishly at the salesgirl. She wore a sullen expression, and clearly, cared nothing for his custom. Regis abruptly returned to the mini-sweater. It would have fit Audrey nicely, he thought, holding out its purple and turquoise striped arm. Especially around the—

'This for a portfolio?' The photographer peered at Angel through tight, round frames. She was thin with a wideish face. Her hair rose up in a foam of springy curls. Angel nodded. 'Ok, well, you know the fees. They're on the card over there.' She frowned as she studied his face. 'You're wearing make-up. Do you do drag?'

Angel narrowed his gaze at the woman. 'No. I do not.' He cast a glance about the studio. 'Where can I change?'

The photographer pointed to a room along the corridor. 'In there. There's a mirror and other bits. Feel free.'

Angel placed a thin cloth bag over his head to protect his costume from make-up smudges. He was nervous. This was his first time trying on the suit. He didn't even know whether it would fit. His skin tingled as he slipped first one, then the other leg inside. He felt the satin cleave to his buttocks, the leather embrace his trunk. There was an involuntary buzzing in his crotch, a slow creep of desire he couldn't explain. Angel closed his eyes and recalled the telephone – conjured up the panic that had gurgled up his throat as soon as the line had gone dead in his hand. It worked. And just in time. Angel removed the bag from his head and hooked the cape around his shoulders. Then he walked over to the mirror and stared.

It was a little slack around the stomach, but otherwise the suit fit perfectly. Angel was amazed. His dream of walking through the gates of heaven with Elvis was nothing compared to this. Standing there, in a Notting Hill studio, Angel knew that Elvis was now in him. His blood was running hotter already. He even fancied he could detect a blue fleck in his eyes. The room darkened, as if signalling the start of a performance. Angel opened his mouth and let out a single note. It started low, like the baritone of a ship's horn, then gathered momentum as it rose a semitone. It opened out, red and hot, brazen as a hibiscus flower in bloom, and swept up the walls in broad, parallel strokes. Angel had delivered a jewel from the depths of his larnyx. It hung in the centre of the room, a star sapphire radiating waves of white sound out and back into itself.

The sky went dark and Regis heard something deep and roaring that rose and seemed to turn him inside out. He gasped, dropping the sweater, and looked up at the clerk, whose aloofness had evaporated along with the colour from her face. She was translucent now, looking like a very cold, very crisp ice cube. Regis looked past her, to the building across. Lightning flashed, reflecting bright blue-white in the second storey window. 'Jesus, that was close,' he whispered.

He ran out to the front of the building, scanning it for damage. He wasn't the only one. A few shopkeepers and a lady walking her dog stood alongside Regis, craning their necks at the windows. But no one appeared, no one even bothered to come out of the building. So they looked at one another instead, widening their eyes and shaking their heads. The dogwalker, who was standing next to Regis, kept squeezing her lips together like a fish. 'Oooo,' she breathed, 'haven't seen anything like that before. Goodness, what the world is coming to. Too many of them greenhouse gases. Electric storm, I suppose. Reminded me of the Blitz.'

Regis drew closer to the old woman, bending his ear toward her. 'The Blitz?'

'Oh yes.' The lady nodded, 'Those were troubled times. Sirens going off, blackened windows and then the sky lighting up like a projectionist's screen.' She smiled at Regis, then pulled at the leash. Her Jack Russell had parked himself between Regis' ankles. 'Billy,' said the dogwalker in a stern voice, 'not there, my love. Not there. Come over to mummy, there's a good boy.' She turned her face toward Regis again. 'Don't mind him. He's just getting old.'

Regis shook a finger and smiled. 'Oh no, not a problem. He can sit wherever he likes.'

The old woman paused to study Regis' face. 'You're not from around here, are you, love? American, aren't you?'

Regis nodded.

'Been here long?'

He shook his head.

'Ah, terrible, this is. You arrive and first thing you see is the wrath of God.' She laughed. 'Or maybe it's a sign. From Him.'

'Him?'

'Yes, yes. Maybe it's his way of saying a quick hello, you know? Only, he can't do it subtly because he's the Lord, after all.'

Regis tipped his head slowly from side to side. 'I guess it's possible.'

'Oooo,' she pulled another fish-face, laughing. 'I'm not saying it's a miracle, you know. Nothing like that!'

Regis grinned. 'Hey, you never know.'

'Ah, a believer.' She laid a hand on his forearm and winked. 'Have a nice trip, love. Come here on a Saturday. Come to the market. You'll like it better then.' She waddled away, her Jack Russell trotting behind her.

Regis gave her a quick wave, all the while keeping an eye on the door. Angel hadn't emerged yet. F-stop, thought Regis, a photographer's studio. If he was having his picture taken, he might be in there for a while.

Angel closed his mouth, bass roaring in his ears. The jewel dropped with a clink to the floor. He blinked at the photographer, who had appeared at the changing-room door. As he watched, she split apart at the nose – a strange mytosis that sent her floating left and right before collapsing her back into a coherent whole. She was mouthing something about a thunderstorm. Yes, he thought, she had heard it, too – his voice, an elemental force, scything through clouds, spanning horizons.

Angel shook away his dizziness, ignored the pin-prick neon dots that were supernova-ing just above the surface of his eyes. He cleared his throat. 'Can we start now?'

Regis sighed. He looked up the road, which was flanked by metal girders – street stall skeletons – and wished it was the weekend. At least he wouldn't look so obvious, so out of place. He pulled out *Interview*, walked up the road and settled in a nook on an abandoned crate. He still had a decent view of the building from where he was sitting, and it was comfortable. All he had to do was wait.

Waiting. In the past, this had never been a problem for Regis. Waiting had meant re-visiting the map of pursuit, predicting a minimum of three possible scenarios, ordering and re-ordering his thoughts. But his mind wasn't racing this time. It was soft and wet like newspaper in the rain. The truth was that Regis had lost interest. He was going through the motions, dragging out the mission, trying to make a decision about whether or not he really wanted to do this. But it was too late. He'd already accepted the contract. On paper anyway. Yet his body rebelled against that decision, thwarted him at every step by moving that much slower, that less precisely.

He turned a page. Fuck Audrey Kim, he thought. This was the first time he'd allowed himself to think the words. It felt good, like a cat stretch for the soul. He repeated the phrase, this time breathing it out slowly: 'Fuck. Audrey. Kim.' That felt even better. He inhaled deeply through his nose and exhaled through his mouth, whispering in a monotone. 'Fuck. Audrey. Kim.' He sighed. Regis wasn't really angry at Audrey. That anger had swallowed itself up weeks ago, erupting occasionally as an itch around his neck or a vicious headache. But the fact that he could even think these words, let alone say them, meant that Regis really didn't care about Audrey anymore. That she meant nothing to him. That he was free.

The wind rustled the pages of his book, blowing a few of them forward. Regis didn't mind. He considered it strange that at this moment, the thought of Audrey did nothing to him. Yet only thirty minutes ago he had picked up a sweater and imagined her body moving in it. Perhaps this was how it happened. Though the process was gradual, there would always be the cusp: the point at which white became black, love became hate, hurt became relief. In his experience, the cusp was a well-travelled zone, a place that saw a lot of to-ing and fro-ing. You would almost arrive at one end, only to find yourself transported to the other without warning. Regis couldn't say for sure whether he'd made it clear to the other side. Perhaps that, too, was gradual – a slow-motion landing. Perhaps only his shadow had fallen across the line. So, he would have to wait for his body to join it.

Regis turned another page, and noticed dark brown spots gathering in a swarm on the paper. It was drizzling now. He closed the book and turned his face up to the sky. Grey-white and inscrutable, it seemed to be bored with itself. Regis felt the drops against his skin and on his tongue. Cool pin-pricks of water, channelling the city's dirt into his pores. He leaned back, stretching his arms out and behind his neck. When he raised his head again, he saw the skip walking past.

Regis didn't react. He merely followed him with his eyes, giving him the advantage, as he always did. Angel seemed preoccupied, staring at a piece of paper and looking up at the houses as he went. Not long afterward, and still within view, Angel paused in front of a small shop. He peered into the front window, then made his way inside. Regis walked up to the place, a design studio, then returned to his crate and opened his book.

The photographer was good. Angel ended up with a fine set of promotional shots which were turned into some impressive publicity by a designer friend of hers. Given a fat incentive, the designer knocked up two quick postcards. Angel had them printed, blowing up a few for posters, and he set off to do the pub rounds.

Despite the flash publicity, Angel had a hard time getting

people to take him seriously. Most laughed nervously and nodded, before sending him away with a 'We'll have a think about it and see, yeah?' But Angel was determined. He had his experience at the Pineapple Ring and Santa Eva to draw on. There the crowds had been huge and roaring, the bookings steady and numerous. He needed a break. Just one performance would do it. So Angel tried the Horse and Saddle in Ealing. It was a small place, with a mixed clientele – a selection of ages and ethnicities. The proprietor, Eddie, was a friend of a friend of a friend. But that wasn't what shifted things in Angel's favour. Eddie was looking for someone to fill in for a cancellation that Friday night. He invited Angel into his office, and asked him to play one of his recordings. He smiled when he heard Angel's voice coming through the speaker: 'In the Ghetto'.

Regis was exhausted. He waited for a good fifteen minutes before entering the Horse and Saddle. It was small and he couldn't see Angel anywhere, but he thought he heard his voice. He ordered himself a rum and Coke and took a seat at the bar. Aside from a few old gents rambling about 'Andy Cole', and a middle-aged woman loosing intermittent gales of laughter, it was fairly quiet.

Regis examined his coaster which had the word *Young's* stamped on it along with a picture of a lamb. *Agnus Dei*, he thought to himself as he fiddled absently with the small cardboard circle. There was a lull – lasting perhaps a few seconds – and through that gap the words: 'In the Ghetto'. Another roar erupted from the lady in the corner and the men resumed their conversation. The song was lost, though the melody hung in Regis' ears. He kissed his teeth.

What did Elvis know about the ghetto? Rural poverty, yes, but the *ghetto*? Regis shrugged. Elvis was ok, he thought. He wasn't really the rip-off artist people accused him of being. Not like the skip who, at that very moment, was peddling his talent for ripping off a dead singer. For some reason, this really rankled Regis. He hated look-a-like contests and drag artists. To him it was art for the lazy – in other words, artless. It was the same reason why he had no stomach for Andy Warhol. Only people who were really unhappy with themselves went into that kind of business. Imagine that, he mused: making a living out of impersonating someone else. What a head fuck.

Eddie stared at the picture of Angel: a sneer on his face, eyes masked by aviator's shades, cape flung over one shoulder, one leg out to the side in an angular stretch. He was impressed. 'Looks good, mate. Sounds good, too. Where've you gigged in the past?'

Angel grinned. 'I've been living in LA for the last few years. Performed at a local club, the Pineapple Ring, and my church, Santa Eva.'

'Church?' Eddie looked dubious.

'Yeah. It was a small congregation to begin with … but all that changed after I arrived. People came from everywhere. Just to attend mass at Santa Eva. It was amazing.'

'And you sang Elvis songs … at church?'

Angel nodded. 'The recording you were listening to was made at Santa Eva.' He leaned forward in his chair and reached for the cassette. 'You know, in some communities in America, Elvis is a saint.'

Eddie's brows puckered and rose in two perfect arcs. Slowly he nodded. 'Guess it's not surprising … So, why did you leave?'

Angel shrugged. 'London. I missed it. It's my home, yeah? LA is … LA. It's not … real.'

'Does it matter? Sounds like you were having a great time out there. Why bother with reality if life is as sweet as you say it was.'

'I don't know. Guess I just woke up one day and saw it for what it was. Once that happens, you can't go back.' Angel drummed lightly against his thighs with both palms. 'So, do I have a gig?'

Eddie smiled. 'Yeah. This Friday night. I haven't seen you perform before, so I can offer you about fifty quid. Suit you?'

Trussed

Angel sighed. He didn't care about the money. But he didn't want to appear too eager. 'Fifty? Nah, nah. I'd say more like eighty. I'm doing two sets of forty-five minutes each, remember?'

Eddie studied Angel's face for a full minute. 'You're lucky I'm giving you this chance.'

'You're lucky I walked in, given you need a spot filled.'

Eddie's face hardened for a few seconds. Then he sat back in his chair. 'Ok. Seventy-five. Happy?'

Angel smiled.

The skip sauntered out of the pub with a grin on his face. This, Regis saw through the mirror behind the bar. He returned to his drink, staring at the ice cube at the bottom, recalling the salesgirl at the knitwear shop in Notting Hill. He chuckled, then drained his glass and left. Out on the pavement, he hunched away from the wind and picked up his pace. Angel was about two blocks away, but it was dark. Regis didn't want to lose sight of him. He kept his head down, kept his hands in his pockets. The wind was picking up, dragging ragged bits of newspaper into shopfront alcoves.

Angel walked up Ealing Broadway, keeping the wind at his back. His mind wandered. He had a gig this Friday. Even he hadn't imagined it possible to land a break that easily. The pavement was slick, reflecting shopfront fluorescents in radioactive patches. He thought of his photo session, wearing the suit for the first time, the song that beat its way out from his lips, the dizziness. Then he stopped. His eyes darted left and right. Something about the street was wrong. His heart broke out into a frantic rhythm. He started walking again, more quickly, then stopped.

Regis was keeping a brisk pace now, but when he looked up again, he stopped. The skip was standing still, tensed. Shit, thought Regis. Angel started walking again, and Regis let him go before venturing forward. Suddenly the skip dashed into the middle of the street.

There was someone, something, a shadow. Someone was following him. Angel couldn't turn around. Darting into oncoming traffic, he hailed an approaching cab and jumped in. As they sped away, he caught a glimpse of a large, dark man in a mid-length jacket. The man didn't appear to be paying any attention to the taxi, but something about his stance, about the fact that he had slowed down, looked unnatural.

Regis looked into a shop window, keeping sight of the cab in its reflection. He shook his head slowly, from side to side. The skip knew he was here now. Regis would have to stop procrastinating and make his move. He wandered back toward the Horse and Saddle, and saw in its window a poster of Angel, dressed in a superfly jumpsuit. Regis laughed to himself. Angel was performing on Friday. He would corner him then.

'Shit,' hissed Angel, pulling at his hair. 'Shit, shit, shit.'

'What's that?' The cabbie made eye contact with Angel through his rear-view mirror.

Angel tried to steady his breathing. 'Ah, nothing, mate. Just … forgot something.'

'Hope it's not your wallet, innit?' He laughed.

Angel forced a smile. 'Nah. No worries, mate. Just drop me in South Harrow, yeah? Moat Farm Lane?'

They continued in silence. Angel sat back in his seat and stared glumly out the window. Rain spattered the pane, warping contours and melting colours. Buildings slid by: silent, stubborn, suspicious. Eventually, they turned off Ealing Road into Harrow, and Angel felt himself relax slightly. He closed his eyes, trying to bring back visions of that afternoon's photo shoot. But all he saw was a thick, solid looking bloke in a thigh-length mac staring him down. Angel sat up with a start, opening his eyes as wide as he could, trying somehow to dislodge this latest apparition. His eyelids prickled, felt dry. Angel refused to scratch them. He shook his head, willing the image to come tumbling out like sand from a shoe. Surely he was imagining things. The man on the street could have been anybody: a local, a drunk, a madman. What was it about him that had made Angel run? Maybe the King was warning him. It wouldn't have been the first time. Angel recalled how he had had that dream – the dream that had led him to Santa Eva. Elvis had been his guardian then. Why not now?

Angel felt suddenly comforted by this thought. If Elvis was warning him, it meant he didn't want him to get caught. He was on Angel's side. Nothing could go wrong. By the time the taxi pulled into Moat Farm Lane, Angel had recovered his composure. He handed the cabbie his fare, topped with a generous tip, and stepped out into the night.

The house was dark save for a blue light flickering in the living room. Angel rolled his eyes. As he opened the front door, he heard a nasal voice – a journalist commenting on Clinton's successful re-election. He peered cautiously into the room, trying to keep out of view.

'Anh, Angel. Come. Come.'

Angel crouched down to unlace his shoes. 'In a minute, *Thathi*.'

His father nodded. 'Yes. Yes.' He paused. 'You know, that Junius Jayawardena died on the first.'

'Who?'

'Former Prime Minister and President of Sri Lanka, *men*. Late 1970s and '80s.'

Angel blinked. 'Whatever.'

'You-all don't care what happens there.'

'Why should we? They're just a bunch of *yukkos* anyway.'

His father chuckled. 'That Junius was mad, *men*. Saying it was right to kill those bloody Tamils. He must have had lodgers in his brain.'

Angel frowned. 'What?'

'Lodgers. Lodgers.'

'Lodgers?'

'Yes, *men*. They come in and upset things, don't you know.'

'Right.'

'Mmm.' His father's attention returned to the screen. He snorted. 'Anh, that bloody Neil Hamilton …'

Angel went upstairs. He went straight to his room and deposited his gear on the bed, then turned an eye on Vinda's door. The light was off. She was out. Probably getting pissed again, he smiled to himself. No direction, he thought. Vin – Asma, his baby cousin, now grown up and beautiful. But hard. Everything about her was pointy and abrasive. Angel felt something bitter rising in his throat. Asma was four years younger than him, but she seemed a lot older. Angel looked up to her in a weird way, but he also found her irritating and ridiculous. What was all this 'Vinda' shit? She'd been insisting on that for ages. Why the fuck she wanted to name herself after an Indian curry was beyond him. 'Stupid bitch,' he muttered. She was, from time to time. Like when she made fun of Elvis.

She never believed in him – in Angel. Always snickered whenever Delia Aunty said that Elvis had chosen him. What did Asma know? Back then, all she did was clasp her hands and roll her eyes to God, pretending to be pious. Angel knew what she was – what she did. He knew that she'd fucked that poncy Ryan in school – didn't even wait until after hours, had to do it between classes so everyone would find out. As she got older, it got worse. His friends said she'd screw any English guy for a bag of chips. That wasn't exactly true. He'd seen the boys she went with. Cool guys who drove MGs and wore designer gear. Some of them even liked her – a lot. But she didn't care – just took what they gave her and pissed off.

Trussed

When Angel told her he was moving to LA, Asma had asked whether he intended to find Elvis. She'd had that look in her eye: cruel, hard, reptilian. She was really saying that he had to go because he wasn't good enough to go to college. That he was going to LA to pursue some mad, childish dream. She thought him a fool, but she was wrong. She was blind.

Angel wasn't sure how long he'd been staring at Vinda's door when he heard footsteps on the landing. Hastily, he closed his door and sat on the edge of his bed. It was probably her. There was a tick as she turned on the light, then the creak of her floorboards. She didn't sound drunk to Angel. There was some traffic between the bathroom and her room, a flush, running taps. Eventually, he heard another tick – the sound of a light switch being flicked down – and silence.

Angel undressed and turned out his own lights. Standing in his boxers and T-shirt, he went over to the window and looked out. The street was dark, but the road was uncharacteristically busy. One car after another drove by. After about half an hour, Angel thought he saw the same car drive by twice. Instinctively he ducked down, then raised his head inch by inch until his eyes were just above the ledge. There was nothing there. Just a rustling tree. It had been a small car, possibly a Fiat. He frowned, but didn't dare stand up again. Instead, he crawled to his bed, swung up and pulled the sheets tight over his head.

Back in his car, Regis dropped his head against the rest and yawned. From the corner of his eye, he surveyed the Peries home. A light was on in one of the second-floor windows, and another strobed blue from the living room downstairs. Regis closed his eyes. He was hungry. He wanted to drive. He wanted to sleep. He opened his eyes and engaged the car engine. At that moment, he saw a smallish woman walking up the pavement toward him. Regis watched her approach as he began pulling out into the road. She had dark hair and toffee-coloured skin and looked upset about something. Regis blinked. She was closer now, and he could see that her face was sharp and angular, that her frame was slight but strong. She looked straight at him, unseeing. She must have been ill, walking, it seemed, with difficulty. To Regis she was striking: beautiful, resolute, vulnerable. And she had entered the Peries walkway.

Regis was already on the road now. As he drove forward, he saw her opening the front door to the Peries house. This was something he hadn't expected: a beautiful woman entering the net. He drove absently for a while, disturbed by the warmth flooding through his gut. He couldn't understand why he felt this way. She was just a woman. There were more attractive women in LA, anyway. Lithe, full, whatever – you could have anything you wanted. True, Regis hadn't had anyone since Audrey. Unless you counted Carol – but that was work. And Anthuria. Poor Anthuria. Plain of face, ample of bottom, and so desperate for affection she'd be or do anything you wanted.

How Regis had ended up at Anthuria's he couldn't remember. Maybe she called him. Maybe he called her. The ex-wife of one of his mechanics, she used to come to the shop from time to time to flash some back at the boys. Of course everyone looked. Some even touched. But Regis had always thought her a sad girl, whose dignity had been pounded to a fine and faintly coloured powder.

Days after things ended with Audrey, Regis had found himself in Anthuria's bed, staring up at her pillow-creased face. It was awful. She cried and showed him her bruises, then asked him to hold her. Regis was in no mood. He himself was feeling brittle and raw. He couldn't cope with Anthuria's need. It had been a bad idea. In the end, nothing really happened. They went through the motions for a few minutes, then stopped and lay quietly on their backs. Not touching, staring up at nothing, Regis feeling the ground spin, Anthuria letting her tears run into the pillow.

Regis turned the car back and around the block. He drove

down Moat Farm Lane again, slowing down as he passed the house, looking closely at the windows. Nothing. He circled again, peering through the glass, and saw the silhouette of a man drop from view in one of the upstairs windows. But no sign of the woman. He sighed, feeling suddenly tired. Tomorrow, he thought, and headed back to his hotel.

When he saw her again, it was morning and her breath was hitting the air in smooth little clouds. Before he knew it, he was on the tube, watching her as she scanned a newspaper. He observed her foot bobbing absently, her hand emerging from a pocket to deposit a cracker in her mouth. She still didn't look well. There were dark circles beneath her eyes, and her lips looked slightly grey. Crumbs dropped from her mouth, hitting her chin and dusting her chest. She brushed them off with a flaccid gesture, then pulled out a can of something and took a small sip. It was a straight journey: South Harrow to South Kensington; no changes. They arrived in less than half an hour.

Outside, Regis was amazed by the buildings that reclined, like palaces, along the street opposite. Older than anything he was accustomed to, they were ornate, imposing – like something out of a fairytale. He almost forgot the woman as they walked up the steps and into the Victoria & Albert Museum. Standing in the Grand Entrance, surrounded by marble pilasters, Regis felt awkward and out of place. And yet, it reminded him of a visit, some years back, to the Bradbury Building in Downtown LA. That had been a quiet revelation: light spilling through a glass-ceilinged Victorian court, dark brown wood, filigreed wrought iron, caged elevators, and silence. The Grand Entrance revealed a similarly complex interplay of light and substance, but unlike the warmth that had suffused Regis' body as he entered the Bradbury, the V & A exuded a cool, intellectual sophistication that was somehow disquieting.

He walked gingerly between glass-cased artefacts and thick

tapestries, holding his breath in astonishment while keeping the woman in his sights. One moment he was scrutinising a royal bed, the next he was amongst violins, cellos and clocks. Regis stole into a pocket in the raised room, turning his gaze first on the crowds milling below and next on his subject. She was lost in thought, staring into the faces of grandfather clocks, frowning occasionally, and chewing, from time to time, on a cracker. Regis couldn't help but smile. She was so serious, so engrossed in the objects before her, that she didn't notice the spray of crumbs building, like sediment, across her chest.

Regis decided she had a slightly odd face. Overly defined, like a caricature, yet curiously attractive. Perhaps it was her resemblance to the skip. There was no specific element that he could identify as Angel's, but the overall effect – the shape of the face, the cut of the jaw – suggested the two were related somehow. He couldn't tell what her body was like under the coat. All he could gather were the obvious things: her hips were wide, her shoulders broad, she wasn't tall. She was neither fat nor skinny. When she walked, she took proud but compact strides, head held aloft, eyes fixed straight ahead. Despite her obvious discomfort, she managed to compress her movements so that each was a finely executed action. To Regis, she seemed completely oblivious, cloaked in a mantle of meandering thoughts, unaware of the effect she might have on other people. This made her different from many of the women Regis encountered in LA.

He wished he knew her name.

They were on the tube again, this time rattling slowly eastward along the District line. Regis despaired of the dirt that was depositing itself consistently along the surface of his skin. He could feel it tickling his throat and gathering in the ducts of his eyes. He didn't like the Tube, though he had to admit it was the most efficient way of getting around London. If only it was cleaner. He couldn't really compare it to public transport in LA. LA, like most of America, was built for cars – its light railways bought out long ago by oil companies and paved over to make way for the almighty tyre. Regis embraced the road – loved to blaze his Soft Tail down the PCH when the mood took him. But he never forgot his childhood fascination with the Red Cars, the Pacific Electric Railway that once ran from Long Beach deep into the San Fernando Valley.

Bill, his mother's brother, had ridden those Red Cars and spun tales for his sister about how nimbly they took to their tracks. She, in turn, took these tales and twirled them like ribbons for a young Regis. As a result, Regis spent many an afternoon drawing pictures of red trains full of Chinese, Japanese and Mexican farmhands. Born in 1958, Regis never saw the Red Cars. They stopped running in the early 1960s, clearing the way for more freeways to be built, for more cars to be bought and sold. Regis never saw his Uncle Bill either; he died of suffocation when he went out to buy a pint of milk during the Great Smog Attack of October 1954.

Los Angeles had its problems, thought Regis, but London's air wasn't that much better, especially underground. No wonder everyone looked pale and heavily pixelated – like low-resolution images of themselves. No sun, clammy, polluted – at least the sky was blue over LA, even if occasionally tinged with yellow. But then there was the architecture. Regis had never been across the Atlantic before, had never seen Europe beyond the television documentaries and travel magazines. So when he got into central London, his heart leapt; he was suddenly and dramatically enveloped in history.

Crossing the Thames along what he later realised was the Hungerford Bridge, Regis stared to his left, keeping well back from the woman. From his vantage point, he could see Big Ben itself, regal though studded with scaffolding. Parliament fanned out next to it in delicate creamy spikes. Bridges seemed to extend indefinitely along the water's width. Regis looked down. Through the grating below his feet, he saw the river, green and undulating. A plastic bottle bobbed against a piece of driftwood. Trails of scum foamed gently along the water's surface. There was a sneeze. He looked up and saw a young homeless man sitting at the end of the walkway. Regis passed him by with a shake of the head, and hurried down the staircase, hoping he hadn't lost the woman.

On the esplanade, Regis saw the woman moving quickly down the steps to a large building – the Royal Festival Hall. He followed, taking in the width and emptiness of the space. Cutting through a spray of cymbal crashes, he headed straight through the building, keeping his eyes on the woman. She took a seat at an empty table by the windows, took out her paper and began reading. At that moment, Regis wanted to sit next to her, ask her who she was and what she was looking for. After all, to him, she seemed to be tracking something, following an unseen path that rose up to meet her feet and compelled her onward.

But Regis resisted temptation and sat several tables away from her instead. Someone had left a paper on the table: the *Camden New Journal*. Regis began flicking aimlessly through it, glancing from time to time at the woman. She was eating now. And making notes with a pen in her newspaper. Regis returned to the *Camden New Journal*. It bore all the marks of a local rag: stories about garbage collection and local crime rates. He sped through a piece about housing discrimination – an Indian woman winning the right to be re-housed – and sighed. As far as he could tell, London wasn't so bad. LA, on the other hand, was crazy. His parents had only managed to leave South Central in the early 1980s. When he was a child, he remembered his father sighing and telling him they could pass as many Rumford Acts as they liked, but South Central would still be the only place a black person could live in LA.

Through the corner of his eye, Regis saw the woman spring from her seat. Abandoning her belongings, she dashed across the hall toward the bathroom. Regis approached her table and surveyed the objects strewn across it. A pen, the classified section of a newspaper, a discarded sandwich. He leaned closer to the table, putting his paper down for a minute. Her bag was sitting on the chair, stuffed with packets of crackers and some kind of soft drink. Regis wanted to reach inside and pull out something that would put a name to her face. He positioned himself closer to the bag, but as the shadow of his hand fell over its mouth, he saw her. She looked drained and distracted as she emerged from the opposite end of the hall. He turned abruptly, walking along the windows before crossing over into the bar area. She hadn't noticed him, but Regis decided to leave the building immediately.

He was annoyed with himself. In the old days, he would have known her name before he'd even left LA. He would have mapped out the family, predicted the dynamics, had a list of names, ages, occupations. And yet, here he was, having followed her the whole day, and he didn't even have a name. But he knew she was pregnant. There was no other explanation he could think of to account for the general pall of nausea that dominated her face, and the stash of crackers and carbonated drinks. He had seen no evidence of a man. She seemed a loner to him – someone comfortable enough with herself to forget about the company of others. The fact that she rarely looked at other people convinced him of this. Or perhaps she was hiding something.

Images of the woman effervesced in Regis' mind as he made his way back to South Harrow. She looked lonely, he thought. And hurt. In fact, she seemed the very opposite of the skip. In spite of his crime, Angel was brazenly seeking attention, searching out a stage to raise his profile. He was arrogant in the extreme. She, on the other hand, was subtle, prudent and low key. And of course, she was cute.

6 Gig

By the time Friday finally arrived, Angel had stopped drawing open the curtains. He'd called in sick on Thursday morning, and quit Imperial Mini Cabs that evening. He couldn't risk being jacked out of his car by some crazy bounty-hunter. He'd heard the stories. He knew what he was up against. As long as he stayed inside, he'd be ok. He wagered that the agent wouldn't break into a home in the UK. He probably hadn't made any contact with the authorities here, so Angel felt safe in his bedroom, at least. His mother berated him for being a layabout, but Angel was unmoved. He remained where he was, venturing to the kitchen and bathroom infrequently and only out of necessity. He didn't even bother to nag Vinda, though she hadn't really been around anyway. This morning, he thought, he would ask her whether she would come to the Horse and Saddle. Later, he decided a note under her door would do.

Angel opened his cupboard and stared at the garment bag containing his suit. Despite all his previous reservations, he decided to wear it that night. He was excited. His first proper performance in what seemed like months. But there could be a hitch. His pursuer might make an appearance. 'I need you,' he whispered, eyes fixed on the hanging bag. 'You have to help me.' He removed the suit from its protective sheath and laid it out on his bed. There wasn't much light in Angel's room, but the suit seemed to glow from within, scintillating like snow beneath moonlight. He knelt down, bent his forehead to the knee of the jumpsuit, and closed his eyes. 'Help me,' he prayed. 'Help me. I need you.' The room was silent, but for Angel's measured breaths. Everything was in shadow, cloaked by the opacity of his thick blue curtains. Then he felt something. Warm and tingling against his forehead, like hot water flowing between his eyebrows. He screwed his eyes shut even tighter and saw the outlines of a face, followed by a body. Mutton-chopped and lush of lips, visored, wearing the selfsame suit: it was Elvis. He didn't say anything, just sneered and jigged a thigh. It was a sign. Elvis would be there for him tonight.

Hours passed as Angel did voice exercises and ran through his songlist. He spent at least ninety minutes in the bathroom, showering, scrubbing, shaving. Another forty-five minutes went into his make-up, a thickish foundation to hide any blemishes and subtly lighten his skin tone. Last, he donned the suit, and miraculously, the fit was even better than before: it shrank back to the memory of his contours, contracting snugly against his waist. Angel stood for a full fifteen minutes staring at the way it rounded his seat and flared out at the shins. He practised throwing the cape back dramatically over his right shoulder and crouching down to greet an adoring crowd. *Ooo, ooo, ooo, I feel my temperature risin'*. The words shot from his lips, unprepared, unrehearsed, but perfectly intoned. This was better than cocaine, he thought, better even than sex. He was high on himself. He was invincible.

Fired with confidence, he rang Carla. He found her number inscribed on a green post-it, crushed into the nose of his holster. Smoothing the square of paper with a thumb, he smiled at the portly numerals, their curled ends and weighty centres.

'Oh, Angel! So you are calling me, then?' Carla giggled.

Angel was relieved. 'Of course. I … I haven't been well, that's why I didn't ring right—'

'—Oh yes, yes,' she broke in. 'It doesn't matter. I was away anyway. On business, you know.' She paused. 'So, how are you now? Feeling better?'

Angel caught sight of himself in the mirror opposite and grinned. 'Yes. Much,' he observed the bulk of his thighs, steel-smooth and bullet-tight. Heat stirred in the pit of his stomach. 'So … do you have any plans for tonight? I've got a gig. Will you come?'

Angel expected a 'yes'. After all, he was wearing the suit now. Nothing could go wrong. But Carla said she could make only the first half of the show. Still, in the same breath, she asked Angel to drop by afterward if he was up to it. In fact, she sounded so excited about seeing him, Angel knew it was all down to the King. Elvis was exercising his legendary doggedness. If he could convince Richard Nixon to meet him, unannounced, in 1970 and get the president to give him a special badge from the Bureau of Narcotics and Dangerous Drugs, then bringing Carla within the shadow of his cape was a simple manoeuvre. Elvis had declared her to be Angel's; it would be so.

Angel gave his reflection a final, admiring glance, breathed a prayer to Elvis and swept out the door.

The Horse and Saddle was brimming with the usual Friday night crowd. A mix of university students, married couples, old-timers and – it being Ealing – at least a handful of under-aged teens. Angel went in through the back entrance, hidden beneath a great, dark coat. Eddie was there to meet him, grinning.

'Right on time, mate,' he said, grasping and shaking Angel's hand. 'Lots of people out there. Been drinking fairly steadily, so you're bound to get some enthusiastic dancers.'

Angel nodded. He wasn't up to small talk. He handed a recording to Eddie – his backing tracks – and fished out his microphone. Inside his head, guitars were rolling, chords meshing, all to the steady throb of a blood vessel somewhere below his right temple. Something was flinching and growing inside him. Something hot – like acid reflux – was working its way up his oesophagus. Angel rubbed his belly, which had become uncomfortably distended.

'You've got fifteen minutes, mate.' Eddie returned from wherever he'd disappeared to. 'Everything all right?'

Angel half-smiled, willing Eddie to leave the back room. Alone, Angel gulped for air, hoping to get rid of the weight in his stomach. He opened and closed his mouth four times. On the fourth try, he let loose a bubbling burp that simultaneously cleared his windpipe and flattened his stomach. Angel patted his chest and took a few deep breaths. He called Eddie in to check the sound on his mic and the levels on the recording.

The pub was packed when Regis arrived. He'd followed the skip to it earlier, but took a walk around the area, recceing possible escape routes first. This time he came by car, expecting to leave with the skip in a few hours' time. There was the small problem of involving the local police (and Scotland Yard), but Regis thought he'd bother about that later. He was sure he would be able to cut a deal with Angel to suit both their needs, without having to resort to outside forces.

When he entered the Horse and Saddle, he was surprised by the diversity of the crowd: young, old, black, white, Elvis freaks, college kids. He slipped in and felt at ease. Laughter rose in arcs above people's heads, voices clashed and mingled, and through all this the beer flowed easily, like a brook through a breeze-blown meadow. Regis scanned the room, keeping fairly close to the entrance. Then he saw her. Not too far from him, on her own, smiling to herself and drinking something clear and bubbly. Regis walked toward her. She didn't notice. He stood next to her, feeling his nerves begin to fray.

'Uh—'

That's all he managed to blurt before the music tore up the

room. Out came Angel, sparkling, sweating, quaking with energy. The woman was now grinning and bobbing her head.

The crowd went mad. *Lord almighty, feel my temperature rising*, sang Angel and his audience replied: *Higher, higher, it's burning through my soul*. It went on like that until the end of the song, Angel sweating, roaring, launching open-palmed karate jabs to the air. He saw everyone, and no one, though at some point, he caught a glimpse of Asma singing frantically along, a bag of crisps in her hand. Carla, too, was there, eyes shining, lips full and smiling. Angel winked at her and kept going: 'Blue Suede Shoes', 'A Little Less Conversation', 'Fever'. Teenage girls were howling, laughing, jumping up and down. Three men by the bar wreathed arms and serenaded one another. There were at least two men in the room with fluffy sideburns and ponderous midriffs, and a trio of elderly women nodding their heads at an alarming pace. The stink of beer and gin filled the room, but Angel barely registered it. His blood ran black at that moment: sixteenth, eighth, quarter notes flowed freely through his veins, coalescing somewhere in his bronchial passages and rushing up and out his throat like a school of glimmering moonfish.

Regis was taken aback. Well fuck me, he thought, the shit is actually good. In spite of himself, lyrics shot up from his diaphragm and hit the air, right on cue with everyone else. He looked over at the woman, and she darted a smile at him, nodding to the rhythm. Regis was suddenly dancing next to her, both of them dipping heads toward one another and singing.

Regis was confused. He couldn't figure out why this was happening. It was totally out of character for him. He tried to remember how little he liked Elvis, how even less he liked the skip. But the vibe in the room was infectious. And this was his only 'in' with the woman. He decided it had to be her. In his day, Regis had done far stranger things to attract the attentions of a lady. He told himself it was also his job to meld with the crowd. This made him feel even better.

They danced. They sang. They mugged at one another. 'Blue Suede Shoes' got everyone twisting and pointing fingers to their toes. 'A Little Less Conversation' set off a Mexican wave of gyrations across the room. Regis was having a blast. When the set ended, he turned to the woman with a grin.

'Hey, not bad.'

She smiled. 'No. I'd forgotten how good he is.'

'You've heard him before?' Regis feigned surprise.

'Yeah. Oh God, but back then it was just a pain.'

Regis offered a puzzled frown.

She laughed. 'When we were little, he used to sing in the shower – or worse, in front of the mirror.'

'When you were little?'

'He's my cousin,' she said. 'Can you believe it?'

Regis looked at her. 'What's wrong with that?'

The woman paused and shrugged. 'Nothing, I guess. It was just a bit weird when we were growing up. But now … well, look at everyone.'

Regis nodded. 'No one's complaining, that's for sure.'

The woman peered up at Regis, eyes searching. 'You know, you look familiar for some reason.'

Regis dropped a beat, nerves vaguely tickling. He'd been careful the other day; he was sure she hadn't seen him. Still, it was safer to ward off the questions now. He laughed. 'You trying to pick me up?' He considered his feet for a moment, then looked up and smiled. 'Hey, I'm Bill, by the way. What's your name?'

'Bill, huh?' said the woman, studying his face. 'That's a solid, American name … I'm Vinda.'

'Vinda?' Regis scrunched his face. 'Does it mean anything?'

Vinda grinned. 'Depends on who you are, I guess.' Her eyebrows did a double-skip.

Regis nodded. He smiled at the sight of that brow signalling what he took to be a clear and tempting invitation. They sipped from their drinks, looking up at one another from time to time, and around the room. People were knocking back pints, laughing loudly, showing off their Elvis moves. In the far corner, a drag king, sporting a pompadour and Greaser jacket, demonstrated a series of pelvic thrusts. 'Hey,' Regis nudged Vinda, 'look at that. She's even got the sideburns.'

'Where?' Vinda searched the crowd giddily. 'Where?'

'There. Over by the corner,' Regis pointed with his eyes. 'Near the woman with the purple top.'

'Cool!' Vinda looked delighted. 'She's the best of the lot. I mean those two guys—' she jabbed a finger quickly to her right, '—are just appalling. They look like a couple of Hell's Angels in toupees.'

Regis glanced at the men. With their enormous paunches and veneered coifs, they did look like a parody of something you'd find in an LA biker bar. On the other hand, they would have easily disappeared into the landscape in Memphis or Vegas. 'Well, at least they try.'

Vinda rolled her eyes. 'Sometimes it just isn't worth it, you know?' She blinked, shifting her gaze to the inside of her glass. 'So, whereabouts in America are you from?'

'Los Angeles.'

'LA! Really?' Vinda's eyes were shining. 'You know, Angel was there for a while. He was working and gigging out there. Small gigs, mainly, I think. Nothing on the Sunset Strip or anything.'

Regis leaned forward. 'How long was he there for?'

'Oh, maybe a few years. I don't remember exactly. It feels like ages.'

'Is he going back?'

Vinda shook her head. 'I don't think so. He says he's had enough of America. Says he found LA a bit too superficial and that he misses London. Can you believe it?'

Regis frowned, tipping his head slightly left and right. 'Yeah, I can. London's beautiful. LA is … LA.'

'You know, that's exactly what he said: "LA is … LA".'

'Have you ever been?'

'No. Not yet, anyway.'

'It's a great place in some ways; a dive, in others. But London's fantastic.'

'Well, how long have you been here?'

'A few days.'

'Give it a few years and tell me how much you love it then.'

Music rushed from the speakers and everyone started to cheer. Angel swept into the room, cape flashing behind him like a comet's tail. He leapt on top of the bar, rolling his hips and flexing his thighs. He was belting out 'Jailhouse Rock', sending the crowd into a twisting frenzy.

Even Regis was awestruck. He realised, then, what mass at Santa Eva must have been like, how Theresa could not have helped herself, why everyone had let Angel walk into their lives and take whatever he wanted.

By his second set, Angel seemed to have entered a higher plane of reality, though, admittedly, he owed much of that feeling to his new position on top of the bar. He threw in a couple of ballads, crowd pleasers, inviting some of the ladies to join him on his pedestal. 'Love Me Tender' reduced one stiff-haired ladette to tears, 'Can't Help Falling in Love' left a young Japanese student swooning. There was no doubt in the room; Elvis had come again.

Regis looked around him and was amused by the dewy eyes and flushed faces. Only he and Vinda remained fairly untouched, Vinda looking slightly – and suddenly – pale, and he feeling generally aloof. He bent toward Vinda. 'Are you ok?'

She nodded, swallowing and looking expectantly into her glass.

'Do you want another? I can get you one.'

She shook her head. 'Shh. I think he's going to sing – yes – he's going to—'

We're caught in a trap, broke in Angel. Regis looked up.

Angel was shimmying along the bar, jumpsuit dazzling under the lights. Vinda seemed to forget her discomfort and started bobbing up and down. Regis looked at her sideways, watching her cheeks flush and her hair flop in all directions. Something about the determination with which she caught the rhythm and channelled it through her body made Regis uneasy. She looked possessed, and yet it seemed a controlled possession. Regis couldn't figure it out. And the fact that he couldn't inexplicably made him smile.

Angel was in raptures. His skin was on fire, his mouth dripping liquid gold. He launched into 'Suspicious Minds', eyes squeezed shut, tongue delivering notes like sparks from a firecracker. *So, if an old friend I know/Stops and says hello* … He opened his eyes, dimly surveying a swaying group of college kids. Rolling his head back, he blinked, then hunkered down and drew a pointing finger across the crowd until he found himself staring at his cousin and, next to her, to his horror, the man: tall, dark, in a mid-length jacket. The stranger was smiling at Vinda, but the moment Angel's gaze fell on him, the man looked up sharply, like an eagle with a mouse in its sights. *Would I still see suspicion in your eyes?* Angel's heart was thudding painfully in his chest now. The man was no more than a metre away. The set was almost over. There was no escape.

Regis looked up and found the skip staring directly at him. Terror flickered in Angel's eyes. Regis narrowed his gaze, locking the skip into his eyeline. Angel was off the bar now, and moving through the crowd. Regis kept him in his sights, gradually making his way to the exit. He said nothing to Vinda.

Here we go again/Asking where I've been. Angel began a quick backward strut toward the opposite end of the pub. He cupped one, then another lady's chin, crooning gently. *O, let our love survive – or dry the tears from your eyes.* Fans pressed against him, drunk and desperate. Angel managed to keep a wall of women between himself and the man. *When honey, you know/I've never lied to you …* He was nearly there. He could see the man's head bobbing up and down, making for the entrance. Angel kept singing and backing away. *We're caught in a trap/I can't walk out …* He barely had time to finish the number, but he did. The pub erupted, and Angel fled into the back room, searching for a way out. He was panicking now, wondering why Elvis had forsaken him in his hour of need. From what little he could tell in the few seconds he took, there was no other way out but the back exit. 'Fucking fuck,' he spat, then, without a second thought, blasted through the door and dashed down the alley.

Outside, Regis made for the back alley, side-stepping rubbish and empty beer bottles. When he got to the door, he found it wide open and swinging on its hinges. The skip's cape was flashing in the distance. Regis sped behind it, crunching glass and tin cans underfoot. For a moment, he gained pace, the glitter of Angel's suit getting brighter, the cape almost within reach. He stretched out an arm, grasped air. He lunged with his legs, lengthening his stride, pushing his feet forward. His right sole landed on a can, slid to the side. His body followed. Regis stumbled, almost fell, kept running. But the skip had gained an advantage. Each step Regis took sent the glimmering cape further and further away.

Regis stopped, bent over, held his thighs. He was panting, gulping air, feeling the wind stiffen his sweat-soaked shirt. He could not believe he'd let the skip get away – let him take the advantage. Next time, he thought, unbending himself. But even as he thought this, doubt crept into his mind. He turned around and walked back down the alley.

Angel could hear quick steps behind him, but the 'Howling Wolf' suit had transformed into a second, slick skin that massaged his muscles and heightened his aerodynamics. He was an Olympian speedskater, shooting nimbly through the back streets. At one point the agent seemed to gain on him, almost getting hold of the very edge of his cape. But Angel doffed him off, suddenly elated by the knowledge that he couldn't be caught. There was what seemed like the sound of hoof-beats at his heels, but Angel opened his mouth, sucked in more air, and ran harder.

By the time he'd made it to a main road and hailed a taxi, he felt certain there was no one behind him. He couldn't go back home, though. The man would be waiting for him there. Then he remembered his phone call, Carla's invitation. He leaned forward and asked the driver to take him to Aberdeen Road.

Carla smiled when Angel arrived at her doorstep, glittering under the moonlight like LA at night.

'I wasn't expecting you so soon,' she said. 'You know, you didn't even speak to me at the intermission. I looked for you before I left, but you had disappeared. What happened?'

'Sorry.' Angel suddenly felt breathless. 'I wanted to see you, but … things …' He felt his chest shudder. Putting a hand to his heart, he exhaled sharply. Pain rushed up between his rib-cage and an odd, uncomfortable heat radiated from his groin. 'I …' His breathing was laboured. 'I … need … to sit … down.' He sank to the ground, body sagging on one of the steps, and pointed at the cab. 'I … sorry … Carla … ?'

Carla looked from Angel to the taxi and quickly ran to it, wallet in hand. A minute later she led Angel into the house, supporting him at the elbow as she sat him in a chair in the kitchen. 'What's wrong, Angel? Do you need a doctor?' She poured him a glass of water and sat next to him.

Angel shook his head. 'No … be … fine.' He gasped. 'I'll pay you back.'

Carla rubbed his back with her palm, trying to calm him. It seemed to help. 'You know,' she began. 'I'm glad you rang … it's nice to see you again.'

Angel tried to meet her gaze, but the room was on a tilt and turning. A wave of nausea swelled at the back of his throat and the right side of his skull began throbbing, threatening to peel away from the rest of his head. 'Car—' A spasm ripped through Angel's belly, jerking him forward. He clutched at the table, feeling his stomach yawn wider and wider. He could feel it stretching open, hear it heaving a sea of storms. And then it struck him. A hunger like no hunger he had ever experienced. Angel suddenly felt hollow. Air whipped through him like lemonade through a straw. He was certain that if he didn't eat at that very moment, he would detach from the chair, like dandelion fluff, and dissipate into the air. He swallowed dryly, mumbling to Carla. 'I think … I think some food would help.'

Carla, who for the past few minutes had been staring at Angel with mounting panic, roused herself. 'Yes. Of course. What would you like?'

Angel looked up then, sharply, without a pause. When he spoke, he scarcely recognised his voice. 'Do you have any peanut butter?'

I have to eat. Nausea is sliming a slug's trail up my throat. I don't bother to tear the croissant into polite morsels; I sink my teeth into the whole. I'm in my room and no one is watching, so it doesn't matter. I finish the croissant in two bites. Luckily I have another one.

Trussed

Angel hasn't been home for two days. He didn't come back after his gig at the Horse and Saddle. Agnes Aunty isn't really worried – not yet. She's used to Angel coming and going at odd times. And I reckon he's at Carla's. He'll ring when he's ready. He should, too. Yesterday, someone from the Catacombs phoned asking whether he was available to perform at their cabaret night on Tuesday. That's Tuesday as in tomorrow. I should have stayed out of it, but I've always wanted to go there – see what actually happens inside instead of gobbling up all the rumours. So I said yes.

Now I have to find Angel. I've enjoyed these forty-eight hours without him, without his gormless prattle and infantile jokes. But I meant what I said to Amrik – Angel isn't really *that* bad. It's just that he thinks he's better than everyone else, especially me. And so does everyone in the family. I can't deny he's got a great voice, that he's a born performer. When he decided to go to LA, I was stunned. I thought he was crazy, but I admired him, too. But when that thing with Ryan happened at school and the rumours went round, everyone believed I was guilty – no one gave me the benefit of the doubt. And yet Angel was running around, shop-lifting beer and records and no one cared. He would sing 'Jailhouse Rock' and everything would be forgotten. I would pick up my rosary and deny the vicious attacks on my reputation, but no one heard.

I sweep croissant flakes off my chest and pad across the hall to his room. As I enter, I find myself coated in stale airlessness. I dry heave twice before making it to the window and throwing it wide. I pull open his curtains, dousing the room with light. Elvis is on the dresser, smiling at me through open tubes of make-up and bits of paper. The cupboard door is open, a garment bag hangs inside, unzipped. Angel's jeans lie spread-eagled on the carpet.

The number, I think, but zero in on the open cupboard instead. The garment bag smells like wax and lavender and is pristine on the inside. I move it to the left, peering into the cupboard's corners. There are a few shirts and trousers, a small black sports bag, an old video camera case. I step back, returning the garment bag to its original position and browse the dresser.

Its surface is interrupted by so many screwed-up bits of tissue and paper, the former blotted with blood, the latter gathering dust. I press open each one, like a fortune from a cookie, and read. Most are receipts: one from a design studio in Notting Hill, another from Boots. One is written in Angel's hand and has the word 'Elvis' repeated three times on it. I scan the ground below the dresser: more crumpled tissues, a shred of plastic, a blob of cream, a twisted piece of green paper. I pick it up and open it. It's a note from Carla, written in a florid hand, and containing the number I've been looking for.

Angel opened his eyes to find Carla lying next to him. His 'Howling Wolf' suit was draped over a chair behind her. He looked at the clock. It was 2 am. He was hungry. Edging out of the bed, he stood, naked, at its foot. He stared at the suit, his skin crying out for it, wanting to surrender to its grip. But he dared not disturb the slumbering Wolf. Instead, he slipped down to the kitchen, the tiles cool beneath his feet. He opened the fridge, throwing yellow light onto his skin. There was almost nothing in it, apart from a tub of hummus and some carrots. Angel turned to the cupboards, opening them one by one. He found a half-full jar of crunchy peanut butter. It was the same jar he had eaten from when he arrived at Carla's after the gig. He was surprised – and relieved – to find it wasn't empty.

Planting himself on a stool, Angel set about finishing what he had started the night before. He dipped a spoon into the jar and sucked on it, comforted by the sweet-salty stickiness coating the roof of his mouth. It felt good dissolving against his tongue. Angel wanted to call home, but feared the agent was still lurking about the house. He wanted to tell Asma to stay away from the man. He recalled how easy the two appeared to be in one another's company and wondered whether they'd actually spoken. He raised another spoonful of peanut butter to his mouth. They probably hadn't – and even if they had, Asma didn't know anything. He relaxed on the stool, impervious to the chill of its chrome. He swung his legs and traced patterns along the tiles with his big toe.

Scraping the bottom of the jar, Angel thought of the Horse and Saddle. The crowds had adored him, their gratitude tumbling forth in fervent displays. Angel lapped up that energy, consumed it. But his stomach yearned for more. The King was a febrile presence, coursing through his muscles, heating him from the inside out. Even now, he was sweating.

He was also wide awake. He roamed through Carla's flat, picking up objects and examining them. The King was in him, but for how long? Was he a worthy host? Angel paused by a blue vase. He wrapped his hands around it, feeling the tightness of its circumference, the absoluteness of its circularity. He was worthy. Of course he was. First Delia Aunty, then the dream, Santa Eva and finally the suit. He was on the path to greatness and that path would henceforth be strewn with gold. His mind raced. He was anxious and wound up and full of the King. He put the vase down, his body suddenly molten. He was taut, poised to act.

He woke Carla.

The sheets hung in white braids from the bed, their ends frayed and fanning out on the oak floor. Carla knelt, hair in tangles, arms thrown over the mattress. Behind her, Angel shifted the pressure from his knees, relaxing onto his heels. One hand trailed down her back, the other was placed flat on the floor as support. They were panting, their bodies slick with sweat. The sun, which had risen an hour ago, charged through the blinds, cutting gold slivers into their glistening skins. Angel's arm trembled. He stretched out on the floor and pulled Carla toward him. One of her feet was still trapped in the sheet.

He held her against him, fighting against the sensation that he was not here, but somewhere outside looking in. Even as he pushed into her, his mouth upon her breast, it was as if he were only a conduit – a bridge between Carla and Elvis. And yet he felt himself melting, pouring into her, devouring her scent with his tongue.

Angel glanced to his left. He was lying by the chair which was holding his suit. As he looked at it, threads of uncertainty unravelled inside him. His blood chilled. Perhaps this was only a suit – a finely crafted jumpsuit – and nothing more. After all, its components were no mystery: leather, satin, a few gems. He grazed a cuff with a fingertip. He might even be able to determine the precise mix of material if he put his mind to it.

He rubbed the edge of the cape between thumb and forefinger. It was silky, slippery even. He tightened his grip. His fingers grew warm and the warmth spread through his forearms, into his shoulders and down his back. Soon his whole body was hot and humming. Doubt gathered its threads and withdrew; loaves bloomed in its stead. Elvis had come again. And Angel was his vehicle. He put his hand on Carla and her eyes opened with his touch. Angel pulled her on top of him and somersaulted into her eyes.

When Angel returned from the shower, Carla was speaking to someone on the telephone, nodding. A bead of fear trickled down his spine. She held the handset out to him, smiling. He stared at it, brows crimped, and swallowed.

Carla pushed the phone into his hand. 'Take it. It's for you,' she said. 'Someone called Vinda, about a performance?'

Vinda was two blocks ahead. She was walking with someone else – maybe her boyfriend. They were heading for King's Cross station. Regis was surprised when she came out of the flat. He'd been standing across the street, clutching his copy of *Interview with a Vampire*. She was wrapped in a long black shawl, wearing spiky-heeled boots. Her hair was pinned up, hanging in two braided arcs at the back – like the scalloped edge of an elaborate gown. As she strode, fishnets flashed in the moonlight. Regis swam toward them.

He had been watching the Peries house for three days. He wagered that if he stuck to Vinda, eventually she'd lead him to the skip. Either that or Angel would come back to the house. If he was going to run again, he'd need his things. When Vinda emerged from the house that evening, Regis had to make a decision: follow her or stay put. Something about her manner convinced him to take the first option. She'd looked nondescript, in jeans and a jacket, and was carrying a bag. She might have been bringing it for Angel. Regis convinced himself of this because he couldn't face sitting another day in front of the house. He wanted a change of scene. Vinda gave him the excuse he needed.

And what an excuse. Walking up Gray's Inn Road behind Vinda, Regis was enmeshed in her stockings – trapped by the swish of thigh against fabric. Standing on the tube, he cast sidelong glances at her legs, meditated on the tiny diamonds of flesh flickering in the light. He was careful to stay out of sight, taking up a position a little way down the carriage, keeping his back to the couple. They were oblivious, huddled together, talking and laughing.

They didn't stop talking, even when they reached their destination – something called the Catacombs. There was a long queue of people, many with arrow-tipped studs through their lips or noses. But Vinda and her friend walked right up to the front of the queue, said something to the doorman, and were swallowed up inside.

Regis looked from the bouncer to the line of punters stretching behind him. There were a few 'normals' in the crowd, but the majority were costumed in anything from plastic baby-dolls to rubber body socks. Regis eyed the doorman once again. He was tall and black like him. Regis strode up to him and smiled. He had a fifty-pound note folded into his palm. He reached out and shook the bouncer's hand. The man glanced at the note, smiled back and ushered Regis through.

I hold Amrik's hand as we walk in. We are in a tunnel and descending, descending further into darkness. The thump of music pulses underfoot, sprints up my calves and thighs. It becomes hotter as we go deeper, so hot that I pull the wrap from my shoulders, let the air settle on my bare skin.

'You look unbelievable, darling,' says Amrik. His eyes are wide. He hasn't stopped saying this to me since I put on the outfit at his flat. 'Even I'd fuck you if I could.'

I hold up an admonishing finger. 'I'm not here to fuck, am I?'

Amrik shakes his head. 'Well, you should be ... You look un*believable*.'

I link my arm through his. We come to a fork. The music is louder on the right, so we head that way, each step relaying rhythmic jolts up our legs. I lean into Amrik.

'What are we doing here?'

'Not fucking.'

I nudge him with my elbow. 'No really. Why are we here?'

Amrik looks at me. '*You* wanted to come here.'

It's true. I did. But as I navigate this labyrinth of thunking music and naked desire, I feel only Derek's breath in my ears, clammy and stinking. I am wearing the costume I wore at our first appointment: a low-cut bodice of black and red, only this time I have drawn a heart-shaped beauty mark on my breast. Derek's grin hovers before me: shiny, mocking. His breath chokes me, his flesh suffocates mine. Bile scorches the back of my throat. I steady myself against Amrik and keep walking.

People line the walls, their writhing bodies silhouetted in blue-white light. A woman pulls out a dildo and thrusts it up a man's backside. As she does this, she chokes him with a silver lamé collar, teeth bared against his ear. I am shocked by the violence of the movement, the vulnerability of the man's position. But his face is wreathed in ecstasy. I clutch Amrik tighter and hurry forward. 'Did you see that?' I whisper. Amrik rolls his eyes and grimaces.

Suddenly, the walls fall away and music blares from all sides. We are standing in a vaulted cave, lights strobing above us. Music rushes into us, flattens our anxiety. Two women clad in identical nun's habits, thongs and stilettos, whirl on the dance floor. I slip on my mask, a silk confection of black feathers that wraps around my eyes, and join them.

Amrik cups his hands around my ear. 'What time does he come on?' he shouts.

I shrug, mouthing the words 'I don't know', and raise my arms. The music is breathy, high-speed, delinquent. I move with it, forgetting my nausea, ignoring the corset squeezing against my ribs. It envelopes me, transmogrifies into an embrace. I undulate within it, sloughing thoughts of Derek to the ground. My skin is alive and open. Amrik dances behind me, runs his hands down my hips. He's wearing a tight T-shirt, leather trousers and some of my black eyeliner. His head, which he has recently shaved, is covered in glitter.

Amrik is a firefly in the darkness, appearing and disappearing at intervals. One moment he's next to me, the next he's gyrating with a handsome, sculpted blonde. Meanwhile, my heels dig into the dance floor, gashing holes in Derek's skin, winching apart his jeering mouth joint by joint. By the time the track has melted away and the applause begins, Derek has been shredded underfoot, battered by a throng of daggered heels.

Angel opened his arms to the applause, satin and leather taut against his muscles. He opened his mouth and notes unfurled from it like silk from a spool. He'd spent two days without anything, aside from Carla, touching his body – two days walking around her house in nothing but his skin. Aside from Howling Wolf, he had nothing to wear. He avoided the suit, stroking it from time to time and recoiling from the yearning that crept over him. He was afraid. Sometimes he would beg Carla to fold it into her closet, out of sight. But whenever she tried to, he shouted, commanding her to keep her hands off its precious surface. When Vinda rang to tell him about the Catacombs, he had no choice but to wear it. Immediately, Howling Wolf enfolded him, colonised every skin cell. For a moment, Angel panicked. Then warmth fizzed in his belly and his nostrils filled with the aroma of oven-fresh bread.

Before mounting the stage, Angel snorted two lines of coke. Carla had offered them to him, before cutting a couple for herself. His brain, eyes, skin – everything was tingling. He surveyed the crowd, which writhed and hollered as he sang. A woman bared her breasts to him. A man danced on the end of a silver collar. Another, in leather shorts and an Elizabethan ruff, pogoed up and down. Everyone was tangled in the other, linking arms or legs.

Angel dove into them, microphone in hand, still singing. Hands scrolled over his body, kneaded his flesh. Each fibre of the suit suckered onto him. Angel reached out, his palms floating over upturned faces – lips, noses, tongues. Satin and leather melted into his pores. He howled, surfing a carousel of hands. The crowd shouted back, groping him. Howling Wolf flowed through Angel's veins, rose to the under-surface of his skin. And everywhere the hands kept pushing, lifting, caressing, pummeling.

Angel found himself back on the stage, belting out 'Fever'. The crowd snapped their fingers and thrust their hips at him. Angel thrust back, winding his arm in haughty circles. Words issued from his lips, stretching out like plasticine. It was not Angel's voice, yet it came from his mouth and his vocal cords vibrated as he sang. He closed his eyes. Elvis was within and without him. 'Thang you vera muhsh,' he heard himself say. The set was over.

Regis leaned against the bar. He watched as the skip floated over the crowd, arms outstretched in a Christ-like pose. Angel looked tired, the make-up doing little to hide the bags under his eyes. But the energy radiating from him was awesome. Men and women thrust their hands everywhere, tearing at Angel's hair, his armpits, his crotch. He kept singing, oblivious to the assault.

Regis sipped from a glass of rum and Coke. His lip, submerged in the liquid, rested on an ice cube and was steadily going numb. Cool vapours travelled up his nostrils. They contrasted with the dense atmosphere of the club, the sticky heat and smell of sex. Regis had only been to a place like this once before. That was with Audrey. She thrived on the S & M scene, saying it was the backbone of her cartoon drawings. She would sit and watch the crowds with delight, doing mental sketches of the more audacious among them. Rarely did she actually take part, though she did that too, offering up her tattooed back to anyone who wanted it. Regis couldn't watch. After that first time, he let her go alone, asking her to keep her outings a secret from him. It was no use. She couldn't hide the bruises from Regis, or her eyes, wet and shining with wonder. Even as he saw all this, he didn't believe it, preferring instead to think of it as a necessary part of Audrey's creative research.

Regis ordered another rum and Coke. He saw a similar sheen in the skip's eyes – the same wonder and loss. Angel was singing 'Fever' now and the entire dance floor was gyrating in front of him. Vinda and her friend were there, too, slapping their thighs and shaking their arses. Vinda's head was thrown back, light spilling pink and yellow on to her throat. Her friend was grinding against another man's thigh. Regis smiled, relief pinching his cheeks.

He looked over at the skip, who was jabbing his pelvis forward and propellering his arm. Those eyes were dripping wonder and loss, yes, but desperation, too. And confusion. This was not like Audrey Kim, after all.

Regis thought he saw panic. He knew that Angel hadn't seen him – couldn't see anyone with the lights dazzling his view. But the fear in Angel's eyes was unmistakable.

Regis had seen that look before. Years ago, he'd found his

grandmother squatting in her cupboard, urinating into one of her suitcases. 'Reggie,' she'd said, 'this toilet is too damn dark.' When Regis calmly explained that she was not actually anywhere near a toilet, she looked up at him, shocked. Then she looked down. When she met Regis' gaze again, terror bloomed on her cheeks, coloured her eyes. A minute later, her expression was calm. 'Reggie,' she said, 'why're you standing there watching an old woman piss? Can't you wait instead of barging in on me?'

Regis rolled an ice cube in his mouth. Poor old Grandma Gigi. She died not long after, in her sleep. But she'd fallen off that cliff long ago, let herself go without knowing it. Regis crunched into the ice cube, showering cold shards onto his gums. He squinted at the stage. No, maybe that wasn't the skip. Or maybe he wasn't quite there yet. Sooner or later it would happen, though. Elvis freaks always took the same path: they started with admiration, carried through to obsession and ended in the nut-hole. It was true enough – he'd seen it on *Donahue*. There was a battle taking place on that stage – a clash of wills. And one day, Angel would lose.

I am falling. The music simultaneously swallows me up and wriggles through me. I am a breach in time, feeding and excreting dimensions. Bodies whirl, fan, coalesce. Angel's voice keeps us in motion, buoys us. We are spinning on our axes, rotating around one another. The entire floor throbs. Then silence. Light is extinguished. And all that is left is a dense and heaving darkness, wet and impenetrable.

'Oh my.'

Words condense in my ear.

'He's not bad, Vinda. Not bad at all.'

I blink through dampened lashes. The lights are back on, strobing us. People are slapping their hands together, hooting and whistling. Applause hails down like firecrackers on a tin roof. I want to clamp my hands over my ears, shut the noise out. Amrik bobs up and down in flashes, like something from a stop-motion animation film. I grab his wrist and pull him from the mass.

'A drink,' I shout, but he doesn't hear me.

We stand at the bar, gulping down water. Then we order two tequila slammers each and swallow those as well.

'Darling, your cousin was fabulous.'

The tequila is carrying out a pincered attack on my guts. I am momentarily queasy. As it passes, I smile at Amrik. 'Yes,' I say, prickling at the admission.

Amrik licks salt from his lips. 'But I really can't bear another set.'

I nod, relieved.

'Shall we go down? To the dungeon?'

My hand trembles. This is the answer to my question. This is why I am here. I put my glass down. My heart beats its wings, rattles in its cage. 'Ok.' I say. 'Yes. Let's.'

As we turn away from the bar, I see a broad-chested man leaning against it. He is sipping from a glass, frowning to himself. He doesn't look like he should be here. I consider his solid hands and perfectly shaped head. I have seen him before. This thought comforts me. But it alarms me as well and I don't know why. At that moment, he looks up from his glass and everything slows down. Amrik is tugging on my arm, pulling me away from the bar. I am about to follow, but cannot take my eyes from the stranger. A haze hangs between us. We are locked into one another's gaze, each searching an index of data that begins with random tube journeys and ends with miscellaneous shags. Something clicks in my head, pricks a hole in the haze. But Amrik jerks my arm, ripping me from the stranger before the connection is sealed. As we head down to the dungeon, a syllable flashes in my brain. Bill. When I met him at the Horse and Saddle, he looked familiar. I didn't know why. Now I know. He was in a car, driving by the house, and I saw him. And now he's here. This is no coincidence. Angel is in trouble. Again.

I want to turn around, but Amrik has his arm around my waist.

'I want to see you in action, darling,' he says, his breath moist with tequila.

The dungeon is only a few steps away and my courage is still a willing companion. I cannot turn back. Angel's troubles fade with each click of my heels. The stone floor echoes underfoot. Every muscle in my body is poised. Sweat blossoms on my throat like jasmine.

Angel could smell the coke as it fired up his nostrils. He rubbed the rest of it into his gums, invigorated by the electric sparks sputtering in his mouth. He stepped onto the stage, lyrics issuing from his lips in sculpted phrases. Mentally, he was exhausted, desperate for sleep. But his body was in overdrive, kicking here, karate chopping there. He did not know where his skin ended and the suit began. Howling Wolf fused with his body, drilled roots into his organs. Yes, he thought, Elvis was providing him with the energy he needed. And Angel was desperate for that energy – desperate to receive the King in all his glory. He realised that being chosen was a blessing and a responsibility. It did not mean he didn't have a choice. He could reject it – squander it – if he wanted to. Angel thought back to Delia Aunty, Santa Eva, his journey to Memphis, his arrest and exile. He knew his destiny was here; he only had to hold his hand out to it. So he bowed down on that stage and surrendered – offered himself up to his master's will.

He was still singing, eyes closed, as heat spread through his limbs, into his groin. He was saved. As he opened his eyes, he found himself staring into a predator's gaze. The agent was standing, not a metre from Angel, just like before. Angel didn't panic. He didn't call out to the King for succour. He didn't need to.

Angel kept his eyes fixed on the agent. He went through one song after another without a hint of distress. In his mind, he went over his escape routes. The Catacombs were labyrinthine. But the stage had its own exits and entrances. A staircase led directly from there to a side alley. Angel ended his set with a flourish of his cape. And was gone.

He stood by the side door, steadying his breath and anticipating which direction Angel would take. Within seconds, it flew open and something streaked out. Regis was stunned. It moved so fast, he saw only a red blur blazing up the alley. He ran toward it, pumping his legs, feeling his body knit into a single mass. The night air was crisp, the moon half shrouded in cloud. Regis was breathing hard, but refused to stop. Not this time.

They were in someone's backyard now, jumping fences, ripping through clothes lines. Regis was just a few paces behind. He could see Angel's head bounding up and down, his cape undulating behind him. Jewels winked along its length, a constellation of shimmering reds and blues. Regis reached out, his fingertips hooking the edge of the cloth. With a gasp he let go.

Regis' fingers ballooned with blood. Angel was crushing them in his hands. 'No one touches the King,' he hissed. They were standing face to face, glaring at one another. Regis lifted a fist, but Angel struck first using the butt of his palm. He caught Regis on the chin, snapping his neck to the side with a karate jab. Regis went rigid, dropped like a plank. His legs flew open as he hit the ground. Something cool and wet – like a kiss – pressed against his cheek Regis thought of Vinda. She'd seen him in the club, studied him through that silk and feather mask, eyes shining, lips concentrated and full. He regretted not going up to her then, regretted not giving her his real name. He imagined what she must have thought of him that first time, leaving without even saying goodbye. He regretted that too.

What had brought him to London, he thought. The skip? Not really. Regis had been dubious of the case from the start. He should have quit when he wanted to. He should never have walked in on Audrey and Finn. He should never have let her go. ... No, that wasn't true. He was over her. Things couldn't have worked out between them. He knew that now. So it didn't matter after all. None of it did. Not Finn, not Audrey, not even Vinda. And this skip with his passion for Elvis – who was he hurting, anyway? So he took some money. So what? In the grander scheme of things, none of that mattered. Not even Regis.

He was on his side, trying hard to breathe. Air filtered into his lungs in thin rasps. He saw, with a sudden clarity, blades of grass standing stiffly in silvery light. An ant was scaling the tip of one, its antennae wavering above its head. As Regis' eyes dimmed, he noticed the clouds clearing the moon. A migraine, he decided, finally. A migraine had sent him here, in a brown wrapper, like a gun in a paper bag.

7 Fade to black

Darkness. It is stifling down here and my head begins to pound. An airless, tropical heat clings to the inside of my mouth and pastes itself onto my skin. We walk through smells that haven't moved for hours, that linger like stains on a shirt collar. Amrik's hand is turning into a paper mulch in my fist; I let it go.

I am in the dungeon. Tiny bulbs skirt its walls, throwing up low, yellow-orange arcs of light. Figures emerge from the gloom, visible only from the waist down. Breaths rasp against stone as crops scythe through air, strike skin. Even if I want to turn back, I can't.

'Over there,' hisses Amrik. He presses his fingertips into my elbow, guiding me to the left.

A man is manacled to the wall, back exposed. His head is zipped inside leather and pushed to the side. Only his eyes are unmasked. I draw near, study their expression. They are a metallic blue, a desert of dry ice – unbearably cold and desperate. They are Derek's eyes. I unzip the slit at his mouth and bend my ear to him. 'Dresden,' he says.

I nod. Yes. I will rain down a storm of fire to quench his icy thirst.

I step back, survey his torso. It is milky smooth and finely contoured and dusted with tiny freckles. It is not Derek's body. I hesitate. I look to the eyes for confirmation. They are seething, freezing over with grey. Amrik hands me something and withdraws into a corner. I clutch the something, examine it. Its grip is wrapped in a ream of rawhide, reminding me of an old bicycle handlebar. I flick it and a tail of leather sweeps through the air, hits the ground. I hurl it again and it pops, like a fairy light blowing its fuse. I take up my position, trailing the whip behind me.

He flinches with the first cut and exhales with the next. Each strike is accompanied by a whispery grunt. He turns his head, straining to see me, to behold the instrument of his release. Derek's eyes are upon me, willing me to hit harder. My arm. *Every man hath his sword.* And woman, too. I am a warrior, trained in the Virgin's army. Queenie Aunty didn't understand. Yet it was she who groomed me – who told me how the Virgin had crushed the serpent under her feet. She who taught me the *Magnificat* and the mysteries of the rosary. I prayed – begged the Virgin to take me into her fold, to induct me into her army and deliver me from this world of turpitude. I recited the *Magnificat* every day, knew that I was preparing for battle. But she didn't come. And I was left alone, abandoned.

And then I understood. *I* am she who is like the morning rising. *Me.* Ryan was the first -- the first I crushed underfoot. Poor Ryan. He didn't deserve it, not really. Then everyone found out. First the kids at school started talking. Someone told Angel. And Angel, the arsehole, told Agnes Aunty who told Queenie Aunty. No one would look at me. They saw me praying and scorned me. They said I was a hypocrite. I couldn't make them understand the importance – the significance of what had happened to me. Angel never understood. Angel who could do no wrong in their eyes. Angel whose photograph was paired with Elvis' on the family altar. I had to pray. To show them. So they would not believe what was said about me. But they swallowed all the gossip and spat it in my face.

I didn't speak of my transformation after that. I became quiet, stealthy until they, too, stopped talking about the incident.

Trussed

Eventually, they pressed it like clay into a corner of their minds where it fused with the matter around it and slowly disappeared.

While they forgot, I exercised my revealed knowledge, each conquest a validation of my belief. Derek was an accidental choice. A default selection precipitated by boredom. They always say the serpent enters at unexpected moments. I was caught off guard.

The man is moaning now. My whip has etched a string of ideograms into his skin. I stop, approach him, put a knee into the small of his back. Looping the whip around his neck, I press my lips against his upholstered ears and breathe filth into them. He pants louder, writhes in his shackles. I step back and unleash another blur of beatings upon his back.

Derek will pay – blood or money, I haven't yet decided. Perhaps both. This thought is so comforting. As comforting as the knowledge that my ultrasound is the day after tomorrow. Soon that, too, will be over. I cannot think beyond that moment. Beyond that moment is bright white – the kind of light people talk about when recalling near-death experiences.

Someone is shouting, 'Dress ten. Dress ten.'

My arm won't stop. It is powered by a tightly wound spring mechanism. My arm goes up, then comes thrashing down. Once, twice, three times. It goes up again, falls, strikes something. Sweat buds on my skin, runs down my spine. A fever rises in my belly, inhabits my organs. My arm rises and falls, faster and faster in time to my racing heart. I am reading this stranger with my whip – up, down, up, down, pleasure, pain, pain, pleasure – until there is neither one nor the other. Until we are neither one nor another. Then the narrative is interrupted. My forearm is in Amrik's hand.

'Stop,' he shouts.

I stop. The man in chains is still yelling: 'Dresden. Dresden.' Blood dribbles down his back. I drop my arm. The whip skids to the ground.

I wait for his eyes. They are squeezed shut, lids trembling. When they open, I see that they are warm and blue, serene and melting. I am shaking. Amrik is undoing the man's chains. He slumps against Amrik, unable to move. I cannot move either. My body is limp. I want to go to them, want to hold the man's wilted frame in my arms. I force myself forward, put my hand out to him. He takes it and kisses my fingers. I remove my mask. Tears spill from my eyes onto our clasped hands. He is saved. I have saved him.

I am standing in a toilet cubicle, staring at its polished black walls. Silent and discreet as the interior of a confessional, they reflect only the contours of my face. Like a slab of marble absorbing water, these four walls suck the exhaustion and confusion from me, restore my anonymity. But I have carved my signature into a stranger's back. I drew his blood and he blessed me for it. That canvas, cut up and raw, pulsing forth blood, is my shield and my banner. I am amazed. I am appalled. I am ashamed.

Derek's flat is shaped like an 'L'. The room – that room where I woke up – is the short line of the 'L'. To get to it, you have to walk through every room. To leave it, you have to walk through every room. The shame of that room burns me, makes my guts squirm. I twist round and lean over the toilet, balancing my weight on my knees. In that room, there were bruises on the inside of my thighs and raw, shiny patches on my cheek where the skin had rubbed off. The walk from that room to the front door had been stilted – a sentence stammered by a nervous child. Outside, everyone stared, moved out of my way. Yet I was perfectly dressed, my hair tucked into a neat chignon. Only my shirt was a little wrinkled. Perhaps it was the shirt that gave everything away, that said, 'It was a financial arrangement; the customer is always right.' People shifted from my path, neither smiling nor nodding. They made it easier for me so they could be rid of me quicker, lest I should linger or brush up against them. I felt their stares like stones on my back and, despite the tearing pain, moved faster through that pastureland of pin-striped suits and leather pumps.

I am stooped over the bowl, swallowing back mucus. Derek's eyes set into leather. How I wanted to unzip the stranger's mask, see his face as clearly as he finally saw mine. And yet, at the end, the stranger's eyes opened and they were not Derek's. This thrilled and astonished me, compelled me to reach out to him. The stranger had transcended Derek and taken me with him.

Someone walks into the bathroom. I flush the toilet and exit the cubicle. I stand for a while, looking at myself in the mirror while running the tips of my fingers under cold water. As my hands slowly tingle and go numb, I feel the blood run hotter through my temples. Music sweeps in through the door. I examine my face, small and pinched, in the mirror. The lights are a muted gold, giving my skin an unexpectedly healthy glow.

'Asma?'

I shut the tap with a jerk of my wrist.

'Asma Peries?'

A woman with straight red hair and a nose stud stares keenly from the mirror. I offer a blank smile.

'It's Leila. Leila Fenchurch.' The woman blinks at me expectantly, then adds: 'Ryan's sister.'

I gasp as Ryan's features surface like a push-pin sculpture on Leila's face. 'Leila, of course!' I swallow back the fluttering in my chest. 'Sorry.' I roll my eyes. 'Too much tequila. Kills the brain cells, innit?' For a moment, neither of us speaks, each working over the other with our eyes. Leila was only a year younger than Ryan and had been as spotty as her brother. She was thin and gangly then, but the intervening years have given her a more voluptuous figure. Those years have certainly done Leila good, though she is by no means beautiful. Her best features are her feline eyes and impressive bosom – which she is showing off to great advantage in a rubber push-up bra.

'You look great,' says Leila, grinning. She lights a joint and offers it to me. 'What are you doing these days?'

'Oh you know, this and that.' I take a hit and hand it back. 'Nothing hugely exciting. But,' I try to deflect her question, 'how's Ryan?' I keep her talking, hoping she won't remember all the names. What's the use? It's in her eyes. *The Bike. Easy Rider. Recess* – a clever combination of the notions of 'time-out' and 'a musty hollow'. Whispered in corridors, scrawled on toilet doors, words designed to hurt and humiliate. I erased them all with 'Vindaloo'.

'Great. Yeah. He's gone to India with the VSO.'

'Wow, really?' The spliff is back with me; I pause to take a couple of drags. Leila gives nothing away. Ryan probably never told her what happened – how I ended it. But she knew about the rumours. Everyone did. 'I bet he's really loving it there.'

'Yeah. He is. He's into his second year now.'

'That's wonderful.' My face breaks into a genuine smile. At least it feels genuine. Leila has passed me the roll-up again – or maybe I've had it all along. I puff on it, not caring. 'Shame I didn't know he was there. I went travelling after I finished my BA last year, and spent a little time in India. We could have met up. Ah well … What about you? What're you doing these days?'

'Oh,' Leila shifts her weight from left to right foot, toke sticking to her lower lip. 'Just finishing my degree. I'm reading geography at SOAS … next year I'm going to Australia.'

'To travel?'

'Yeah. Travel and maybe work.'

'Hey, that's brilliant.'

Leila grins broadly, handing me the last of the spliff. 'Yeah. I'm really looking forward to it.' She winds a lock of hair behind her ear. 'Anyway, I'll let Ryan know I ran into you. He'll be really chuffed.'

'Tell him I send my regards,' I say, sucking on the joint. 'Maybe I'll see him some time.'

Leila's cheeks dimple as she smiles a goodbye. I place a hand on her shoulder, wishing her luck, then walk out into the music.

Trussed

Like a racing heart beat, it trips through me, drawing me to the pulsating crowd. I am back on the ground floor, above the dungeon and its scoliotic tunnels and humid nooks. I want to find Amrik to tell him about Leila, but he is nowhere in sight and the music is rushing through me, entering the very marrow of my bones. I throw my head back and tabla breakbeats coast up over my throat and off my chin. Through the corner of my eye I see hands undulating in the air, heads nodding, teeth glowing.

The music has me by the pelvis. My knees are loose, my spine lax. Someone puts an arm around my waist, draws me near. I smile at her, offering my cheek to her searching lips. I dance away toward the periphery of the moving crowd. Tabla and sitar have given way to a cascade of electronic blips sutured together by violin strings. His cuts could have been made with a razor. I can still see the stranger's bleeding back. It stands before me, weeping, kissing my fingers. I hold my hands aloft, out of reach, and spin, sucking notes into my vortex. One foot skids beneath me and I steady myself against a jogging shoulder. The ground is tilting and I slip with it. I grab another shoulder and stop.

We are all on the deck of a ship, tossed on churning waters. My insides pitch and roll. I stumble to the side, find a wall, close my eyes. This is worse. I am on a gigantic swing, arcing down, ever down, faster and faster. I open my eyes. There is a queue of people down another passageway. I walk toward it. Taking my place at the back of the line, I crane to the left and right, trying to make out what we're waiting for. After a few minutes, I lose patience and walk up to the top, regardless of the eyes trailing me. I push forward and eventually make it to the head of the queue.

There, I find a group of people, mostly men, milling around something. I lean forward. They are standing around a bath strewn with floating candles and flower petals. Tiny flames flicker along the surface of the water, like spring buds. Beneath them, a fish hovers, still, or perhaps it is merely a shadow. I squint, trying to make out whether it is a creature or a trick of the light. Then I see that it is not a fish – neither is it a shadow. Two hands lie one crossed over the other upon the chest of a naked man. His eyes are closed; he is entirely submerged.

I blink and look up. Only then do I realise that the men surrounding the tank are not simply standing, but urinating into it. I look down at the man, at his still face and serene smile. Like an ascetic who has achieved transcendence, his expression is beatific. Pink petals drift over him like clouds. He is entombed in a liquid sarcophagus. I scan the faces of the standing men, but none of them share the submerged *sadhu's* peace. Most look relieved of a weighty bladder. Someone new takes up a position and looses a particularly torrential gush. His expression goes from pained to sated within seconds. It's Amrik.

'The queue for the men's toilets was too damn long, Vinda,' he says, zipping up. I am tapping his shoulder from behind, darting a querying brow.

He gestures to the entombed man. 'If he's enjoying it, why should I bother?'

'But how is he breathing?' I ask.

Amrik looks at me. 'There's a straw – like a small snorkel, sticking out of the tub. Can't you see it?'

I shake my head. 'No.'

Amrik frowns, 'Well, I'm not going to point, am I? Either you look for it or you forget it.'

I nod, staring harder, but can see neither straw nor snorkel. I don't want to see a straw, anyway. A straw would ruin the saintly image. I prefer to think of the man as a specimen in a jar, an exotic relic that pilgrims pay homage to.

'Let's go,' I say, prodding Amrik. 'All this pissing is stressing out my bladder.'

'Then why don't you have a go, too?' he grins.

I pull him down another artery of this warren. 'You'll never guess who I ran into.'

Amrik leans into me. 'Who?'

'Ryan's sister – can you believe it?'

'Ryan?'

'Yeah. And he's in India now, too. Doubtless scoffing his share of vindaloos.'

'He didn't have to go all the way to India for that.'

'He's with the VSO now.'

Amrik's attention is caught by a well-defined abdomen lurking by the wall. 'Hmmm.'

I squeeze his arm. 'What happened with that guy? Dresden?'

'I snogged him.'

I grimace. 'Through the zip?'

Armik laughs. 'No. I took his headgear off. He was actually very cute. I had to make up for your – well, he was in pain and I had to do something.'

I round on Amrik. 'He asked for it. He wanted it. I did what he wanted.'

'I think we both know you went a little too far.'

'Oh come on. He's wearing a mask, he's chained to a wall. He wants me to beat him with a whip. What does he expect? … He even kissed my fingers.'

Amrik looks at me through the corner of his eye. 'He what?'

'He kissed my fingers.'

Amrik examines the ground, his brow furrowed. 'He didn't.'

'He did.' I think of the man's lips, soft against the cold teeth of the zip.

'He didn't. I'm sure he didn't.'

I clasp my hips, looking directly at Amrik. 'And I'm telling you he did.'

Amrik shrugs.

I sit on Amrik's couch sipping Horlicks. He has given up and gone to bed after I insisted on sleeping in the living room. It's just after 3.30 and I can already hear birdsong. I curl up in one of Amrik's T-shirts and close my eyes. Sleep evades me, throwing up instead gruesome scenes from our night out. The stranger keeps turning his back to me, displaying his wounds. Eventually he is only back, a shank of flesh on a meat hook. It could be anyone's flesh. It could be Derek's. Except I can see clearly, very clearly, the contours of the back's ribcage. Song lyrics are branded on the back. I step closer, trying to read them. Then the back lifts me up onto it. My knees squelch on its surface, skid. I dig my fingers into a bloody furrow and cling on. The back is moving quickly through a sea of backs. I am on a sea of backs, all dribbling lyrics from cuts. They are shouting something, holding me aloft. We parade through a labyrinth of urine-splashed walls and litter-strewn alleys, until the walls melt away and we are in the centre of a roaring amphitheatre. The singing is so loud I cannot make out what they are saying. Lights flare, drenching us in tungsten. I squint at the brightness.

The sun steals into the room through a slit in the curtains. I shut my eyes against it.

'There it is, can you see it?'

I nod. It is tiny, like a bean, and seemingly lifeless. I turn away. My bladder is near bursting but the nurse keeps pressing against my abdomen, sliding the probe around and to the side. It is cool and wet and feels like gelatine against my skin. I survey the room, taking in its varnished wood surfaces and floral printed curtains. Housed in a Victorian conversion, the clinic was easy to miss amidst the homes and shops around Warren Street tube. I walked for ages, looking left and right at the numbers on the buildings. When I found the right one, my heart gave a little leap. Someone would finally give me a date to circle on my calendar which I could walk toward over a bridge of Xs.

Trussed

Aside from a couple holding hands in the waiting room, the clinic was empty when I walked in. I sat in a leatherette chair feeling strangely hopeful, as if a burden was about to be pried from my shoulders. When they called me in for the ultrasound, I sprang to my feet and headed upstairs with a smile.

'It's very small right now. Only a few weeks ... probably about eight or nine ...'

I'm trying hard to listen, but the pressure on my bladder seems to be echoing inside my ears. I breathe slowly, concentrating on my muscles, tightening them against the possibility of a leak. I look to my left, away from the screen, my lips gurning. A heart is beating against my eardrum, like the wings of a hummingbird.

'... twelve weeks.'

I yawn, trying to dispel the patter which is crawling deeper into the cavity of my ear. I blink at the nurse. *Twelve weeks*. What does she mean, *twelve weeks*? As I open my mouth to ask, the nurse smiles and tells me where the loo is. I thank her and immediately hoist myself off the examining table. In just ten careful steps, I am behind the walnut door of a pine-scented bathroom, squatting over the commode and sighing with relief.

A few minutes later I am sitting across from a dour-looking consultant, averting my eyes from the woman's thick-rimmed stare.

'Ms Peries, do you have a partner?'

I study my lap. 'No.'

'Does the father know about the baby?'

'No.'

'Are you in contact with the father?'

I hesitate, running a palm along my thigh. Jason and I haven't spoken for at least two months. Does that constitute no contact? 'No,' I say.

'Were you using any contraception?'

'Yes.'

The doctor casts me a disbelieving glare. 'What form did you use?'

'Condoms. It must have broken without our knowing.'

The consultant is silent. I can hear the air entering and leaving the woman's nostrils in tense puffs. 'You should never,' she begins, her voice flicking sharply like a pocket knife, – 'never allow any unprotected contact.'

I nod. 'So, when can I expect to …?'

'The embryo is at approximately eight weeks. Unfortunately, we don't have an appointment for another four.'

My cheeks blaze. 'But that's another month away.'

'It can't be helped.' The consultant's voice softens slightly. 'Anyway, early terminations are not always successful.'

I wring my hands, muttering to myself. 'Another month.' I sigh. The optimism with which I entered the clinic dissipates as I utter the two words. I can't imagine four more weeks of hiding my condition from my family. I've already gained weight and am looking unmistakably pasty. Agnes Aunty keeps remarking on my sallow complexion, urging me to go to the doctor. Thankfully Angel has returned home, giving her something else to worry about. He still hasn't taken off that suit and has started to stink. This, and his weird appetite has kept Agnes Aunty at bay, thwarting her from pursuing a more thorough line of investigation with me. For once, I am actually grateful to Angel for something.

Back at home, I lie in bed, feeling ill. I have a store of food within arm's reach – all high in sugar and salt. I play one flavour against the other in an attempt to stave off my nausea. Often this is unsuccessful, particularly when I am alone and have nothing else to think about. This time, however, my strategy is working. In fact, the illness brewing inside me is more psychological than physical. I've just finished re-reading the article from last week's *Camden New Journal*. I clipped it and kept it on my desk that first time, reading it at least once a day thereafter. Now it is lying beside me, fragile and wilted, one of its edges just touching my left index finger.

I wanted to burn it the first time. I even went as far as

lighting a match, but somehow couldn't bring myself to destroy the piece of paper. Derek's leer transfixes me, galvanises me in a way I never expected. Most importantly, it makes me forget my capsizing stomach. It gives me an adrenalin rush, powered by hatred and rage.

The moment I saw the piece, I began spinning thoughts in my mind like plates on the end of long sticks. I am a one-woman show, ablaze with ideas that I share with no one, not even Amrik. Not yet, anyway. Derek has been tipped to take silk, an honour bestowed on the most promising of lawyers. I can imagine him sitting at his desk, bloated with self-importance, expertly projecting expressions of care and compassion. I imagine, too, that he is simultaneously smiling inward, thinking about his private den off Great Ormond Street. He must have found someone else by now. Either that, or he's hiring the space out to his colleagues so they, too, can enjoy their bits on the side.

I've been considering staking out the flat, capturing Derek's little interests on film. It would be incontrovertible evidence that I could use to my benefit, if necessary. And of course, it *is* necessary. After all, my word couldn't possibly be enough. I would be considered a tart with a vengeful streak. Who would believe allegations put forth by the likes of me? No one believed me after the Ryan incident, did they? That was different, of course – I mean, I actually did what they all said I did, but the point is, they believed it, despite all the rosaries, despite the *Magnificat*s, despite everything. So why believe me this time? It's the same reason why I can't sell my story to the tabloids. I don't want everyone knowing about this. If I sold them the footage, then what? They would keep digging and the headlines would fly: 'Barrister lured by tart take-away', 'Leading lawyer takes spicy drubbing', 'Spice queen whips lawyer into shame'. And who would believe anything after that? In the end I would be vilified and Derek would emerge a blameless victim.

I could kill him, but the consequences would be too great. I don't want to go to jail for his *panna cotta* arse. It's out of the question, as is physically maiming him, though I've lingered on this, my fantasies throwing up gruesome close-ups that send shivers through my heart.

I reach for the telephone.

'I have a plan,' I say, holding the receiver close to my chest. I am on my side, one eye fixed on Derek's picture.

Amrik yawns. 'Oh, it's *you*. For God's sake, Vinda, it's one o'clock in the morning.'

'Oh, stop pretending you were asleep.'

'I *was*.' Amrik's voice is half an octave lower and several shades more brittle than usual.

'Ok, sorry, but I have to tell you this now. I have to act now. Do you understand?'

'Keep going.'

'He's taking silk. I mean, he's expected to.'

'The D-man is taking silk? Really?'

'Yes. As it turns out, he's a fucking good lawyer.'

'Right. And?'

'Don't you see, Amrik? He wants this more than anything. I know it.'

Amrik clears his throat. 'Go on.'

'So, naturally,' I finger the newspaper cut-out, 'if something were to prevent him from doing so—'

'Yes?'

'Or if someone were to threaten his chances …'

'Yes! Yes!' Amrik's smile is audible.

'Well, that someone could stand to gain quite a bit of dosh, wouldn't you agree?'

'Blackmail!' Amrik's voice returns to its normal mid-pitched clarity. 'Why didn't I think of that one?'

'*You* probably didn't see the article.'

'Which article?'

'The one last week. In the *Camden New Journal*. He won a discrimination case, so there was a write-up on it.'

Amrik spits. 'Always the humanitarian – bastard. ... So your plan?'

'Blackmail, darling—'

Amrik gasps. 'Why didn't I think of this before?'

'We just went over that,' I say, irritated by the interruption. 'Why do you have to be the first to think of everything, anyway?'

'No. No. Not that.' Amrik's breath crackles in the receiver. 'Silk. He's supposed to take silk, right?'

'Yes. That's what I read.'

'I *know* someone.'

I pause. 'What do you mean?'

'Vinda, listen.' Amrik's voice is giddy with excitement. 'Listen to me. Last month, I shagged this boy. Floppy-haired and blond. You know the type. Smooth all over—'

'Yes. Yes.' I urge him on.

'—Anyway.' Amrik sighs. 'Yes, *anyway*, he was the son of a very senior barrister or was it QC? Apparently he sits on the bar council.'

'What—'

'—Wait. So ... where was I? Yes, so, Jamie told me – his name was Jamie, aren't you proud of me for remembering his name? – He told me that his dad was an influential figure in the soundings process. His opinion, he said, carries impressive weight. I can't quite recall why it even came up ...'

'Why—'

'—Oh, *now* I remember – I told him I was a lawyer, and he was trying to impress me. He told me I might make Queen's Counsel one day.' Amrik giggles.

I am speechless. My heart somersaults in my chest.

'Vinda? Are you there?'

'This is fabulous.' I can barely control my voice. 'Fabulous. When do you see your Jamie again?'

'I don't know. I picked him up at Russell Square.'

'Shit!'

'No, not shit. Do you really think I'd let a floppy-haired blond slip my arms without getting his number?'

'You have his number?'

'I have his number.'

'Shit!'

Amrik laughs.

'Amrik, I …'

'Yes.'

'You do know what this means, don't you?'

'I can guess.'

'But will he help us?'

'I don't see why not … he's been ringing, you know. Lucky for you, I've been a little coy. When I ring him, he'll be all too happy to oblige.'

'So he's been ringing.' I am suddenly curious. 'You never told me about him before.'

'Well,' says Amrik, '*you* never told me about the article. You could have said something earlier. When we were at the Catacombs, at least.'

'That wasn't the time or the place, was it? … So, is this boy the Ronan lookalike?'

Amrik gives a smug chuckle. 'Oh no. More like Jude Law.'

'Oooo,' My taste buds start to tingle. 'Jude Law! Lucky you, Amrik.'

'Oh no.' Amrik sighs contentedly. 'Lucky *you*.'

As it turns out, Jamie has obliged Amrik more than once without getting to the point. I am beside myself. I have to know whether Jamie's father will be involved in this year's QC appointments. Amrik keeps claiming it isn't a subject that comes up naturally in his exchanges with Jamie. I've threatened to send him out to buy processed cheese slices every Friday evening for the next month if he doesn't get me the information I need immediately. Amrik just laughs and tells me that Jamie gives very good head. I've tried everything to get Amrik to speed things up. Everything, that is, except bribery.

'You know you'll be getting a share of that money, of course.'

Amrik is chewing on a baguette, fluttering mischievous half-smiles at me. His lower jaw drops. 'What?'

'Come on. Without you, I could never carry this out. You're my partner. You get some dosh, too.'

'How much?'

'Twenty per cent.'

'Of?'

'Twenty grand?'

Amrik's eyes glaze over. 'Twenty grand! Four thousand pounds? For shagging Jamie a few times? … Oh my *God*.'

'Not bad, huh?'

Amrik takes another bite out of his baguette. 'Vinda, you're a genius.'

A few days later, Amrik delivers some bad news. He was wrong; Jamie's father is a banker, not a lawyer. The blond with whom he'd had the QC conversation was an anonymous pick-up. Amrik has neither name nor number.

'I could stake out Russell Square for you,' he offers. 'I'm sure he's a regular.'

I am dismayed. 'But you don't even remember what he looks like, do you?'

Amrik tucks his upper lip into its lower counterpart, making an envelope of his mouth. He furrows his brow. 'Well, his hair was layered at the back … and his nape was shaved.'

'That's it?' I ball my fists against my hips. 'That's all you remember? The back of his head?'

Amrik looks sheepish.

I kiss my teeth. 'Forget him. This isn't a joke, Amrik. I'm not paying you twenty per cent to shag your way through Russell Square.'

Amrik hangs his head.

I grip his forearm, forcing him to meet my gaze. 'I'm leaving it to you to find a contact we can use – a name, an address. That's all we need. Will you do that for me?'

A light glows in Amrik's eyes. 'Of course. Just leave it with me.'

While Amrik does his research, I decide it's time to make myself comfortable in the vicinity of Derek's flat. I spend a good portion of Friday night in Queen Square, eyeing all pedestrians approaching Great Ormond Street. There is no sign of Derek. I realise that from where I'm sitting, I would get little more than a photo of Derek with another woman – hardly incriminating evidence. I have to catch him in the act, but how?

My answer comes the following evening. I start in the square, conjuring up the flat's layout, trying to recall which side of the building it was at. Unable to remember anything precise, I walk up to the building, swigging a shot of Lucozade for courage. I walk in front and along the sides and back of the structure, studying its façade and the windows rising in parallel columns. I notice a fire escape at the back, and remember seeing iron railings and a couple of rubbish tips from one of Derek's windows. I screw my eyes shut and try to dig out the memory. There was a balcony. I remember thinking how unusual this was for a block of flats in London. Derek showed it to me with a sneer, making some comment about the little patch of outdoors the middle classes jostled so desperately for.

'Look at it,' he said, 'they'll pay a hundred pounds more for something the size of a welcome mat, just so they can hang a window box out back or grow a precious stash of basil.' He shook his head. 'Pathetic.'

Trussed

I climb up the fire escape, certain that I will be able to find the flat if I take it slowly. Each step sends a shudder up my hamstrings and sets off butterfly wings in my gut. Shit. I'm terrified. I'm sure I'll get caught. I've left Amrik at home, of course. I can't have him whining about this or that, gasping at the slightest sound. And I don't want to give him an excuse to ask for more money, either. I have plans. Four thousand is as much as I am willing to give up.

At the third storey, I pause, scanning left and right to make sure no one is around. I am lucky. I peek into each window, wondering if I will recognise which is Derek's flat. Certainly not the one with the pinwheel in the window. That's not his style. Which leaves the one directly in front of me. I look down and see two rubbish tips below the window. Two rubbish tips beneath iron grating. This is it. I get down on all fours and crawl toward the window, then raise myself up slowly and look inside. As far as I can recall, the window was curtainless. I thought it strange then, considering the flat's purpose. But I realise that Derek is, paradoxically, a closet exhibitionist. He delights in the idea that someone *might* see him in the act, though he never goes out of his way to ensure it.

As I peer into the flat, I feel my insides constrict. The moisture sucks itself right out of my mouth, and my head begins to throb. I swallow, feeling the base of my tongue rubbing against the hinge of my throat. I imagine a tall, cool gin and tonic materialising beside me, a lime crescent floating amidst its ice cubes. Ahead of me lies the main body of the flat: the living room with its horrid little carpet and white settee. It is the perfect vantage point. I can even see part of the kitchen. My thoughts race. Photographing Derek was my first option, but that would be cumbersome and possibly noisy. I would get caught.

I thrum my fingers against the ledge. It is a decent-sized ledge, wide enough to accommodate a small video camera. My mind turns to Angel. *He* has one. A Super-8 that I've seen him set up once to film himself singing. It's in his closet somewhere. These days, Angel doesn't look at himself in the mirror. I doubt he'll have much use for his camera either. I nod. Video footage would be infinitely better than photographs. Anticipation tears through me. I chuckle. 'I *am* a genius.'

Two nights later I swoop up the iron steps, clad in black, left hand firmly gripping a camera bag. I am beginning to think no one lives in the building, so rare is it to find even a light on at the back. I am thankful for its slight dereliction as well. Chances are, people don't bother to stare out their windows from this side anyway. Most keep the blinds down at night, which comforts me. Still, I am cautious, walking as lightly as possible, and making no sudden movements. I try to melt into the night as best I can, imitating the way a cat might prowl a garden for unsuspecting birds. I imagine its twitching tail, its sinuous grace. Every movement undulates, mirroring the sweep of a cloud or the curl of the wind itself. As I stoop on the balcony to set up the camera, I evoke this image physically, feeling it inhabit my skin.

A light flickers above me. I freeze, grateful that I am already pressed against the wall. I can feel the darkness swallowing me up, extinguishing me in its velveteen embrace. Aside from the chill that is working its way up my spine, I am relieved. The light goes off. I lose no time. I practised setting the camera up the night before. Amrik sat, swilling a glass of red wine, watching as I prepared the camera repeatedly. I refused to stop until I'd successfully completed the operation three times in succession – blindfolded. Amrik rolled his eyes, refilled his glass and asked whether I was preparing to audition for the *Cirque du Soleil*. 'I'm not sure revenge can be classed as a circus art,' I replied, adding, 'somehow, I'm pretty sure people would notice if I scaled the balcony in a canary-yellow bodysuit.'

I am giggling, in spite of myself, and feel like a hyena on the Serengeti. I don't know why exactly, given my heart is leaping. I should be feeling like prey, poised as I am on the landing, muscles twitching at every sound. Instead I am getting high on my own adrenalin. It only takes a couple of minutes to get the camera out of its case, place it on the ledge and turn it on. I adjust the lens, then duck out of view, glancing at my watch and any neighbouring windows for the next fifteen minutes. When the time is up, I pluck the camera from its roost and play back the tape, staring into the eye-piece.

'Shit!' I thump my forehead with my left palm. 'I'm such an idiot. No light. Christ.' I chew vigorously on the inside of my cheek. This is going all wrong. I consider the options. I already practised at Amrik's. I tried filming Uncle Aloy through the living room window. Both occasions were a success, particularly the latter.

I've decided to hang on to the footage I collected of Uncle Aloy embracing a cushion as he watched a late-night film. Dirty old man. Reviewing the shots in my room later that night, I was struck by the veracity of this realisation. Everyone thinks he's so harmless. Well, maybe he is; I don't care. The tape is now at the back of a drawer, ready for use should the occasion arise. Right now, however, I am crouched beneath Derek's window with some dark rushes of nothing. I might as well have left the lens cap on. This dummy run has turned out to be a big disaster. Next time may well be the real thing. I'll have to take my chances.

Forty-eight hours later, I am sitting against the same wall, waiting for Derek's light to come on. It does. The camera is already in its spot, rolling. I do a quick and daring check, glancing quickly through the lens to test focus and magnification. *Every man hath his sword upon his thigh.* Yes. This camera is my sword, polished and sharpened to a fine point. With it, I will skewer the serpent, crush him. I will annihilate him as he has tried to annihilate me. I will leave him chained to a brick wall, his life peeling away from him in brittle flakes. My sword is upon the ledge, poised to strike, yet I quiver. Soon he will be in the living room with her. I don't want to look.

I rock gently in place, steadying my breath, trying to keep my thoughts in check. My nerves are taut and almost humming with tension. There is a burning sensation in my lower back. I can't recall the colour of the rug. Was it red? Or beige? Clay tiles coalesce with fluid ceilings, pompadours with nappy-clad lawyers. My memory turns somersaults over the steel-barred landing, slinkying down the stairs in quiet, caterpillar scrolls. I feel something bilious rising in my throat, and start to tremble. I try to turn my mind to something else, something neutral. The cat. I see it again, snaking through gutters, flexing its tail, twitching its whiskers. It belongs to no one – no collar. And it behaves with all the nonchalance and feral curiosity of a creature unhindered by the comforts of home.

I close my eyes and breathe in slowly. Silently, I begin to tell myself where I am, describing the exact position and location of my body. Starting with the placement of my feet, I move up my thighs to my belly, eventually getting to my chest, arms, neck and head. When I open my eyes again, I am completely aware of myself and where I am, so that turning around and inching up to the window is no effort at all.

What I see is not unexpected. Derek is in his white towel, down on his knees, head pulled back at a sharp angle. Standing over him is an east Asian woman, clad in very high-heeled boots that rise to her thighs. Suspenders link her footwear to an elaborate bodice that laces all the way to the woman's chin. Her hair is pulled into a severe knot, and a pair of narrow glasses perch on the end of her nose. She is glaring at him, flitting a riding crop against the palm of her hand. Derek is in ecstasies.

I take a quick look through the lens of the camera. The shot is good, if a little blurry. I zoom in and sharpen the image. My sword is indeed drawn. Through the lens I can see that Derek's eyes are wet and that sweat is beading on his forehead. He is still as white and soft as I remember him. The woman climbs on top of his back and begins riding him, driving a heel into his thigh from time to time. With one deft movement, she yanks off his towel and begins whipping one of his buttocks. I resist the urge to applaud. The woman has chosen the side closest to the window; the shot is perfect.

I lean back against the wall and consider the rubbish tips below me, the black slats of the fire escape, the monotony of the lot behind the building. No wonder Derek chose a flat here. There is no one around, and those who are, are not worth worrying about. Derek knew what he was doing. I wonder whether the woman is a neophyte like I was. It doesn't look like it. The woman appears quite professional. So what exactly is Derek's game? Does he pretend he's submissive, while determining how to dominate his victim? That must have been it in my case. Or maybe, he just did it to me because I somehow enabled him to. Maybe he saw it in my eyes. Saw my anger and knew that my armour was as flimsy as cardboard left out in the rain.

This woman is different. Hard, proud, contemptuous of Derek. I see it in her eyes – see it, too, in the way she towers over him, indifference flattening her spine and regulating her stance. Even as she straddles his back, meting out little stings with her whip, she seems in the thrall of a full-bodied shrug. Derek can see none of this. Caught up in his own pleasure, he has little regard for the woman on top of him. He feels her arse on his back, her heel needling his thigh, the snap of leather against his skin. That's all he needs. Soon he will be crying, his body flaccid and jiggling as he sobs.

The light dims. I hold my breath and raise my eyes to the window. I reach up and pluck the camera from the ledge, turning it off as soon as I have it on my knees. There is a noise at the glass, the sound of someone tapping against the pane. I flatten myself against the wall, biting back a sickly urge to giggle. I realise I am grinning, much like a chimp caught in the sights of a dominant troupe member. The fear grin. It plasters itself to my face, indicating, in spite of myself, my submission. I am thankful that it is dark, that no one can see me, least of all my aggressor. Perhaps the fear grin isn't meant to be placatory. Perhaps it is merely a nervous reaction, the most natural, comforting movement to still trembling lips. Right now, I don't care about meanings. I can only sigh with relief as the thunder quells in my chest.

Left with silence, I take three deep breaths, concentrating on any sound I can detect from the window. It is double glazed, making it almost impossible for me to tell whether anyone is still there. Eventually, the living room light goes out. I count a full sixty seconds, then pack away the camera and inch across the landing to the stairs. I crouch as far down as possible, convincing myself that no one is at the window, and leap onto the stairs.

Halfway down, I give in to temptation. I turn around to take one last look. I stop. Derek is standing in the window, watching me. I can't move. Sweat bursts from my pores, running rivulets down my spine. Starved of moisture, my body fills with salt.

We stare at one another as my muscles begin to atrophy, fusing with my bone. Neither of us blinks – or so I imagine – as my chest grows cobwebs. Derek's eyes, set not in leather, but peering through layers of glass. Derek's eyes, hard as steel, unmoved by either whip or orgasm. These eyes now stare at me, grow brighter. Like a yo-yo in slow motion, his jaw begins a gradual, unmistakable descent. Shock splinters his face like a damaged windscreen. I cannot hear my heart. A breeze, sweet with the odour of rotting eggs, rises from the rubbish tips and enters my nose. A child's shriek roils over Queen Square, pushing its way into the lots where I stand, pillar-still, gaping at the window. I want to run, fly, de-materialise from this spot. But it is as if I've been shod like a horse, hooves planted upon a giant magnet. My body grows cold.

There is no bloody back to climb upon, no lips to kiss my fingers. Only Derek upon me, immobilising my limbs. Derek drooling into my ear. Derek crying and mumbling and hurling himself into me, tearing me up inside. Derek, who left me at the bottom of his L-shaped flat. He is coming now. Coming down to get me. My sword is slung upon my shoulder, blunt. I can hear his feet on the steps, the thud and shake of iron.

Something flits its way up the fire-escape – a cat. Heat stirs in my calves. Yes. The cat. I look up. Derek is still in the window, face stiff and acidic. A shadow passes overhead. The switch of a tail. My heart starts beating again.

I dive down the steps, dashing through the lot into Lamb's Conduit Street, not stopping again until I find myself in Mecklenburgh Square. There, I stand under a tree and make a quick change, turning my jacket inside out and removing my hat. I let my hair hang loose and loop the jacket through the handle of the camera case. Satisfied, I walk briskly, but calmly, to Gray's Inn Road, ending up, minutes later, at King's Cross station.

I catch the last westbound Piccadilly tube, and am home within forty-five minutes. My heart is still dancing in my chest as I turn into Moat Farm Lane. Adrenalin propels me forward, staving off any signs of nausea. I am itching to review my footage, paranoid that the tape has somehow got damaged, or worse, erased, on the way home. I didn't have time to remove it from the camera. 'Calm down,' I tell myself. 'Just calm down.' But my hand still trembles as I bring the key to the lock.

Safely inside my room, I plug in the camera and rewind the tape. My heart thumps loudly against my ribs as I examine the material I've shot. Though it starts out slightly blurry, Derek is clearly visible, and eventually magnified in all his glory. Most importantly – and something I didn't witness myself – I've caught the exchange: Derek, sweat-stained and shivering, placing £20 note upon £20 note in the bondage woman's surprisingly delicate hand. I have to stop myself from laughing out loud – I've scored my 'money shot'. I creep downstairs and immediately hook the camera up to the VCR. I have three blank video tapes, which I waste no time in filling with Derek's pathetic pleasure. Much later, I am back in my room, painstakingly labelling the tapes, boxing the original and storing it on the topmost shelf of my bookcase.

I pull the telephone toward me.

'Vinda? Vinda … not again. It's effing three o'clock.' Amrik is groggy and annoyed.

'I did it.' My voice is hushed but excited.

'It's three am, Vinda. *Three* am. What is wrong with you? Have you gone completely mad?'

'Silence! Listen. I did it, Amrik. I have a video tape. A *tape*! Can you believe it?'

'Wait. Rewind. What do you mean, "tape"?'

'Amrik,' I snap my fingers. 'Wake up, darling. Listen to me. A *tape*. A fucking *video* tape.'

'Of?'

I let out an exasperated breath. 'Of Derek. The D-man. The jerk-off. Remember?'

Amrik starts. 'The D-man? You have the D-man on tape? … Doing what?'

'What do you think? Licking the heels of a Japanese S & M chick. Totally professional. She was hard, Amrik. Really hard … And bored.'

'I want to *see* it,' Amrik barely contains his mirth. 'I *must* see it. Vinda. Please.'

'Of course. Of course, you'll see it. Don't worry, Amrik. I'm coming round tomorrow and we can watch it then, if you like. I've already transferred everything three times.'

'*Three* times?!'

'Yes, three times. So we can keep a copy for ourselves. And send one of them to Derek.'

'What about the other one?' Amrik is finally showing signs of wakefulness and rational thought.

'That's for whoever else needs to see it … your contact, for instance. Tell me you've found someone.'

'Yes. Yes. It took some digging – but how did you …?'

'A stake-out, darling. I've been living on that bastard's fire escape for the past five nights. Don't you remember? All that practice in your living room?'

Amrik yawns. 'Mmm … Why didn't you ask me for help?'

'*You*? Ask you? You're joking, right?'

'You're lucky he didn't catch you.'

'Never mind, Amrik. None of that matters now.' I glance at the clock. 'I'll see you in the afternoon, ok?'

I fall into a sleep as thick and black as tar. I float, like a leaf on water, drifting deeper into a landscape heavy with concrete and huge, girdered cranes. But something about the texture of the water makes me uneasy. Cloying, yet slippery, it throws rainbowed shadows that grow more and more defined as I range forward. Gradually, I feel the familiar bump of shoulders gathering beneath me and I am surfing a sea of roaring heads, blinded by the light growing ahead. As they draw nearer, I can just make out the great plain of a football pitch lit up by a fluorescent glow. The shouts grow louder and even less discernible. I feel myself slipping. I grasp desperately at whatever is at my fingertips: hair, ears, necks. My body is melting into oil, reducing to a thick and greasy gravy. I look down and see myself disintegrating over a crowd of singing people that loops and snakes endlessly behind me.

The queue at the post office is longer than expected, but I've opted to mail the package from the Russell Square branch because it is often deluged with students and tourists. I feel less conspicuous here than King's Cross for some reason. I spent the last couple of hours at Amrik's, viewing and reviewing the tape. Amrik was horrified by the softness of Derek's flesh, stating there was no excuse for someone of his status to be as ill defined as he was. I laughed hysterically, swallowing back a throatful of bile. We agreed the Japanese woman was exceptionally brutal. By the end, Amrik and I were enthralled by her, shaking our heads in awe.

'She's *so* cool,' I whispered, and Amrik nodded, eyes wide and misting over. I then took Derek's tape, placed it in a padded envelope and got Amrik to address it. We poured out two glasses of white wine and made a toast.

'To the Japanese dominatrix, our queen of the boudoir,' said Amrik. 'May she continue to ply her trade with skill and dispassion.'

I affected a plummy accent, 'Here, here, darling,' and clinked my glass against his.

Standing in the queue, I smile to myself. I hug the envelope to my chest, scarcely grasping the enormity of what I am about to do. The thing is, Derek has nothing on me. Nothing at all. True, he saw me. But what does it matter, in the end? Is he really going to show the tape to someone as evidence against me? He has no option. He will email me, as I have directed him to. He will meet me and hand over whatever I want. I can't believe I didn't think of this earlier. Can't believe that I let it fester so long, corroding my insides, invading my womb with its poisonous breath.

I am at the counter and an Indian lady is blinking at me, directing me to place the package on the scale. I do as I am told. I hand over the required amount, affix the stamps and with a steady hand, drop the package into the mail slot. I've made sure to send the tape by first class. By tomorrow afternoon, the envelope will be sitting in Derek's in-tray. It is marked *private and confidential* so only he will open it. That is the only concession I have made to his privacy. No, not his privacy. I am simply honouring the process. Everything has to be in its place, every move executed according to the rules. After all, the rules are age-old and immutable. I didn't make them up. I, too, have little choice in the matter now.

Outside, the sky is a yellowish grey, like nicotined teeth. I sigh and immediately, a little cloud forms in front of my lips. Soon it will be dark. I consider going to Charing Cross Road, but choose to sit in Russell Square instead. I can't face the Christmas crowds with their steely faces and monickered bags. There will be fairy lights strung across Oxford Street, of course. And window art proclaiming pre-Christmas sales. But I am happy to sit on a park bench and stare into the now dry fountain. No one cruises during winter, so I sit back, relax and watch the light slowly fade to black.

8 Trust

Something wet and slightly rough swept over his cheek. Almost immediately, he became aware of a tickling in one of his nostrils and exhaled gruffly, trying to blow whatever it was out. A warm breeze, smelling strongly of an empty tuna can, washed over him in quick huffs. Regis opened his eyes. A purple-blue tongue hung just above the bridge of his nose, rippling at the ends like a New Year's Eve party favour. Regis didn't want to alarm the tongue or the chow attached to it. Instead, he cast his eye (the one closest to the sky and unhindered by grass) around him, trying to figure out where he was. He couldn't recall how he'd got there – *there* being a place he neither recognised nor cared for. It was cold and damp. It was definitely not LA.

Regis sneezed. A loud, jarring, full-throttled explosion that sprayed the gently lolling tongue and startled the chow. The tongue disappeared for several seconds, reappearing in magenta bursts as the dog barked its annoyance at Regis. Regis rolled onto his back and looked at the animal, sensing the situation to be far from threatening. In fact, the chow had a husky, withered bark, and around its muzzle was a growth of silver hairs. Regis made soothing noises, trying to quiet the dog. Gradually, he turned onto his side and started to get up. The chow went silent and its tail began wagging. Regis wasn't sure what time it was, but from the wetness of the grass and the dim light, he guessed it was early morning. He glanced quickly at the house, praying no one would see him standing there, like a broken tree, in stained trousers and shirt.

He moved quickly but steadily, skirting the house, hoping he could get to the front without having to jump over any fences. But there was no way around the house from the outside. He peeked over the fence and saw that there were other yards like this one, five deep in either direction. He was trapped. He had no choice but to leap his way out. He shook his head. Surely there was another way? Perhaps, he thought, perhaps he should just lie down again on the grass and wait for someone to find him. At least then he could ask them where he was.

Regis tried hard to remember the night before. His throat was sore, as if someone had stitched the back of it, leaving the thread to meld with the flesh around it. He could barely swallow, but as he did, he saw a flash of a sideburn. Just a flash, like a giant, hairy lightning bolt. Something about this vision made Regis reach for his chest. He felt the memory of suffocation pressing against his lungs. He swallowed again, this time glimpsing a tiny Regis surfing what looked like the well-varnished swell of a pompadour.

'What the fuck?' he breathed to himself. 'What in the fuck was that?' Regis was inexplicably frightened then. There was a trembling in the soles of his feet which juddered up the backs of his legs and tunnelled into his intestines. He stood helplessly as his insides liquefied. Any minute now he would lose control, leaving a mess in the garden. Regis lay down by the fence. He was, he thought, nothing more than a muddy plastic bag that had been blown across a pristine lawn.

His belly spat like sausages under a grill. Regis looked desperately at the chow, which had folded itself to the grass and was staring at him through slightly senile eyes.

'Oh shit, dog,' whimpered Regis. 'I've got to get inside.'

The chow blinked, then cracked a smile. Regis drew himself up and started walking toward a pair of French doors. As far as he could tell, there was no one about. He tried the handle and was surprised to see how easily it flipped down. Behind him, he heard panting and the swish of a tail. He inched open the door, sweeping the room with a nervous eye. Stepping quickly inside, he closed the door on the dog; he couldn't risk being given away by an ill-timed bark. He found the small corridor and tried a couple of doors. The first was a closet full of musty coats, shoes and rubber boots. The second was a pot-pourri-scented toilet.

Sitting on the commode, Regis took a moment to survey the bathroom. It was done up in candy-striped pink wallpaper with white fixtures and a coral basin. Curios were arranged fastidiously to the left and right of the sink. Regis studied two miniature frogs, both seated in rocking chairs, one reading a newspaper, the other smoking a cigar. For a second, Regis felt envious of their putative bliss. They looked like they should have been seated before a fire in a Victorian sitting room. Perhaps they had once, but realised a pink bathroom was all they needed out of life. Regis almost giggled then. As his bowels relaxed and emptied themselves, an absurd physical contentment overcame him. He wanted to laugh out loud, but started counting the stripes on the walls, trying to distract himself.

This was a bathroom unlike any he had come across in America – a typical English bathroom, he thought. The toilet was very small, and the water in it, was very low, lower even than the water at his hotel. He gave his hands a diligent wash – not the easiest thing to do given the hot and cold taps were at either end of the sink – while studying the creams and soaps huddled to one side of it. This was the bathroom of a single woman, he mused, elderly and silver-haired, much like Grandma Gigi before she got Alzheimer's. He would have examined the bottles more closely, but the sound of barking outside reminded him of the urgency of his situation. He placed an ear to the door, straining to hear the pad of feet or other evidence of someone in the house. Satisfied that no one had been disturbed, Regis extracted himself from the bathroom and saw, to his relief, the front door not three feet from where he was standing. He sprang toward it, looking neither left nor right, and quietly let himself out.

Out on the pavement, Regis bowed his head and walked. He tried to get as much distance as possible between himself and the house he had just left. When it occurred to him, he decided to cross the street, darting a glance left and right before venturing into its middle. As his foot advanced off the curb, he heard a loud honking which sent him sprawling backward. He almost shook a fist at the car, then realised he'd been looking the wrong way.

'Oh Christ,' he whispered, as memories of the previous night took shape in his mind. That club, with its maze of tortured bodies and sex-filled rooms. Angel fixing him with liquid, rootless eyes. His hand coming at Regis in slow-motion. The thud of bone against jaw, knocking the breath from his lungs. The skip then leaving him choking in the grass.

Regis rubbed his chest. Floored by a skip, he thought. This had never happened to him before. Never. Floored – and by an Elvis impersonator, at that. Something rose in his gullet. Regis scowled. It was charred and acrid and tasted of defeat.

Angel felt it slide down his throat like bourbon. He made a mental note to buy himself another bottle of Pepsi later that day. It would go well, he thought, with the peanut butter and banana sandwich he was ploughing through just then. He hadn't even bothered to find himself a plate. Instead, he ate it right out of the frying pan. Agnes, his mother, was too horrified to protest. She'd grown accustomed to the scent of sizzling peanut butter, had even ventured a taste before recoiling with a shudder. Angel didn't care anyway. He was too busy listening to his rumbling belly. It was insatiable. Like an airplane cabin with a punctured window, his stomach seemed to be losing its contents to a continuous and ravenous suction. But Angel didn't know where it was all going. He hadn't been to the toilet in days.

In fact, his belly felt like lead. It was heavy, bloated, flabbing over his belt. Angel's trim figure was nowhere to be seen. It had been subsumed into a sweaty, heaving mass that grew daily, trapping him inside the jumpsuit that he hadn't removed since the Catacombs the week before. Everyone gave him a wide berth. Aloysius, his father, rolled one of his mole eyes toward him, wrinkled his nose, and said nothing. Vinda simply ignored him, holding her breath if ever he drew near.

Carla had told him to leave two nights after the Catacombs gig, dismayed by his callous attitude toward her and simultaneous passion for fried chicken and peanut butter. Her large eyes grew even larger as she watched him cook his meals. Greasy vapours clung to every surface in her kitchen, casting yellow shadows on the ceiling like LA smog. 'Angel, what is wrong with you?' she would ask, clutching a bottle of bleach.

Angel didn't know what to tell her. His surrender to the King had been absolute. But he hadn't anticipated this kind of suffering. All the fear and uncertainty of the previous weeks returned. Angel was astonished by the pimples that began studding his face like rivets on a Nashville handbag. 'Look,' he said, grabbing desperately at Carla's hand. They tried all kinds of treatments, but the pimples kept bubbling up, white pearls beading in their tiny mouths. Angel wept, watching his face disintegrate before him. He tried to hide the blisters with daubs of foundation, but it was no use. The pimples reared up, their white heads glistening against a chalky brown landscape.

Generous of heart, Carla tried to assuage Angel's plunging ego in other ways. But by then Angel felt nothing, and the terror this should have inspired in him was swallowed up by the incessant gnawing in his brain. Desire had relocated several inches upward, creating vast, empty spaces in his stomach. It grew cataracts over his eyes and poured sand in his ears. When Angel looked at Carla then, he wondered what he had ever seen in her. Her diminished enthusiasm, her withdrawal from him – they meant nothing to him. He had consumed her that first night, so long ago; she was no more than an arid husk to him now.

When Carla finally told him to leave, he simply shrugged. By then, he'd stopped looking at himself or caring. He was more interested in other things. Did it really matter what he smelled like? To his mother, it did. She was repulsed by the scent of rotting hamburger that emanated from her son and saturated everything in his path. She calmly told him to either take a shower or pitch a tent and sleep in the garden. He knew she was half joking, hoping he would peel off the stained suit and wash away the layers of fat he had put on in such a short space of time. But Angel would not be moved. He looked absently at his mother, dragged some of his bedding outside and sheltered it under an old tent.

Angel only went inside the house to fry a sandwich or pee. He didn't need to wash. He no longer seemed to need to crap. He wasn't afraid of the agent, either. Thoughts of him had dissipated the night of the Catacombs gig, when Elvis had saved Angel through the grace of his suit. The agent had no sooner touched the hem of his cape than he crumpled to the ground. Angel would never forget this miracle, despite his subsequent corpulence and chaotic state of hygiene. It was true that Angel had stopped singing. But this didn't bother him. He had more pressing concerns – concerns which led him to dip into his cash reserves and order up whole buckets of fried chicken direct from the KFC to the garden. He tipped lavishly, so no one complained about the smell or the distance they needed to go to deliver.

Angel preferred Sunpat crunchy peanut butter. It seemed to fry well and released a smoky aroma that caused a cloud's worth of precipitation to pool on his tongue. He bought several jars in jumbo sizes, but was already well into his fourth not one week since buying the lot. As he stood alone in the kitchen, downing the last bite of his sandwich, he drew a palm over his stomach. He felt a pang – not of hunger, but nostalgia. Where once he had been able to discern every muscle from upper to lower abdomen, now his hand faltered over a fluttering pudding, his flesh yielding like an underbaked cake. Angel stared at the frying pan, undisturbed by the fat beading and hardening like yellow-white stalagmites on its black pate. He scraped one off with a fingernail and sucked on it. It was viscous and slightly saline – not unpleasant, but not particularly appetising either. He took a knife and etched it off the pan, then smeared it onto a piece of bread and popped it into his mouth.

There was nothing for him to do but sit in his tent and wait for the next delivery of fried chicken. So Angel took to the garden, sitting on an oily bedsheet and mattress, and contemplated the back of his home. The neighbours had begun to stare. Soon enough they would complain about the smell, but not yet. Vinda had already apologised to them, blaming the odour on a non-existent compost heap, thus pre-empting a more organised assault on the Peries household. After all, the community was notoriously uptight, mobilising delegations to the Council for the slightest disruption. Angel didn't bother to justify anything to anyone. He barely spoke. Somehow, his voice seemed to have mired itself in a well of grease.

From time to time, he would feel a note rising in his throat. It would tremble in his inner ear, sparkling and dancing like a faerie, promising something as shimmery and light as the waters in 'Blue Hawaii'. But when he opened his mouth, there was only a belch: deep, resonating, unfurling like a gigantic wave. At first this distressed Angel. So much so that he tried repeatedly to remove the suit. But as hard as he pulled, the fabric cleaved with even greater force to his skin. It was as if he was flaying himself. He had given up after the first day, cutting a hole in the groin area to facilitate going to the toilet. The back end he had begged Vinda to alter, but she refused, telling him to 'stop being ridiculous and remove the damn suit'. Eventually, he tried to do it himself, but only at the last minute. He failed, of course, and in desperation, sat on the toilet fully clothed and simply let go. This, it turned out, was the right thing to do, for to his shock, the back of the suit simply opened up at the key moment, sealing up again when he was finished.

Sitting now in his tent, Angel thought of Delia Aunty: her black hair always shining, shot through with a weft of silver. And the keloid on her chest, like a melting milk chocolate, a scar left by heart surgery carried out before he was even born. He had sent her a copy of his first Santa Eva recording, couriering it straight to Idaho, where she'd moved years ago. A letter had arrived for him in the post some weeks later, inscribed in her florid hand, containing words of thanks and praise. Angel wished she could have seen him on stage, but his invitations came to naught. So he sent her video tapes of his better gigs, and made sure to send her any publicity as well. He sighed. Her face, with its coal eyes and soft-lipped smile, had been his inspiration. But months had gone by, and he still hadn't replied to her letters. And now it was no use.

He wondered why Elvis had chosen to inhabit him in this way. Perhaps he was being punished? Yes. Perhaps. Angel had been bad. Stealing to buy authenticity. This must have been a considerable sin in the King's eyes. So, Angel had been allotted his own private Calvary. He could look forward to the end, beached on a toilet, slack and sweat-stained. Well, why not? If it wasn't beneath the King, how could it be beneath him?

Angel caught a glimpse of his mother in a window. She looked frightened, furtive, like a woodmouse at dusk. His cousin flitted past a pane on the upper floor. Two women who knew nothing about him, he mused. His mother, still ignorant of the miracle that had taken place in her womb all those years ago. And his cousin, who envied and maligned him for his gift. Never mind. Others believed.

Others reached out and touched him like he was the Messiah come amongst them. He'd seen it first in Delia Aunty's face. Then, years later, Theresa had given herself up to him. So had Carla. So had many others. Angel was chosen and they knew it. But who would have guessed that Elvis would come to him like this, permeating his skin and slowly colonising him from the inside out?

Regis walked for days. He was in London, looking for a man in make-up – who, it had to be said, probably wasn't all there. He should have been an easy catch, but from the beginning, Regis knew he'd been lax. First he'd forgotten to bring the Peries family's telephone number. Then he'd let Angel get away from that pub in Ealing. He'd even let himself get distracted by the skip's cousin. He'd fucked everything up, from beginning to end. He couldn't face going back to his hotel room. What for? Who was he, after all? A failed-bondsman, that's what. No wonder Audrey had left him.

He walked with no direction, now wandering west, now lurching east. From time to time, he would flip his chin up and search for clues, but the sky was an interminable grey, as confused and woolly as his mind. He had some money which he used sparingly, buying the occasional samosa or bag of crisps. His wallet had disappeared. When he had woken in that garden with the chow, it was one of the first things he felt for. But its reassuring weight was nowhere to be found.

His appearance quickly degenerated, and a musky, urine-daubed odour followed him wherever he went. Quietly and quite naturally, Regis became associated with the shuffling invisibles that populate the streets of the city, nosing through rubbish bins and bedding down in shop fronts. People would clock him from the corner of their eye, as they would a turd on the pavement, and carve swooping detours around him. It was what he deserved. He was a failure, a reject, a nothing.

Up and down the city he meandered, following the Thames one

day, circling the financial district another. On an unusually warm day, Regis had the good fortune of finding himself in the vicinity of Hyde Park. So he lay on the grass by the Serpentine, breathing in autumn, struggling to find some meaning in the clouds above him. As soon as he fixed his eyes heavenward, a thrill ran through him. This was the first time, since he had been on the street, that he had looked up into a lapis lazuli sky. It was beautiful: as wondrous as those hard blue skies that hung over LA the day before a rain storm.

And just like that a memory fell between Regis' ears: lying by the swimming pool, Audrey at his side, staring up into just such a sky, watching an eagle hovering far above. Seen from such a distance, the eagle appeared no larger than a moth, but its wings were clearly discernible. Regis had reached over and taken Audrey's hand, stupidly refusing to speak for fear of startling the creature. Audrey played along, smiling quietly and flipping down her shades so she could peer in the direction of Regis' finger. They watched it for what seemed like hours before dozing off, holding one another's hands. When they woke up they made love, right by the side of the pool, and Regis thought he could still see the eagle, its wings outstretched, caught in the chestnut of Audrey's widening eyes.

The memory of Audrey washed through him like whiskey on a Sunday afternoon. Quilted, warm comfort – that's what she meant to him. But not love. Not any more anyway. Staring at baby-fat cumulus, the type that conjured images of storks and suspended infants, Regis saw Audrey and Finn again. They were wrapped tight against one another, thick with slumber. Regis wondered what Finn had seen in Audrey's eyes, whether she had given up a sharp-beaked raptor for him, or one of her crazy cartoon beasts. Regis shrugged, accepting he would never know, and realising he didn't really care. Not now. Not here, on this grass, by this water, under this sky.

He closed his eyes. Thoughts pattered through his brain, leaving pawprints here and there that morphed into inchoate remembrances: Elvis in his trademark gold lamé jacket, the rustle of a foil cookie packet, a baying wolf, El Vez, a tattooed back, row after row of brown fencing, fishnetted calves, a tweed cap. Regis shook his head, leaving this medley of images to flutter against the tissue of his brain like bills posted by guerrilla advertisers. He had, the day before, thumped his fist against a clump of newspapers, wishing he had never come here, wondering how he could possibly be homeless in London when he had a clean, tastefully decorated apartment in LA.

But the gap between the one and the other was insurmountable. He didn't deserve that apartment, in the same way as he didn't deserve to go back to that hotel room and shower and smell good again. All he could do was walk. Walking was what Regis did best. It got him from A to B: Venice Beach to Burbank, car mechanic to garage owner, quiet son to family provider. He took everything in incremental steps. Had Audrey walked away from him or had he walked away from her? He wasn't sure. And now, even now, he wasn't sure where he was walking to. Was he walking toward the skip or away from him?

The next day, as he lay on the grass in Hyde Park, he gave up trying to answer these questions. Gave up trying to find his way *some*where. He submitted to the whimsy of his feet, and tried to make the most of the experience of being in a city he had known only in books. So he ended up moving more or less westward. At times, he would end up walking by the side of a highway, and much as he didn't want to be there, he let himself be drawn along. He was like a wagon which, having no other choice, follows its wheels to whatever destination they choose. So Regis walked along the North Circular, skirted the A40 and wandered dangerously close to the precincts of the Harrow School for Boys. Eventually, he found himself a little way south of the school.

As he peered about him, Regis knew he was on familiar ground. There was a green along the side of the road, and some paces down, a hairdressing salon. Nearby was the kebab shop – not the kind of kebab he was accustomed to, but something rather different, served up beneath shreds of purple cabbage. His mouth began watering at the thought of glossy onions and garlicky yoghurt. He searched his pockets for a few remaining coins and felt three weighty pieces of metal drop into his hand. When he examined them, he nearly jumped with joy: three pounds had been lying in his pocket – three unspent pounds.

Regis clutched them tightly and, without thinking, crossed to the opposite side of the street where he continued his progress forward. He passed the South Harrow tube station, and a minute later, stopped in front of the shop. There was no one about, so he walked quickly inside and placed an order. The man at the counter, though astonished, listened without complaint. Out of deference to the man's olfactory sense, Regis waited for his food outside. His stomach was curiously unenthusiastic, though his mind did several gleeful backflips. Once he had the kebab in hand, Regis stared and drooled for a full two minutes. The foil and the bread made him think of car upholstery and the entrance to the Peries home. He felt it somehow derelict of him to be eating this exotic sandwich outside, on the pavement, instead of over a steering wheel.

He shrugged, not daring to remove his eyes from the steaming parcel in his hands, and walked on. He turned off the main road and went up a side street lined with rows of terraced houses. Narrow and tall, they stood alarmingly close to the pavement, cement blocks and the occasional square of grass creating the only buffer. Regis was two bites into his meal when the smell hit him. Oily, peanutty, and definitely shitty. Regis dry-heaved, assuming his pants had gone rancid. He thought the wind might have been blowing from behind, bringing the repulsive odour of his own groin stinging into his nostrils. But the wind was blowing him backward, sending flecks of dried leaves into his eyes. And on it surfed this nettling reek, at once sweet and repulsive.

Regis lost his appetite. And yet, he felt compelled to follow this bad-breathed sirocco to its source. Plunging the kebab into his pocket, he stuffed a napkin against his nose and walked into the wind. He knew then that certain questions inevitably answer themselves if you let them. He would not walk away this time. He continued, even as he felt the hairs withering on his arms. And then, just as the bile bubbled up the back of his throat, he stopped.

Angel sank his teeth into a drumstick, delighting in the crumbs lining his lips. The chicken was hot and moist, its coating crispy and golden. Threads of flesh wedged themselves between his molars; his tongue was slick with oil. The bucket of wings and legs, delivered only five minutes ago, sat on the swell of his stomach, catching dribbles of spittle and chicken juice as they fell. Angel cast a glance round his tent, which was half open to the elements. It reared over the top part of his mattress like an opera shell, fluttering at the edges, just past his knees. Angel preferred it this way. He could look out onto the garden and toward the house, without falling foul of his own body odour. As he stared now, he noticed the rose bush, bare and trembling with the wind. He couldn't remember it being there before, couldn't recall when it had appeared, or, indeed, whether it had appeared in the last few days. He was unimpressed by its frailty, its pathetic nudity compared to the rush and colour of the surrounding trees.

He took another bite, folding his legs tightly beneath him. The meat retained its heat, sizzling on contact with his tongue. Angel heaved a sigh and looked up, training his eyes on the rose bush again. He craved its fragile twists and oblique tremours. But in its stead stood a man, tall, thin and hopelessly lost.

Regis took refuge by the rose bush, hoping it contained a vestige of perfume to shield him from the stench. But it was barren of flowers, leaves and scent; and offered very poor shelter at that. All this ceased to matter to him when he looked down toward the end of the garden. There he saw a blue tent, and in it a shiny figure, like a glow-in-the-dark saint's statue, only darker and with sideburns. Something jolted in his chest when he saw those chops of wiry, black hair. His stomach took an airplane dive, sending half-digested kebab sloshing part way up his oesophagus.

Angel Peries.

Regis had been walking toward the skip all along.

The strength returned to Regis' limbs. He stood up taller and with greater purpose. Despite all the mistakes, all the hours of fruitless pursuit, the whack in the jaw, Regis was still here. That's what set him apart from the others. His doggedness. His unwillingness to give up. His ability to take one step at a time, never losing sight of his goal. This was what Audrey never understood. The fact that things took time. Regis shook his head. Audrey was impatient. She drew her cartoons, fantasised about a better life, but didn't have the patience to bide her time. So *she* walked. Not Regis.

He frowned as each shard of the past days' thoughts regrouped in his head. A migraine had brought him to London, not the contract. He didn't care about the contract. While he was here, he would do his best to complete it, of course. But it was the ache that brought him here and only its dissipation would send him back.

Regis stared at Angel. The skip was engrossed in a piece of fried chicken. Covered in oil stains, his jumpsuit sagged in places; a jagged hole yawned from its crotch. The guy was a mess, his face flaked and peeling, his lips shining like two slugs. Regis approached him.

'So, are you going to offer me some, or are you going to eat it all by yourself?'

Angel stopped chewing. A voice was hanging between him and the rose bush. He looked up. A black man was standing in front of him, smiling and holding out a dirty hand. Angel's first response was an involuntary flinch. He gathered the bucket to his chest, offering him a defiant stare.

The man's lips drooped. 'Oh, so you want it that way? Too bad. I was feeling kind of hungry.'

Angel blinked. The man was American – sounded distinctly Californian, in fact. He relaxed his grip on the bucket and tilted it gingerly toward him.

'Changed your mind, huh?' The man paused for a moment, and seeing no resistance from Angel, reached into the bucket and plucked out a wing. He toasted Angel with it, and brought the piece tentatively to his lips. 'I'm Regis, by the way.'

Angel continued to watch the man called Regis, eyes fixed on his mouth. Something about him inspired memories of dread. But those memories were sluggish and dull, his heart having long since slipped their thorny grip. 'I'm –,' he stopped short, crinkling his brow.

'—Angel,' supplied Regis. 'Yeah, I remember.' He looked down at his uneaten chicken, then held it aloft, bringing a tissue to his mouth. 'I've seen you before, you know. At a bar somewhere. And a club. You do Elvis, don't you?'

Angel thought back to the Catacombs – to the last time he strode on stage, jumpsuited and throbbing with energy. That had been a decisive moment, a moment of simultaneous victory and submission. He looked at Regis and recognised him as the man who had given chase to him. He stared at him, unfazed by this realisation. He felt he needed to clarify something to Regis, to make him understand what had happened that night. He opened his mouth. 'Elvis is upon me.'

Regis looked at him blankly.

'Elvis is upon me, within me, without me.'

It was worse than Regis had imagined. He'd suspected Angel's sanity, but assumed it was more a case of the 'crazy artist' than full-on madness. Now he wasn't so sure. Regis had fallen into mechanical mode, homing in on his subject, preparing to take his captive. He approached Angel to feel the situation out, to speak to him for the first time. But Angel had the glassy look of someone hovering outside himself. For a moment, Regis, too, detached from himself and floated upward. While considering the situation – one barmy Angel and a stinking pseudo-homeless man, both holding breaded chicken limbs between their fingers – he was struck by a sharp and enormous realisation. The ache was gone. Like a final drop of sweat evaporating from a brow, it had gone. Regis paused, waiting to see whether it would return, heavier and more debilitating, bringing Audrey with it. It didn't. There was nothing there. Not an iota of pain or regret. Nothing.

In a flash, Regis knew he wasn't bringing the skip back with him to LA. The guy was fucked in the head. It wouldn't be fair. Hector's would be pissed off with him, but it wouldn't matter in the end. Regis had enough of chasing other people's misfortune. He was tired. He wanted to have a shower, change his clothes and go home.

'Excuse me, but what do you think you're doing in my garden?'

Regis started, dropping the piece of chicken onto the grass.

'Hey!'

Regis turned around slowly, raising his arms in a gesture of surrender. He looked at the woman standing before him. Her hands were placed firmly on her hips as she narrowed her eyes at him. They stared at one another for a minute before she gave a surprised yelp.

'I know you. You're Bill. Bill from the pub. You were at the Catacombs, too. And before that, I saw you in front of our house. What do you want from us? What – what's going on?' She looked from Regis to Angel. 'What –'

'It's Regis.'

'What?'

'My name. It's Regis.'

The woman shook her head, face screwing up with disbelief. 'Regis?'

'Yeah. And you're Vinda, right?'

She continued, unhearing. 'You told me your name was Bill.'

'Well, it's not. It's Regis.'

'Ok, Regis/Bill/whatever, what the hell are you doing in my garden?' With a sudden movement, she took a step backward and surveyed Regis up and down. 'You stink,' she exclaimed. 'I thought it was my cousin, but ... listen, what the fuck is going on here?'

Regis drew a deep breath. He wanted to sit down, maybe by the rose bush or perhaps next to Angel in his tent.

Vinda turned to her cousin. 'Angel— Elvis. Can you tell me what's going on?'

Angel stared at her serenely, before rotating a small drumstick between his fingers like a hamster studying a sunflower seed.

Her jaw went rigid as her gaze returned to Regis. 'If you don't start talking right now, I'm calling the police. Is that clear?'

Regis sank to the ground with a sigh. 'Ok,' he said finally. 'But can I have a shower first? Please?'

Vinda looked at Regis, his filthy clothes and dirty fingernails, and shuddered. 'Go there, over by the tap. I've got a hose. You'll have to strip and wash off out here first before I let you into our bathroom.'

Bill – Regis – is sitting across from me. He is wearing some of Angel's old clothes – sweats and a T-shirt. They're tight, emphasising his broad chest and barrelly thighs.

'Thanks,' he says, as I slide a cup toward him. It's a lazy, laid-back sort of thanks that makes me smile. He is so big and his face is so wide and smooth. It's safe.

I was shocked to find him in our garden. He was not the person I saw in the Horse & Saddle or the man I recognised in the Catacombs or, for that matter, the man I'd seen in the car. He was dirty and dishevelled and smelled almost as bad as my cousin. I thought he was trying to hurt Angel, thought he had a weapon in his hand. But it was only a piece of fried chicken.

'I can't believe you're here,' I say, not believing I turned a hose on him either.

He grins, looking calm, if exhausted. 'It took a long time for me to get here.'

We are in the kitchen drinking tea while Angel scoffs chicken in the garden, and Regis tells me that Angel is on the run. I tell him Agnes Aunty and Uncle Aloy are also on the run, hiding out at Brent Cross for the day.

I'm not surprised. About Angel, I mean. Ever since I've known him, he's been operating on the fringes of dodginess. I remember his hand, sticky with currants, holding out a scone he'd pinched from the local bakery. I was ten; he was fourteen. He was standing there, breathless, his eyes shining like wet sharkskin. We'd split the scone in two, savouring it slowly, our lips coating with flour. It should have gone down in lumps, clinging to our throats. But it didn't. Instead it sat snug in our bellies, as comforting as thick socks.

'What happened?'

Regis shakes his head. He tells me it was the suit – the 'Howling Wolf' suit – that made him steal the money. 'But that's not the whole story,' he adds. 'It was the whole Elvis thing. His obsession with the so-called "King"'. Regis' nostrils winch up with distaste. 'It was obsession that got him in the end. He's been done by it.'

My mind draws a teenage Angel, belting out Elvis tunes, telling us all he will be King one day. And me, staring at his hair, wiry and untamed and impossible to pompadour. I remember him coming to me years later, whispering that he was going to LA, hope and excitement filling his stomach, catching his breath. I wanted to hug him, tell him it was a brave thing to do. But my eyes closed up, watched him through safety glass like a bank teller does a client. I must have said something bad because his face crumpled like a piece of foil.

'Obsession can jail or free us,' continues Regis.

I bite my lip. 'So which is Angel?' I ask. 'Captive or free?'

'In his case,' says Regis, glancing toward the backyard from the kitchen window, 'I don't think there's a difference any more.'

I go alone in the end. There are no placards, though Amrik warned me there might be. A bus brought me from Brixton station to a room full of green chairs and chintz walls. There was the initial waiting area: a reception room with nothing more than a row of seats and a woman behind a counter – much like an Indian take-away shop. But beyond that place is what feels like a living room, with large armchairs and a television. I am too nervous to watch, my head too full of careering thoughts.

They admitted Angel a few days ago. He'd been walking around with soiled garments for weeks, without any of us intervening. I was too busy staking out Derek's place to notice. So I sacrificed my cousin. I pretended it wasn't happening because I was too scared to bring attention to myself. As if anyone was paying attention to me. Even after Bill – Regis – told me what he'd done, it took another week. I couldn't focus. I was obsessed with getting that footage of Derek. Every now and then I shouted at Angel, telling him to take a shower. I guess I didn't realise how far he'd gone. I thought if I scolded him enough, he'd snap out of it.

But it was obvious Angel needed professional attention. He kept telling me he was 'Aylvis' – like that, in an American accent – saying 'Ayasma, Ayasma'. Poor Angel. He was covered in eczema, clutching at that stinking suit. His stomach was bloated from being constipated for days, while the rest of him, his cheeks and eyes, had sunken in.

And now he's gone; his assessment showed him to be delusional, paranoid and a danger to himself. So he's 'recovering', on a ward somewhere, shifting his frail body in some hospital bed. Agnes Aunty cried when they took him. Uncle Aloy kept nodding slowly, muttering something about 'lodgers in the brain'.

I stare at the others: women, young and old, some far along, others barely showing, if at all. We exchange strained smiles and leaf absently through magazines. I am glad I'm alone. After all, only I will be allowed into the last room, and that is where I will need someone the most. What's the point of bringing someone, only to leave them downstairs, in the take-away zone?

The email arrives the day after I post the package. *How much do you want?* is all it says. I reply with an e-card of a bouquet of red roses. The message, a poor pastiche of a nursery rhyme, reads:

> *Four and twenty blackbirds were never quite enough.*
> *The Queen demanded four be snuffed,*
> *and three gold rings instead be stuffed.*
> *And all of it brought with care*
> *on Monday noon to the square*
> *which bore her name,*
> *upon the frame,*
> *– a demand and not a dare.*

I don't expect a reply, but a day later, there is a terse message from Derek: *What?*

The idiot. I send another card: *TWENTY blackbirds plus THREE GOLD RINGS. Queen Square. Monday. 12 PM.* Adding in parentheses: *(What happened to your love of semantic minutiae?)*

Derek sends another email: *I saw you.* To which I reply: *I saw YOU.*

We say little when we meet. Derek is in his usual pinstripes while I hide under a heavy, hooded parka. It is raining. He tries to smile, but the coldness of my stare drains the blood from his lips. My sword has done its duty – tears a hole in his armour.

'I got your card,' he says.

'Yes. Obviously.'

'I don't do doggerel, you know.' His lips, drawn tightly against his teeth, are an ash-purple.

I say nothing. *Who is she that looketh forth as the morning*. Me. I am she.

'Anyway, I ... I think I have what you asked for.'

I blink slowly, willing him to continue.

'Twenty thousand, yes? ... I ... can give it to you now, if you like.'

My nostrils flare, betraying my annoyance. I scan the benches around us wondering whether he is setting me up. Maybe he's called the police. It certainly looks like he's stalling. I narrow my eyes at his pink nose and body, one cold, the other soft and sagging in the drizzle.

He looks at me for a moment, then removes an envelope from his pocket. A man is sitting on a bench directly across from where we are standing, chewing on a sandwich. What is this man doing eating a sandwich in the rain? I glare at Derek's out-stretched hand, backing away.

Derek looks puzzled. 'Oh, so now you don't want it.' He puts the envelope back in his pocket and turns up his collar. 'Just take it, Vinda.'

'Shut up,' I spit. 'Follow me. Come on.'

Derek's face flushes. 'What? Why?'

'It's raining.' I grab his arm. *I will cut his throat*. 'Come on.' I lead Derek quickly through the square, keeping an eye on the bench-man. He is still eating, staring straight ahead. I pull Derek against me as we come out onto Southampton Row. He tries to pull away. 'Do as I say,' I hiss, 'or I'll scream this whole place down.' Derek goes slack, nodding dumbly. I want to turn around to see whether the bench-man is behind us, but seeing a black cab, I hail it and drag Derek in with me. As the cab pulls away from the kerb, I shove a hand into Derek's coat and extract the envelope. The thickness of the packet, the crispness of the bills, I will remember these vividly. I quickly and furtively count them, making sure it's all there. I glance up. The cabbie isn't looking, but I can see myself in his mirror. The brown of the envelope meshes with my skin. My lower lip is wet and glossy with spit. I frown. *I am not she.* The envelope is fat in my hand. *Every man hath his sword.* I have no sword. My eyes are sunken, my face sallow. *Who is she that looketh forth as the morning. Who?*

I fold the whole envelope into my pocket. Half a minute later, I bend forward and direct the cabbie to stop at the next block. 'The gentleman will be going to Chancery Lane,' I say as I let myself out. Without giving Derek another glance, I shut the door against him and disappear into a thicket of umbrellas.

I don't deposit all of it at once, but make the first credit – four thousand pounds – that same day. After hiding the rest of it in my room, I drop in on Amrik in the late afternoon, and hand over the promised twenty per cent.

'Oh Vinda, darling!'

I smile.

Amrik is ecstatic. 'Darling, Vinda! Four grand.' He counts it over and over again, hungrily. 'Four thousand pounds. Good Lord. That was easy as anything.'

I bristle. 'Oh yeah, really easy.'

'Sorry, my dear. Of course it wasn't easy. But you certainly got what we deserved in the end.'

We both laugh, me gasping until tears sprout from the corners of my eyes. 'Amrik,' I say, clutching my sides, 'I used that address you gave me.'

Amrik stops laughing. 'You did? I don't remember giving it to you. You said to hang on to it, until you asked.'

'I did ask, remember?'

Amrik nods, not remembering.

I dab at my eyes, trying to stifle another fit of hilarity. 'You did an excellent job, Amrik. What would I do without you and all your academic contacts? I asked you to find me an address and you did.'

Amrik gives the air a little slap. 'I didn't do much, really. It all happened by accident, you know. The right invitation to the right dinner with the right academics. You know how it is.'

I offer a mischievous smile. 'Of course I don't. But luckily for me, you do. Ah, Christopher Riesling. Sought after for his opinion when selecting new QCs. Husband of a colleague of your professor. Sweet, like the German dessert wine, and hopefully, as generous as its bouquet.'

Amrik ruffles his brow. 'What do you mean?'

'I sent him the tape, of course.'

'You sent the tape?'

'I sent the tape.'

'Vinda! But, Derek gave you the money.'

'Yes.'

'So—'

'—So what? Do you honestly think he should take silk? Someone like him? He's a psycho, Amrik.'

'Hmmm …'

'Hmmm, indeed. He's mad. Clearly.'

Amrik nods, eyes widening.

'So,' I sit back. 'How are things with Jamie?'

Amrik bites his lip for a moment, then relaxes. His eyes take on a dreamy sheen.

'Why don't we take him out for a slap-up meal,' I say. 'Let's say, in about a week? Our treat.'

Amrik grins. 'Oh yes. *Let's.*' He hugs me, and I feel curiously free.

'Asma DeZoysa.'

I look up. A nurse is smiling at me, holding out her hands like all those statues of the Virgin Mary I prayed to in my childhood. 'Yes.' I follow the nurse, clasping the gown to my body.

Has it only been three and a half weeks? But that's almost a month – a long time. I peer across the hall, shaking my head slowly. An assembly line of abortions made easier with padded green chairs and the soft drone of a television. We are divided: pre and post, by a blue curtain. And we will meet, in staggered time, in the one chair, the one set of thigh rests, the one nurse, the one doctor.

It is cold. Goosepimples rise immediately on my thighs. I start to shake.

'Asma, just take a seat. It's ok.'

But it isn't ok. The seat is comfortable, yes, like a posh, leather recliner. But the room is dark and icy inside.

'Are you cold, Asma?'

'My bum. Yes, my bum.'

Someone switches off the fan. The nurse nods. The doctor smiles. And I remember then the sign that gave it all away. The smell of white lilies when I removed my underpants at night. Sweet and slightly ticklish: the scent of conception.

I will be gutted, like a fish, scales scraped off, innards scooped out. The pain has to be better than constant hunger. I cry, spasming as they plug something into me, letting it dangle out so it wiggles comically against my buttocks. Something burrows through my vagina: a huge, rippling wand of plastic. Then a mosquito bite on my cervix, and the sucking begins. The hoovering. The sound of liquid throbbing up plastic. *Who is she?* My hands go numb. *Who?* Everything must out – the snake, the valve, the hoover, It. *Who? I am not. Who? The morning rising. Who?* I scream in spite of their admonitions, and want desperately to bite a pillow, but they won't let me. *I am not she.*

'What made you think you could do this under local anaesthetic?' asks the nurse. 'Do you think you can do it?'

I say nothing, only feel the necessary invasion. Rasp my breaths, wishing I had someone to hold my hand, and force my pelvis to relax.

Trussed

I emerge ravenous and shivering. Feel a hollow kind of soreness around my cervix, like gums recovering from Novacaine.

They had to cut him out of it. Staff referred to the scalpels they used as the 'jaws of life', and cracked rude jokes as they slit through the black and red pelt of the 'Howling Wolf'. Angel cried out in agony, feeling his flesh tearing away from the bone. They worked quickly, cutting the costume into sections and peeling it away from Angel's skin. Tassels dropped uselessly to the floor; satin fell away in strips. And the leather. Even the leather wasn't saved from the swish of the blades, leaving hair-width parings scattered along the ground. Staff remarked at how quickly the epidermis had fused with the fabric, then cringed at the glue binding the two elements together: a paste of sweat, dirt, dead skin particles, body oils. But Angel continued to howl, flailing his limbs, crying, 'Forgive them. Forgive them, Elvis, for they know not what they do.'

When it was all over, Angel sat in a chair, colon freshly irrigated and skin tingling from the scrubbing received at the hands of a strong-armed nurse. Covered in cream, he felt naked, in spite of the hospital-issue pyjamas. And he was miserable. He could no longer feel the King within him, no longer felt the hunger that drew him larger and larger upon him. He was bereft, cast out from the bower of Elvis. He had lost his voice. When he opened his mouth to ask someone what had happened to his beloved suit, nothing came out. Not the tiniest sound – not even a wheeze. He wrote a petition, demanding the return of his 'Howling Wolf', and received a sympathetic note in reply. Weeks passed without the suit materialising. Like his voice, it was gone. So Angel sat, eyes perennially staring past the sash windows, conjuring a landscape that rolled and swooped like a giant pompadour. It was awesome, multicoloured, decked out in rubies and emeralds and diamanté stars. And Angel felt himself coasting the wave, crouching over it, surfing it, as a gem-studded cape billowed out like a sail behind him.

Regis knew he would have to say something to Hector. He had a copy of Angel's mental health assessment for their information. That should be enough, he mused, then shrugged a shoulder. The plane was due to land in forty-five minutes. He was eager to get back to his apartment, pour out a rum and Coke, and relax on his sofa. He was a simple man, after all. The skip's cousin had given him a hard time, subjecting him to an icy hosing down before admitting him to the house. That first blast of water sent his heart beating wildly. He had gasped, trying to steady his breathing while his testicles shrivelled in the wind. But the shower that came afterward was ambrosial, marine scented and hot. Two weeks of wandering, walking, wasting time, coasted between his toes and down the drain. He had felt rejuvenated, renewed.

He didn't go back to LA right away. Instead, he took a holiday. Just a few days to walk the streets of the city as someone who had a right to be there. He returned to Kensington Park Gardens to marvel at the architecture, was seduced by the gorgeousness of the V & A and the Natural History Museum, walked the circuit round the Royal Albert Hall, was awed by the Houses of Parliament and Westminster Abbey, and tubed it to Brixton to walk up Electric Avenue.

The Peries woman – Vinda, whom Regis had followed so insistently all those days ago – was no less attractive, particularly as she turned the hose on him. Regis had wanted to giggle at that moment, but exhaustion slackened his lips. They spoke for a long time, Regis giving an account of Angel's activities in LA, Vinda later offering Regis advice on what to do before he left London. 'Call me Asma,' she said to him before he left, and he offered her a puzzled smile in return. Asma/Vinda – given different circumstances, thought Regis, they could have been friends. But she seemed all boxed up inside herself, hiding in the shadows that fell darkly beneath her eyes.

Looking out his window now, Regis could only see darkness. He smiled, thinking of his apartment: the clean tiled floors, those delicate curtains that swooned with the breeze at night-time. A gift from Audrey Kim, who, at that very moment, was doubtless surfing blank pages with pen and ink, while Finn held his balance on Malaga's waves. Regis smiled again. He would sit on his sofa, watch television, have a drink. He might ring his aunty with the ridiculously small windows and stinking cat. He would go to Hector's and tell them he'd had enough. He would visit the garage and find out what new music his buddies had brought in for him. He would get on his motorcycle and ride to San Francisco or into Death Valley. Then the plane tilted to the side and Regis saw LA spreading out like a jewelled dancer over the tip of its wing.

Angel is home for Christmas. It's been over a month now. He's managed to patch together a gold tinselled jacket that glimmers when he rolls his shoulders or bends forward. I want to crown the tree with him, so he can flash and twinkle alongside the time-delayed fairy lights and glittering baubles. Instead, I bend toward him and grin.

'Hey, how you been?'

Drool staggers down his chin as he smiles.

'Good, then?' I give him a tight bear hug.

He seems to nod. Agnes Aunty sweeps forward and wipes his mouth with a tissue. '*Ané*, Angel,' she begins, a note cracking in her throat, then she runs a finger over his forearm and laughs softly. 'All this Elvis nonsense!' She dabs her eyes. 'What to do, no? This boy was mad from the start.'

Uncle Aloy nods toward his son, pointing at the television. 'See there? Jimmy Stewart, *men*. And he thinks he can see a large rabbit. Bugger has lodgers, I tell you.'

I stare from Agnes Aunty to Uncle Aloy to Angel. They are somehow knitted together by an unseen yarn, locked into their own version of the Nativity. No goats, though. Or sheep. Or shepherds or kings. None of that. Just me to watch over them like some misguided star. I think of all the Christmases I spent with my parents, sat round a turkey or leg of lamb. Silent, but for the slow mastication of mouths over plates. We pulled crackers, of course. And exchanged gifts. Often we visited Agnes Aunty and Uncle Aloy, and I giggled as my aunt loudly admonished my uncle for saying something puerile or stupid. I wander into the kitchen to check the food, smiling with the memory.

Sitting on a stool at the counter, I smooth my hands over its cool, grey surface. Months ago, Mum and Dad sent me invitations to spend Christmas with them, but like every year before this one, I declined. Next year, I wrote them both, next year would definitely be a possibility. There are gifts from them sitting under the tree, wrapped in brocaded, shiny red paper. I sigh. I sent them identical cards: a bear, wearing a woolly red hat, holding a candy cane.

I sent one to Amrik as well. A few days ago I rang him up, telling him that Vinda doesn't exist any more. I had the dream again, I said, only this time, I wasn't in it. Or I was, but only for a moment. The crowd was the same, though less swampy and more human – a long queue of men and women marching through the streets toward a brightly lit field. I was on their shoulders again, but disintegrating at every step. My skin began to crisp then turned a matt, papery brown. My innards simply melted into a brick-coloured sauce. I was nowhere and everywhere, dribbling down fingers and wrists, bubbling on lips. Then I was gone.

The crowd opened their mouths in unison, belting out their song. The words, this time, were unmistakable. They were chanting 'Vindaloo', clutching greasy paper bags and brandishing football scarves. I found myself suddenly sitting up in bed, heart pounding, knowing that the name 'Vindaloo' would end up being shouted high into the rafters of football stadiums up and down the country.

'You're being ridiculous,' Amrik said when I phoned him shortly after waking. It was 5am, and he was in no mood to listen to my dreams.

'Sorry, I know it's early – too early in the morning. But this is a sign, Amrik. It's over. The whole business has … dissolved.'

Amrik grunted and mumbled something about the time, so I replaced the handset in its cradle, turned over and went back to sleep. When we spoke again, I had to remind him about our conversation. He pressed his lips together, rolled his eyes and finally relented, saying that my dad had had a terrible sense of humour and should have left my naming up to Mum.

I am grinning now, remembering how much money is in my account and under my mattress. I haven't decided what I'm going to do with it all. But at least I have a choice. The first thing I need to do is get a job. Then, maybe, I can buy my own place. I've got enough for a decent deposit. I could do it. I really could.

I tilt my head upward, inhaling the scent of roasted potatoes and plum-glazed turkey. From where I am sitting, I can hear familiar Yuletide sounds: Elvis – the real Elvis – singing 'Blue Christmas', Uncle Aloy's incessant muttering, Agnes Aunty's cyclical shouts of 'Stupid old man.'

I chuckle, then close my eyes and breathe in. Regis is right. Obsession can do you in. Make you a captive or set you free.

Rosemary and port fill my lungs. The scent is electric, setting off little explosions in my brain. Without warning, the words to 'Waterloo Sunset' rise in my belly bringing with them promises of paradise. I swallow slowly, caught in the pause. Yes. I can almost taste it.

Acknowledgements

The definition of 'nomenclature' is taken from the *Compact Oxford English Dictionary of Current English Second Edition, Revised*, Catherine Soanes, ed. (Oxford: Oxford University Press, 2003).

Clare Short's quote is taken from
http://news.bbc.co.uk/1/hi/uk_politics/3020955.stm

Quotes on pp 1, 2, 25, 26, 175, 205, 206, 208 are based on The Song of Solomon (3:8, 6:10, 8:10), *The Holy Bible*: King James Version.

Song lyrics appear courtesy of the following.

'Suspicious Minds'
Words & Music by Francis Zambon
© Copyright 1969 Sony/ATV Songs LLC, USA. Sony/ATV Music Publishing (UK) Limited. Used by permission of Music Sales Limited. All Rights Reserved. International Copyright Secured.

'Burning Love'
Words & Music by Dennis Linde
© Copyright 1972 Sony/ATV Songs LLC, USA. Sony/ATV Music Publishing (UK) Limited. Used by permission of Music Sales Limited. All Rights Reserved. International Copyright Secured.

Thanks to Pete Ayrton, Kate Pullinger, Kellee Nunley, Scott Harvey, Elise Moser, Rajeev Balasubramanyam, Ajay Madan, Jeevan Deol, Anita Sharma, Karen McCarthy and an unknown officer from the Los Angeles Police Department. Special thanks to Neil and my family – immediate and extended – without whom this book could not have been written.